Death
of a
God

S. T. HAYMON

D0180172

BANTAM BOOKS
NEW YORK • TORONTO • LONDON • SYDNEY • AUCKLAND

DEATH OF A GOD

*A Bantam Book / published by arrangement with
St. Martin's Press*

PRINTING HISTORY
St. Martin's Press edition published 1987
Bantam edition / May 1990

ISBN 0-553-27266-7

Published simultaneously in the United States and Canada

Bantam Books are published by Bantam Books, a division of Bantam Doubleday
Dell Publishing Group, Inc. Its trademark, consisting of the words "Bantam
Books" and the portrayal of a rooster, is Registered in U.S. Patent and Trademark
Office and in other countries. Marca Registrada. Bantam Books, 666 Fifth Avenue,
New York, New York 10103.

PRINTED IN THE UNITED STATES OF AMERICA

O   0 9 8 7 6 5 4 3 2 1

Author's note

Anyone who knows Norfolk will recognize that Norwich is the starting point for my city of Angleby. But only the starting point. The city and its inhabitants are the figments of my imagination; and no reference is made to any living person.

S.T.H.

DEATH OF A GOD

Part I

Question

1

The storm broke without warning. One moment the day was bright, brittle with the sunshine of early spring; the next, rain lanced down from clouds split by lightning into convulsions of angry air, thunder blundering about the sky like a drunken giant trying to find his way home in the dark. Fingers of wind tweaked tiles from rooftops, whirled desiccated bits of this and that, the detritus of winter, upward for a brief resurrection before the rain beat them back to earth again, doubly dead.

The rain hit the ground at a sharp angle and turned the slope into a series of rivulets, now separating, now coalescing, as they found their way downhill. Amidst all the hullaballoo only the three crosses planted a little below the summit held their stillness and their silence, the three figures that hung upon them motionless and unaware. Water dripped from their soaked hair, their eyebrows, noses, chins; glistened on their contorted bodies and on their faces, two of them with eyeballs uprolled to heaven in agonized supplication or incredulous surprise (it was difficult to decide which), the third, the central one, chin sunk on bony chest, inscrutable, a shell from which the spirit had departed so thoroughly as to leave behind scarcely even the semblance of one-time life. A pigeon, thrown out of gear by the sudden change in the weather, landed clumsily on the horizontal of the central cross, a little above a pierced hand; found no comfort there and took off again, beating a laborious way towards better shelter. In the lightning flashes, hailstones which had impaled themselves on the crown of thorns which encircled the down-drooping head shone like pearls.

Detective-Inspector Benjamin Jurnet, sheltering in the

3

doorway of Mucho Macho, the menswear shop on the eastern side of Angleby Market Place, peered out at the downpour and observed sourly, 'God save us from trendy bishops! Wouldn't surprise me if His Grace and the blooming Parks and Recreation Committee hadn't laid this on as well, the two of them between them. Wasn't there a storm when it really happened?' Quickly correcting himself, glad that neither Miriam nor Rabbi Schnellman was within earshot, 'When it was supposed to have happened?'

'In that case, boyo, compose yourself for a long wait.' In his ripe, Welsh Chapel voice, Detective-Sergeant Jack Ellers, Jurnet's companion and colleague, launched himself into an approximate quotation: ' "Now from the sixth hour there was darkness all over the land until the ninth hour. The temple veil was rent in twain from the top to the bottom, the earth did quake and the rocks rent"—and that's to say nothing of graves opening and giving up their dead.' Finishing sunnily: 'Not to worry, though. Not even God in all His glory's going to open Angleby graves without a union card.'

The rain had begun to ease, the giant lurching off to the north as if he had suddenly remembered it was the Norfolk coast he had been making for all along. Stall-holders in the Market Place emerged from their lairs and began taking off the covers they had hastily spread over their piles of fruit and veg, their sheets and pillow cases, video cassettes and girlie mags. They poked with broom handles at the striped awnings bellying with water. By the time the two detectives had crossed the street and ascended the main alleyway between the stalls, dodging the not always fortuitous cascades dislodged by the prodding brooms, a tentative sunbeam was brightening the gilded numbers on the City Hall clock.

Jurnet's opinion of authorities ecclesiastical and municipal alike was not improved by a closer view of the crosses on the hill. They had been inserted into one of the flower beds in the narrow strip of public garden which terminated the business part of the Market Place at its upper, western, end. Daffodils in pinched-looking bud clustered about their bases. The pigeon—was it the same one?—had returned to its former resting place on the central cross. It croo-crooed a little in a self-satisfied way, the pink and green on the back of its neck handsome in the strengthening light; probed about with its beak under one wing, and defecated on the arm of the crucified Christ.

'Bugger off!' Jurnet shouted, clapping his hands. The bird, inured to the much greater clatter of the market, regarded him beadily and did it again.

Jack Ellers, referring, not too delicately, to the fact that his superior officer, albeit with no notable result to date, was studying to convert to Judaism, remarked cheekily, 'Shouldn't have thought, Ben, it was your pigeon any longer? Besides, in the Holy Land, if you think about it, it'd have been a lot worse than pigeons. Ravens or vultures, more likely.'

'Don't let on to the Bishop, for Christ's sake, or he'll be phoning the Zoo aviary before you know it!' Impatient with his own ill humour: 'And it's nothing to do with religion, either. It's simply—well, it's a matter of taste,' he finished lamely.

'*Darling, you are growing o-old, Silver threads among the gold*—' The little Welshman trilled a few bars and regarded his companion's dark good looks with a blend of pity and amusement. 'Comes to even the sexiest of us sooner or later.'

'That'll be enough of that, Sergeant!' Jurnet returned his attention to the silent figures looming above him. Forcing his feelings into marketable, if makeshift, order: 'All I meant is—if it was just somebody's cock-eyed way of celebrating Easter I wouldn't say a word. As you say, it's none of my business any more. But you can bet your bottom dollar, however else they may or may not have looked on Calvary in whatever it was AD, none of 'em looked the spitting image of a bloody pop group that happens—just happens—to be playing the town this week!'

'Not just any old pop group, laddie. One from Angleby! Return of the native son loaded down with gold and platinum discs to the simple Council log-cabin where it all began, with skiffle learnt at his Mammy's knee. That's the whole point, boyo, don't you see?' Hard to tell if Ellers were serious or still fooling. 'It's called making religion relevant to the young. Not their fault the Apostles, poor sods, hadn't so much as a Jew's harp between the lot of 'em, even if Jesus did say to Peter, "Thou art my rock and roll," or words to that effect. Personally, I think the Bishop's on to something.'

'Hm! Next thing you know, he'll be chucking the organ out of the cathedral and plugging in a synthesizer.'

'Do wonders for the collection, I'll tell you that! Did you hear that his holiness is attending tonight in person? With purple hair, I shouldn't wonder, now that bishops don't go in for those ducky purple pinnies any more. His worship won't be paying for his ticket himself, that's for sure. What they're changing hands for, you could pick up the crown jewels for less.'

'Just as well I hadn't planned to go. Miriam's the one buys their albums day they come out. Keeps them over at her place, thank goodness, so I don't have to suffer.'

Jurnet continued his gaze upward, deliberately concentrating his attention on the two outer figures of the trio. Since setting in motion the long-drawn-out process of conversion he found any encounter with Jesus, in whatever shape or form, an embarrassment, on a par with running into your old headmaster when you were out on the town with a bird on your arm in fishnet tights and a black leather mini.

One of the outer figures—naked except for a plaid jockstrap—was of a black man, with a noble physique and strongly etched features which must have been even more striking when not distorted by the pangs of crucifixion. Water still dripped rhythmically from the coloured beads which ended each of his clustering braids. The second subsidiary figure was as tall, but of slighter build; white, a neat, efficient body topped by a face of equivocal charm. With him, even the terminal agony seemed under control, informed by an intelligence already detached from the suffering flesh. The full, sensual mouth was open in a silent scream which could just as easily have been a grin at the absurdity of his own predicament. Only a clown, it seemed to be proclaiming, with no respect for the fitness of things, could have allowed himself to be crucified in baby-blue boxer shorts with a pink stripe down the sides.

Both figures were strongly modelled, every muscle and

tendon made explicit: stomach sucked in, the flesh taut over the arching ribs. By contrast, the central figure was a mere sketch, arms and legs seeming a bit too long, hands and feet a bit too large; otherwise, only a hint of nipples, no discernible navel, a blank oval of face obscured by straight reddish hair falling to the shoulders.

Could be, thought Jurnet, forcing himself to look, to make a judgement, it was this very lack of definition which made the image so compelling. Clever bugger, whoever had thought it up. Clever too, to have ducked out of making the Christ figure actually look like the third member of the pop group. Not even the Bishop could have stood for that. If it just so happened, drawing on your own imagination, you chose to fill in the blank with the features of Loy Tanner, the lead singer and darling of the charts, the responsibility was yours and nobody else's.

Only why, then, taking into account all that had been deliberately left out, had its maker fashioned a figure full frontal, not so much as a G-string, and equipped with a set of tools formidable enough to set any pagan fertility god drooling with envy?

2

Jack Ellers exclaimed in the accents of a stage copper, 'Hello, hello, hello! What have we here then?'

A small white van, driven too fast, had come hurtling round the corner into the roadway on the further side of the strip of garden. Abreast of the statuary, the driver slammed on the brakes and the vehicle slid, protesting, to a halt. Across the side of the van, a rainbow painted in psychedelic colours arched over the words, printed in Gothic black-letter: *Second Coming*.

The man who emerged from the driver's seat was a surprise and a discomfort. Not a dwarf exactly—too tall for that—but a grotesque, a massive torso set upon stumpy legs that moved as if in perpetual apology to the splendid body above. The face was dark and Italianate, the black hair curly and vigorous. The man wore an anorak over a shirt of bright checks, his levis hacked short by a hand that had scorned to disguise its anger at the need for the alteration.

As the two detectives watched, the man rumbled bow-legged to the rear of the van, unlocked the doors, and took out a metal ladder and a large, patterned beach towel, both of which—with no regard for the daffodils—he tossed over the low wall which closed off the garden from the street. Jurnet, on the point of lecturing him on this want of respect for municipal flora, bit back the words as he observed the effort with which the man himself painfully negotiated the insignificant obstacle.

Once over, however, he propped the ladder against the cross where the black man hung, positioned the towel over his shoulder, and then scampered up the rungs with a surprising, simian ease, the grim face relaxing with the

8

pleasure of, for once, doing something physical well. He took the towel in both hands and, bending forward, rubbed the braided hairdo energetically, the beads clicking like thrown dice, and then began a brisk towelling of the arms and chest, leaning dangerously out from the ladder to reach the parts furthest away.

Alarmed for his safety, Jurnet stepped forward and grasped the uprights, placing a steadying foot on the bottom rung.

So far from exhibiting gratitude, the man's face darkened.

'How is it some geezers never learn to mind their own bleeding business?'

'It *is* my business, chummy. Detective-Inspector Jurnet, in case you're interested. Someone give you permission, then, to muck up these flowers?'

'Move off, man, will ya? You're making me nervous. The Bishop give me permission, if you must know. Got it direct from God, I shouldn't wonder.'

Jurnet shook his head.

'Not in the Bishop's power, chum, to give you permission or not, as the case may be. Not even, with all due respect, God's. Property of Angleby Borough Council, paid for by the citizens of this fair city. My advice, if you doubt my word, come down from that ladder before you break your neck, go over to the Bishop's Palace and stamp on some of His Lordship's flowers and see how *he* likes it.'

The sun had come out strongly again. A myriad tiny rainbows glimmered in the drops which still bedewed the bodies of the crucified men. The sight seemed to excite the man on the ladder to a frenzy. 'Jesus!' He cast up his eyes despairingly at the bleached sky, and back again to Jurnet. 'Stop me getting on with my job and we'll bleeding sue you!'

'Oh ah? Sue me for what, would that be?'

'You're the ones know the names. All I know is, stop me getting these three dried off proper and you'll be lucky to leave the court with the shirt on your back. They cost a bleeding fortune. Jesus!' The man wailed again as the sun seemed to grow brighter, to aim its shafts at his charges with brassy malice. 'Look at that, for Christ's sake!'—pointing to a small, mottled swelling on the negro's left thigh.

Jurnet tilted his head, took a look. 'Nothing but a bit of roughness. Could be anything.'

'Could be, you mean, because he's been left out wet in the sun because some toffee-nosed dick won't let me get him dried off proper! Or could be because the fucking Israelite what made the three of 'em comes from some place it hasn't rained since the Ark and hadn't a clue what'd happen if they got wet and then dried quick by the sun. Ten minutes more of you holding me up and the whole bleeding bunch'll look like they've broke out with leprosy.'

'You don't say!' Jurnet repressed a sudden impish conviction that the Israelite in question had known more about the English climate than he had let on. Then, as a Jew-to-be, atoning: 'Why didn't you say so before? Any more towels in that van? We'll give you a hand.'

'Queenie!' the man called, and the passenger side of the van opened, letting out a blare of pop music and a girl. The girl was very young, wispily blonde. Except for a quiff of fluorescent emerald rising spikily above a childishly bulging forehead, there was nothing special about her. What was special was the something in the man's voice when he called her name. Jurnet recognized that something —felt it reverberate deep down in his own throat as it did whenever he himself spoke, whenever he so much as thought, the name of Miriam.

The girl came out sulkily, as if the something meant nothing to her apart from boredom and irritation. She listened to what the man had to say, reached back into the van, jeans stretched tight over meagre buttocks, and straightened up with two more beach towels in her arms. With a flashy ease that could have been intended as a deliberate taunt to one who had just accomplished the same manoeuvre with so much effort, she skipped over the low wall, and walked unconcernedly to the foot of the ladder, mauling more daffodils as she came; surrendered the towels without curiosity into the waiting arms of the two detectives, and turned to go back the way she had come.

Jurnet said: 'Mind the flowers, love,'—an admonition to

which she made no answer other than to grind her dirty white track shoes even more remorselessly into the wet earth.

Back at the van, the passenger door re-opened, the music came tumbling out again. The girl stood on the pavement, one hand on the door handle, swaying to the guitars and the insistent drums. Singing along with them in a child's voice, piercing and off-key:

> *'Behold thou art fair, my beloved, behold thou art fair.*
> *Spun gold thy hair,*
> *Thy lips a thread of scarlet, mouth most sweet.*
> *How beautiful thy feet,*
> *Jewels the joints of thy thighs,*
> *And thine eyes,*
> *Like doves soft and grey,*
> *Mirrors of the day,*
> *Fair as the moon, bright as the sun, and as fine.*
> *I am my beloved's, and my beloved is mine.'*

'She one of your group, then?' Sergeant Ellers inquired, drying the feet of the Christ figure with a tender regard for the spaces between the large, splayed toes.

'Queenie?' Again Jurnet, doggedly working his way up towards the baby-blue boxer shorts, registered the tone, the something. The man on the ladder paused in his work, his head a little to one side, listening. He smiled lovingly, his face transformed but not foolish. 'That'd get us in the charts, I don't think! Queenie's our—' he hesitated, as if seeking the right word, and came out primly with: 'our general assistant.'

'That's nice.'

The smile disappeared. The ladder teetered alarmingly. 'What you mean, nice?'

'Touchy, aren't you? Nice. What I say. Just making conversation. You better look out up there, you'll be ending up in the Norfolk and Angleby in plaster.' The little Welshman stood back to admire his handiwork. 'Kneecap's as high as I can go, unless you got another ladder with you.' And to Jurnet, mischievously: 'You're the beanpole, Ben. OK if I leave the working parts to you?'

Jurnet did not deign to reply. The whole business had begun to give him a disagreeable feeling. What the hell had prompted him to act the Boy Scout—perform a *mitzvah*, as Rabbi Schnellman would put it, a good deed that was always, at the same time and by definition, a religious duty? Down below in the market some of the traders had come out from their stalls and were gazing up at the two detectives' efforts with undisguised amusement. Suppose some influential member of the Angleby Jewish community, suppose the Rabbi himself, should happen to come by? A fine religious duty for a trainee Jew to be out on the Market Place for all to see, drying off Christ's balls before they blistered in the sun!

The thought had no sooner lodged in Jurnet's mind than, being the man he was, he had persuaded the owner of the ladder to descend from it and pass it over to him, as being the one out of the three of them best fitted by nature to reach every furthest crevice of the three pendent bodies. Concentrating his attention upon the still damp surfaces as areas to be dried and nothing more, he worked onward and upward, towelling the outsize genitalia of the middle figure, the terrible eyeballs of the other two; gently dislodging the last of the wet from the crown of thorns. Sergeant Ellers held the ladder still, the short-legged man watching with no noticeable appreciation of what was being done for him: occasionally shouting up brusque reminders like, 'Behind *both* ears, for Pete's sake!' and 'That left armpit, man—I could wash my socks in it!'

Out on the pavement, beyond the low wall, the girl was still singing.

'Set me as a seal upon thine heart, a seal upon thine
    arm.
Nothing can do us harm.
I suck thy breasts, I breathe thy breath,
Our love is stronger far than death.
Our limbs like leafy boughs entwine.
I am my beloved's, and my beloved is mine.'

3

Headquarters, that haven from the hurly-burly, that retreat among brothers who—even those who were in a position to slap you down and frequently did—were always on your side when it came to the crunch, seemed doubly welcoming to Jurnet as he and Ellers came out of the ambiguous sunlight into the no-nonsense of fluorescent strips that bathed one and all in the same dispassionate light. Even the little Welshman's: 'Fine thing if the Super was looking out of the window and saw us,' could not defuse this feeling of wellbeing.

'Even if it was in his line of vision—which it isn't, as you well know—helping distressed citizenry's the answer to that, Sergeant. What His Nibs is always on about.'

'Distressed? That bugger? Didn't even say ta. And I'd thought two complimentary tickets at least.'

Jurnet regarded his chubby subordinate with genuine surprise. 'Don't tell me you, the pride of the eisteddfod, would actually *choose* to spend an entire evening being deafened by that aural pollution, even for free?'

'There you go again, showing your age! Life on this planet didn't come to an end with the Beatles, boyo, nor the Stones neither. Not that, if Shorty George back there *had* come across with the goods, I'd have felt able to squander them on myself. Flogged 'em—reluctantly, mind you—and with the proceeds bought a mink for Rosie, a Jag for me, and laid up the rest for the twilight of my days.'

'Crazy!' commented Jurnet, making for the stairs. 'Don't know about you, I think I've earned myself a cup of char—' Reminding himself, not too seriously, on the way down to the canteen, to ask the Rabbi if it was OK, *mitzvah*-wise, to reward yourself for something it was your plain religious duty to have done anyway.

13

The long, low room was crowded to overflowing, reso-
nating with a cheerful noise that Jurnet absorbed with
satisfaction, lowering himself into it as into the comfort of
a hot bath. It was the real thing too, the Lord be praised.
None of that tense mock-merriment such as preceded a
match between Angleby United and one of the League
big-shots—which was to say an advertised encounter with
alien invaders arriving decked out in knuckledusters and
broken-off bottle-necks in the club colours.

Not that demos were much better. These days, it seemed,
you couldn't even take to the streets in aid of endangered
woodlice without it all ending in tears and bloody noses,
chiefly those of the police. As it was, PC Blaker, who rose
respectfully from his egg and beans at the table to which
the two detectives brought their brimming cups, and had
to be urged hospitably to resume his place, could not
conceal his gratification at being detailed for crowd control
outside the University.

'The hall there only holds 1,700, and that was sold out
the day they put the tickets on sale. There'll be thousands
coming along just to stand outside. Wanting to be part of
it, the only way they can.'

'Can't see why you're so cock-a-hoop.' Jurnet helped
himself generously to the white sugar Miriam wouldn't
have in the house, and leaned back comfortably. 'Could be
hairy. Like the Bacchantes in those Greek myths. Thousands of screaming dollies ready to stop at nothing to tear
limb from limb the phantom lover they've been having it
off with in their technicolour dreams and at last is there in
the flesh—the mind boggles. Better you than me.'

'Oh no, sir!' The young constable's face, rosy with ear-
nestness, was also a little pitying. 'That was in the old days
of inhibitions and frustrations.' He studied the two faces
across the table, as if to decipher therein the signs of stress
which must surely disfigure a generation come to maturity
before the sexual revolution. 'Nowadays, when they can
have a lay any time they fancy, they're not bothered. And
with Second Coming it's not like that, anyway. It's not just
pop, see. It's a whole lot more'n that.'

'Oh ah? They sound pretty old hat to me, these days of
keyboards and players who can actually tell one note from

another. Two guitars and a set of drums—the Beatles minus one.'

'Oh no, sir!' PC Blaker exclaimed again, growing even rosier. 'There's never been anything like Second Coming, and never will be. Messianic's what they call it. The way all their songs come out of the Bible, for one thing. And the way they make you think, not just about booze and boobs and all that, but—' petering out in a stammer of embarrassment—'about what life's all about—'

'Christ, laddie!' Sergeant Ellers said. 'You make it sound like a prayer meeting in the Welsh valleys.'

'Oh no!' The other looked quite shocked. 'If you only listened to one of their albums—really listened to it—you'd understand better than I can say. Tonight, for instance, it'll be a piece of cake. You'll see. The kids outside'll just be standing quietly, not so much as the smell of trouble. All they want is to see him, actually see him live. That'll be enough to make it worthwhile.'

'Him? There's three of them, aren't there?'

The young man answered in a tone which, for all his awe of his superiors, imperfectly concealed what he thought of such a foolish question.

'Loy, sir. Loy Tanner. My Auntie Sandra', he added, aglow with pride at being the purveyor of such information, 'knows a lady whose sister-in-law used to live in the same street as Loy's mum. Only she won't say where it is. Somewhere over Gallipoli Street way, my Auntie thinks, except she won't say—the lady, that is. Says people have a right to their privacy.'

'That's a real lady! Only—' the detective frowned, finished the last of his tea, and thoughtfully spooned up the sweet mush remaining in the bottom of the cup—'it's funny, if she's living down there, the media haven't sniffed her out. With all due respect to your lady snout, you'd expect a pop star's mum to hang out a bit up-market from Gallipoli Street.'

'That's what she says,' PC Blaker insisted, crestfallen but sticking to his guns.

Jack Ellers, taking pity, interposed soothingly, 'Could be someone else of the same name. Goodness knows we're not short of Tanners in Angleby. Look in the phone book, they're ten a penny. On the other hand, could be that Loy

Tanner's only a stage name. Most of those pop stars seem to be Joe Muck or Siddy Piffalovitch in real life.'

'He *is* Loy Tanner!' The young policeman's eyes had become suspiciously bright. 'His great-great-grandfather—or however many greats it was, I don't know how many—was *the* Tanner, the famous one in the history books. The one they hung from the top of the castle all those years ago.'

'Was he indeed?' said Jurnet, getting up from the table. 'Not to worry, son. They don't do that any more, even to pop singers.'

The ground floor was crowded with young constables, eager as if they were waiting for the coaches to arrive to take them on a police outing. Some one was whistling a tune which Jurnet recognized as the one the green-quiffed girl had sung, holding on to the van door, swaying, lost in her dream. The detective's face lost its expression of contentment as his mouth twisted a little at the corners. '*I am my beloved's, and my beloved is mine.*' Whoever could lay down the law with that degree of certainty hadn't met Miriam.

Sergeant Ellers, practised at recognizing the signs of incipient melancholy in his superior officer, said, 'We must be crackers, haunting the place even when we're off duty, especially a day like this, strictly for the kiddies. Rosie'll think I've got my eye on some nubile WPC, can't bear to let her out of my sight.'

'Oh ah.'

The little Welshman persisted. 'Look—if Miriam's off somewhere on business, why don't you join me and the missus for supper? It's osso bucco—and Rosie always says the sight of your lovely Latin kisser across the table lends the finishing touch when she cooks Italian. So what do you say?'

'Not tonight.' Jurnet roused himself enough to recognize the oblique reference to the fact that, though carefully behind his back, the boys at Headquarters were prone to refer to him as Valentino. 'Ta all the same. Miriam's not off anywhere. I don't know what gave you the idea. Went up to London for some trade show or something, but she'll be back by now and expecting me—'

'In that case, why not make it the two of you? You're not

planning an evening of culture at the University, so you tell me, and after a hard day's graft Miriam can't be feeling all that like cooking—'

Such delicacy, thought Jurnet, the mouth untwisting a little in grateful appreciation, from one who knew as well as he did himself Miriam's approach to—or rather, bellicose recoil from—the culinary arts: a male conspiracy to keep women from fulfilling their God-given potential.

He smiled at the chubby little man, not afraid to let his affection show. 'Another time, OK?'

The two had cleared a way for themselves almost to the door when the duty sergeant, burrowing through the pack, called across the backs and shoulders which still barred his way, 'Mr Jurnet! Ben! Hold on! Got something for you!'

Arrived at his goal, the man straightened his tunic and smiled indulgently at the high-spirited youngsters all about him.

'You'd think it was Christmas instead of nearly Easter! Someone hang up a bunch of mistletoe, I shouldn't care to answer for the consequences.' Handing over an envelope, small and flat, without superscription: 'Bloke handed it in just after eleven. I got the exact time logged, if you need it. Foreigner, by the way he spoke. Peaky. Looked like a puff of wind would blow him away. Said it had to be given into your hands personal. Made quite a song and dance about it.'

'Foreigner, eh?' Jack Ellers leaned over for a better look. 'If it's a bomb, not enough jelly there to take off more'n a finger or a nose.'

'Not worth bothering about,' Jurnet agreed, reaching into a pocket for his penknife. He selected a small blade, slit the envelope open and took out its contents.

For a moment the three stood staring down at what lay revealed. Then the duty sergeant said with a laugh that was only slightly soured with envy, 'Somebody up there must love you, and no mistake.'

The two bits of green pasteboard took up little room in the detective's hand.

Two tickets for Second Coming in Concert at 8.30 p.m. at the University.

4

Jurnet parked his car as directed in the walled enclosure which was all that remained of the ancient manor upon whose site Angleby had seen fit to raise the concrete ziggurats of its university. The enclosure had once been a kitchen garden. Old nails still protruding from the eroded bricks showed where espaliered apricocks had once ripened under Tudor suns. Under the chill March moon the meticulously aligned cars looked like rows of some weird vegetable, of the marrow family it might be, laid out to ripen off in the alien light. Miriam got out of the front passenger seat and waited for Jurnet to lock up, her breath steaming, the white coat she had bought that day in London wrapped close about her body in generous, expensive folds.

Jurnet came round the car and kissed her with passion, even though she *had* got him out on a night cold enough to freeze the balls off a brass monkey, let alone those of a plastic god hanging on a cross in the Market Place. Their combined breaths ascended the frosty air like a cloud of incense until she pulled away in laughing protest: 'We'll be late!'

'Have you got the tickets?' she had demanded earlier, when he had hardly got his key out of the flat door. 'Mara said she'd get Leo to drop them off. I meant to tell you this morning and then, in all the rush, it went clean out of my head.'

He had shut the door, pocketed his key, taken off his coat and hung it on the gimcrack stand that was all the furnishing of the shabby little hall. In the even shabbier living-room the table was still piled high with the patterns and fashion magazines among which, at breakfast time, he

18

had contrived to find room for his mug of instant and piece of toast. No smell—not even of the dehydrated chemical messes which, reconstituted according to the directions on the packet, turned themselves, when heated by Miriam's unwilling ministrations, into hydrated chemical messes—drifted in from the kitchen.

'Well?' she had urged. Even tight with impatience, her mouth, Jurnet noted with pleasure, could not disguise its lovely, generous curve, at once so revealing and so misleading. He sat down in a lumpy armchair and began to unlace his shoes.

'Who's Mara? Who's Leo when he's at home?'

'You don't listen to me. Mara's one of my knitters, of course, the one I'm always praising to the skies. Leo's her husband—Leo Felsenstein. He works for me too, when he's feeling up to it. For God's sake,' she cried, 'did you get the tickets or didn't you? If you did, you'll have to put those shoes straight back on again, if we're going to have time to eat.'

'Actually,' announced the detective, fishing the tickets out of his pocket and holding them out for Miriam's eager fingers to snatch at, 'I was just going to slip into my sequinned Hush Puppies, get out my medallion, and give myself a quick heliotrope rinse. I wouldn't want to let you down with the beautiful people.'

'Moron!' she murmured, appeased, scanning the tickets absorbedly. Satisfied they were what they appeared to be, she bent down and kissed him lightly on the top of his head, her mind on other things.

'Beautiful people! You talk like a dinosaur! And you a copper with your finger, supposedly, on the pulse of the masses! You simply haven't a clue what gives today, have you?'

'Enough to know those tickets are changing hands for a king's ransom. So what did you have to do to get your hands on these two? Flog 'em a couple of sweaters at cost price? Take out a second mortgage? Sacrifice your maidenhead?'

Miriam said, 'You left out fellatio. I tried them all, actually—but no dice. Then, just by the merest chance—you could have knocked me down with a feather—Mara and I were talking, and suddenly, out of the blue, just for something to say, no more than that, I said something about Second Coming and how much I'd have liked to have heard them live at the University, only getting tickets was out of the question, when she came out quite casually with the fact that Loy Tanner was her son.'

Jurnet hooted. 'You mean he's really—what was it?—Loy Felsenstein, not the descendant of our local hero! Well! Well!'

'I don't mean anything of the sort. He's Mara's son, not Leo's. Tanner was her maiden name. She also told me that Leo was the only husband she'd ever had.'

'I see. My apologies to Loy boy for having slanderously accused him of being born in holy wedlock. They lynch people nowadays for less. Did Mrs F. also confide in you how come she lives in Gallipoli Street, knitting sweaters for a female slave-driver, when her son must be a millionaire several times over?'

'How did you know about Gallipoli Street? Sebastopol Terrace, to be accurate, but the same little two-down-two-ups. And she did, as a matter of fact. Confide.' Miriam's dark brown eyes, large and, as a rule, rather melancholy, brightened with pleasure. 'I felt quite honoured. I don't think she can have let on to anyone else, or the papers would have got on to it and never let her alone. What she said was, it's completely her own decision, living where and how she does. Apparently Loy's forever trying to get her to accept money from him, but she always says no. Not because she's proud, or because she's got anything against money as such, but because she's afraid of what might happen if she says yes. She said she's had some bad times in her life, so she knows how precious happiness is—how hard to get, how hard to hold on to.

'Like hanging on to one of the lifeboats after a shipwreck, is how she described it, with, all the time, the people who've managed to get seats inside the boat hammering on your knuckles to make you let go in case the extra weight overturns the lot of you into the sea. She says she and Leo are very happy the way they are, and she doesn't want to take any chances by making things different, the way more money would be bound to. She says

they have everything they need, and it may surprise you
to know that they actually enjoy working for me. That was
how the tickets came up. Since I'd said I was a fan of
Second Coming, would I care to accept a couple of tickets
for the concert as a mark of their joint appreciation of a
lovely boss? Apparently Loy was insisting on sending round
tickets for the two of them, only she thought the crowds
would be too much for Leo, and even if she felt like going
herself—which, actually, she didn't—she didn't fancy leaving him on his own for the whole evening.' Miriam broke
off, then added soberly, 'She's a remarkable woman. Made
me feel like a materialistic heel. If I had a son rolling in
the lolly, I wouldn't say no to a chunk of it.'

Jurnet commented, 'When the time comes, we'll have
to break it gently to the little fellow that his mummy's a
gold-digger.' He felt around for his shoes, and levered his
knackered feet into them, feeling a small surge of regret at
being, like them, caged up again for the night. 'Just hang
on to those seats, that's all.'

Miriam looked at him, surprised. 'I'm standing here
with the tickets right in my hand.'

'I meant the ones in the lifeboat, actually.'

5

They were too old, Jurnet decided. Himself certainly, his thirties sliding slowly but inexorably out of sight like a coffin in a crematorium, furnace-ward. But Miriam too. Delicious, still young enough to be called a girl without anyone cocking a cynical eyebrow; but she'd been around, as they said, she knew the score. More than her new coat, or the Gucci bag dangling from her shoulder, proclaimed a winner: it was implicit in every movement of her slender yet voluptuous body, in the assured posture of the head capped with a mist of bronze hair so artlessly natural it had to cost a bomb to keep it that way. More than all of this was an assurance—aristocratic was the only word for it— born of an ancestry ancient enough to make half the crowned heads of Europe look like a bunch of immigrants just landed on the Essex marshes. If Jews, Jurnet reflected, moving along at her side with a proper deference, didn't know where they were going these days any more than the rest of the human race, they sure as hell knew where they'd come from.

Almost all the others of the close-packed crowd inching slowly towards its goal of the Middlemass Auditorium were drearily, stridently, or touchingly young; so chuffed to be moving purposefully for once that it seemed almost a pity, the detective thought, they ever had to arrive, to find themselves confronted all over again with a new situation upon which a stance had to be taken, even if it was only what to do with your anorak once you got inside. A few, Jurnet's experienced eyes told him, had fortified themselves against all such decision-taking with a preliminary joint, and now floated along, smiling foolishly, but there was none, so far as he could see, with the yellow skin and

22

the pupils which, to anyone who could read the signs, spelled smack, the big H. Seemingly, young Blaker had known whereof he spoke when he had predicted so confidently that there would be no trouble the night Second Coming came to town.

The Middlemass Auditorium, set down among lawns a prophylactic distance from the brutal bulk of the main University buildings, looked terrific in the moonlight. It could have been an aircraft hangar until you came inside, into an immense vestibule set about with the world-famous collection of ethnic statuary which Sir Cedric Middlemass, the supermarket tycoon, had donated to the University among his many other benefactions.

For all their much-proclaimed liberation from the burden of sexual shame, the youngsters coming in from the frosty air all too obviously found these gods and goddesses from far-off places, with their protuberant jaws, exuberant breasts, and tumescent sexual organs, an embarrassment. They passed by with eyes averted, not looking at one another either.

Miriam, whom nothing could daunt, giggled, and nibbled at Jurnet's ear as if the proximity of such a predatory pantheon had awakened the praying mantis in her.

'Can you imagine actually having them about the house? My guess is, Lady Middlemass said to Sir Hubby, "Either they go or I do!" So the poor man, loving his wife, had this place built to house them. I mean, you could hardly leave them out for the dustman to take away.'

'I could,' Jurnet said.

The Auditorium proper, apart from two garlanded figures which sat at either side of the proscenium arch with enormous hands on their knees, grinning at the incoming audience with the ferocious jollity of crocodiles viewing the arrival of their next meal, was blessedly free of ethnic artefacts. It was a place of cool plastered walls, and terraces which cascaded gracefully down to a stage, empty at the moment save for three stools, some amplifiers, a formidable set of drums, a couple of guitar stands, and several young men in jeans and T-shirts acting importantly amid a battery of microphones. An older man, nattily got up in a white polo-necked sweater, slacks that were a shade too tight, and a camel-colour hacking jacket whose side slits, whenever he moved, gaped like the beaks of ravenous nestlings, went to and fro speaking what appeared to be an officious word or two to now one, now another, of the young men who continued with their tasks without making any apparent acknowledgement of his existence. The backcloth to the stage was made of some dense black material decorated with an enormous rainbow. When the cloth moved, as it did from time to time, stirred by some draught or by bodies moving behind it, the rainbow, sewn all over with sequins, glittered and rippled in a scaly way that Jurnet, for one, found distinctly off-putting.

'And why a black cloth?' he demanded, ramming himself into his grey-upholstered seat. At least the seating was comfortable, that was something to be thankful for. If he had only thought to bring along a pair of ear-plugs he could have been in for a tolerable evening, even managed to snatch a bit of shut-eye. 'Never yet saw a rainbow in a black sky!'

'Magic!' pronounced Miriam. She had taken off her white coat, and with it the air of knowingness which so often troubled her lover: *what was it she knew that he didn't?* In her red dress, very short, she looked as young as the kids all about her. Her eyes, bright with excitement, were wide and wondering as a child's. If there was any difference between her and the teenagers breathlessly awaiting the appearance of their idol, it was, thought Jurnet, that she looked too innocent. Looking about him, the detective decided ignorance was OK, even something to be cultivated lovingly like a pot plant with its own finicky likes and dislikes in the way of light and water. But innocence! Acne was more socially acceptable.

Miriam said, 'This is a night when anything could happen, rainbows in black skies included. For heaven's sake, Ben Jurnet—' she smiled with a radiance nicely calculated to take the sting out of her words— 'can't you forget you're a policeman, just for once?' She leaned forward in her seat and pointed approvingly downhill: 'Why, even that golden oldie in the front row, the one in the Fair Isle pullover, keeps bobbing up and down like a yo-yo—'

Jurnet followed the direction of her finger and commented, 'Not surprising. It's God who's jerking the string. That's his Lordship the Bish.'

'The Bishop! Got up like that?' Digesting her, at first, disapproving surprise. 'Well, there you are, then! If even he can enter into the spirit of the thing, why can't you?'

The Bishop, benignly tonsured by time, in tweeds but with a pectoral cross to show that his heart was in the right place, was dividing his pleasantries between his chaplain, a young man with the terrible defensive jokiness of the lesser clergy and more teeth than he knew what to do with, and a grimly unresponsive middle-aged woman whose ample upholstery of bosom and bum was encased in a floral stretch cover at the end of its tether.

Miriam, appalled, exclaimed, 'That's never the bishopess!'

'Name of Lark, can you believe it? Chair, as they say, of the Parks and Recreation Committee.'

Jurnet bent forward for a better look. The ageing trendy in the hacking jacket had come down from the platform and was making himself pleasant to the distinguished guests. The Bishop bounced up and down co-operatively, the only one in the whole audience, the detective decided, who looked as innocent as Miriam. Parks and Recreation sat unmoved and unmoving.

On the stage, the gleaming array of drums and cymbals stood about on their insect-like supports, waiting for the kiss of life. Yet, strangely, the beat was there already. Stealthily, so that one could never have noted its beginning, it filled the air, as explicit as if the great Lijah already sat enthroned there, commanding the bass and the tom-toms, the snare and the hi-hat, to jump to it, babies, let's get the show on the road.

In the circumstances, then, when a deep, gong-like note resonated through his head, pierced his solar plexus, and fanned out into the space between his shoulder blades, Jurnet did not at first think to seek its origin outside himself. It was the beat, the beat. Only when Miriam nudged him and whispered, 'Lijah Starling!' did he realize that the drummer had indeed arrived and was greeting his subjects.

Black against the black backcloth and dressed in black

from head to foot, there he was, the noble figure Jurnet had last seen convulsed on a cross in the Market Place, resurrected, white teeth flashing, braids click-clicking, pink palms moving tenderly to adjust the angle of a cymbal, the tension of a snare.

There was no applause, except from the Bishop's chaplain, forever doomed to do the wrong thing for the right reason: none of the delighted screeches of recognition Jurnet remembered from the old days. Only a small collective sigh.

Not long now.

Next to appear was Johnny Flowerdew, the bass guitar, dressed in black like the drummer, but his whole appearance, nevertheless, so studiously undramatic as to appear, in that context, quite shocking. His guitar tucked under one arm like a tennis racquet, he raised his free hand in desultory salute to anyone who might be about, crossed the stage and plugged the instrument into the electrics with the absent-minded ease of one popping a slice of bread into the toaster.

All in all, it was a little gem of comic mime, a momentary lessening of tension nicely calculated to deepen the intensity of what was to come. Jurnet felt Miriam's hand seeking his own, which he surrendered with an astonished thankfulness, as if the two of them had never held hands before.

I am my beloved's, and my beloved is mine.

Save for a weak bulb or two over the exits, the lights went out, onstage and in auditorium alike. In the distance a drum began to beat—impossible that it could be Lijah Starling playing with his shiny toys. The sound came, or seemed to come, not just from far away in distance—from outside the hall, outside the University—but from far away in time.

Far. Farther. Farthest.

In the beginning was the beat.

The drumbeat grew louder, nearer. Out of the darkness the bass guitar hailed its approach with deep, happy notes of recognition. The guitar became playful; teased the approaching drum, dared it to hurry up, go faster, come. The rainbow on the backcloth gleamed softly for a second

or two, then burst into a brilliance which bathed the black
face of Lijah Starling and the white face of Johnny
Flowerdew in impartial orange. Jurnet passed his tongue
over his dry lips.

Cheap, noisy, brainless, were adjectives which occurred
to him fleetingly, glancing off his consciousness like tan-
gents off a circle, touching but not intersecting. His fingers, entwined with Miriam's, had become hot and a little
sweaty.

Cheap, noisy, brainless, he reminded himself, without
conviction.

In the beginning was the beat.

And the beat was God.

A rustle went through the audience. What began as an
inarticulate whisper expanded into a cresting wave of sound,
its tone something between a petition and a demand.

'*Loy!*'

It was the damnedest thing. There he stood, all in white
between his black-clad companions, his back to a rainbow
returned to its original scaliness; a gangling youth with
pale, pinched features, nothing to write home about, the
only note of colour his straight, reddish hair falling to his
shoulders—hair that could have used a comb to advantage,
to say nothing of a wash. *That's* the great Loy Tanner?
There he stood, this bleached object, this nullity, possessed of a beauty so intense and so strange that the
beholder, drawn by some invisible magnet, was absorbed
into its strangeness and its beauty, dazzled by its wonder,
racked with the pain of its transcendent loneliness.

'Loy!' cried a voice among the multitude of voices crying
'Loy!' as if their owners had beheld the heavens open. It
came as no particular surprise to Jurnet to discover that
the voice was his own.

Loy Tanner sang. His voice, like everything else about
him, there in the Middlemass Auditorium that cold March
night, was beautiful and strange. Etched against the backing of drums and guitars, it rose high and true as a choir-

boy's, except that it was no child's voice which enmeshed its hearers in a web of honeyed sound and held them there, collaborators in their own extinction. There was no perceivable showmanship, no acknowledgement, even, that an audience was there at all. He sang, strumming his guitar as if absent-mindedly, swaying slightly backwards and forwards—much as, Jurnet suddenly recalled with no sense of incongruity, Rabbi Schnellman every sabbath in Angleby Synagogue rocked to and fro on his heels whilst he chanted the praises of the One Lord, blessed be He.

Except that Loy Tanner's song was directed to a very different address.

> 'The woman clothed with the sun,
> She is the one!
> She holds me,
> Enfolds me
> In a close embrace.
> Face to face,
> I feel the heat of her flame.
> She calls me by my name.
> She illumes me,
> Consumes me,
> The woman clothed with the sun—
> The one!'

6

Outside, in the one-time kitchen garden, the cars were frosted under the freezing moon. They started sluggishly, moved off uncertainly, as if, like their occupants, reluctant to resume the life they were made for.

As Jurnet edged his vehicle along at walking pace between the crowds still patiently waiting, Miriam said suddenly, 'Go by the Market Place, would you mind? I'd like to take a proper look at those crosses.'

'OK. If you want. Though why—'

'I've never seen them close to, and I should think they'll be taking them down after tonight.'

'If you want,' Jurnet said again, contriving to make his ready compliance sound grumpy and disobliging. The detective was feeling deeply angry with himself. For the best part of two hours of twang, bang and boom, of indifferent tunes and crude vulgarizations of Biblical texts which deserved a better fate, he had been—like Bottom in *A Midsummer Night's Dream*, and with as little say in the matter—translated. That all about him were fellow-asses in similar case was no consolation. When the lights came up in the interval he had seen them moving their heads about, vaguely smiling, unable or unwilling to surface out of the cheap but potent fantasy in which they had been submerged.

Down in the front row the head of Mrs Lark the Chair nodded slowly to and fro like the head of one of those china mandarins, black-pencilled moustache and all. The Bishop's chaplain, in an attempt to regain his poise, blew a trumpet voluntary into his handkerchief. Only the Bishop, so jolly earlier, looked thoughtful, touching the cross on his breast every now and again: even a little scared.

Miriam had kept her head turned away, withdrawn her hand.

'So you enjoyed it after all,' now, in the car, she stated calmly, out of the depths of her lovely coat. Her instant grasp of the situation only put Jurnet even more at odds with himself. 'Don't look like that!' Miriam protested. 'What's wrong about enjoying a really first-rate group? No need to act as if you've just come out of a blue movie and you're wondering if you oughtn't to make a clean breast of it to the Superintendent.'

'Not a question of enjoying or not enjoying. Question of being used, manipulated. Brainwashed.' Jurnet glowered at the chapped young faces illuminated by the car's headlamps. 'Look at 'em! Waiting for the great Loy Tanner to come past like he was Princess Di or Christ walking on the water. Pathetic! And you know what? Chap other side of me said actually the group have got a couple of caravans parked somewhere in the grounds, so he isn't even coming. Always travel like that on tour to avoid the crowds, he said. Never put up in hotels. *And* all the fans know it. So what do these kids think they're doing, standing about getting pneumonia for nothing?'

'They must think it's for something, or they wouldn't be doing it,' the other pointed out reasonably. 'It's a free country. It's not yet an offence to be young and besotted, thank heaven. Personally—' Miriam stretched herself luxuriously, her right hand momentarily touching the detective's thigh—'I feel great—used, manipulated, brainwashed and all. An evening I'll never forget, if I live to be a hundred.'

Suppressing a sudden wild desire to press down the accelerator, charge through the waiting ninnies to get there faster, Jurnet said, 'Let's go home and go to bed.'

'Lovely idea. Only by way of the Market Place, if you please.'

The city centre, as always, once the workers and shoppers were gone for the day, was empty, with the air of a civilization suddenly deserted for some awful, unfathomable cause, an urban *Marie Celeste*. Not all that long ago,

Jurnet remembered, feeling unaccountably bereft, people had actually lived on those upper floors above the shops; so that, long after closing time, squares of light had spilled out into the dark, people passed to and fro behind window panes. On warm nights, when the windows were open, you could hear music as you walked along the street, or the ten o'clock news, voices raised in anger or love. Now, there was nothing but the shop-window dummies, their mindless eyes giving back the orange of the street-lights.

Scarcely a car either, since the Council had belatedly awakened to the treasure it possessed in the medieval city and promptly put it into pickle in the middle of a one-way system based, so the natives swore, on the maze at Hampton Court. Even Police Headquarters, that ever-open eye, presented a dark face to the Market Place, all its nocturnal business—after-hours entrance, car park, garage and all—concentrated round the corner in Almoners Hill. On the Market Place itself, cats with amorous intent stalked the skeletal stalls, sliding like shadows across the cobblestones.

Everywhere, that is to say, that bilious dinginess which, in the city, passes for dark:—everywhere save in the strip of garden at the top of the market slope, where floodlighting threw into terrible chiaroscuro the three figures hanging on their crosses. In that theatrical projection of white light and black shadow their situation no longer seemed cause for pity. Scornful and irreverent, they confronted their surroundings with a massive contempt. An air of violence seemed to have gathered about them like winter fog. A promise of resurrection? More a threat.

Solicitous of the long-suffering greenstuff, Jurnet parked his car further along the road where, earlier in the day, the bandy-legged man had parked his van, and ushered Miriam through an official opening in the wall, flanked by some dwarf cupressus. Still fiercely at odds with the contradictions in his own nature revealed to him by Second Coming in concert, the detective kept his eyes resolutely away from the tableau which occupied his lover's absorbed attention. What the hell was she doing, anyway—she, of all people—gazing up worshipfully at the primal cause of Jewish grief through the ages? Bruised by the night's happening, he ached with longing to lie with his head between her breasts.

More in anger than love he said, for the umpteenth time, 'Let's get married.'

'Oh, Ben!' She did not deflect her gaze, her tone preoccupied rather than tetchy. 'How many times do I have to say so we shall, just as soon as—'

'I'm a Jew—I know! As *soon* as! That's a laugh! Rate things are moving, I'll be lucky to make it before the Messiah comes.' Taking Miriam by the shoulders, and twisting her about so that she was obliged to face him: 'Look—it isn't as if you're a pillar of the synagogue. You drive on the sabbath, you don't fast on Yom Kippur, and you're crazy about snails—so what's it all in aid of, this making of conditions? Some kind of fancy brush-off?'

The other chose not to take offence; said simply, turning back towards the crosses and tilting her head the better to study the faces of the crucified, 'In 1290, I think it was— anyway, not long before all the Jews in England were kicked out for good—they took a boatload of Angleby Jews, more than three hundred of them, saying they were going to deport them to the Low Countries. They sailed down the river to the estuary; and there, waiting for the tide to change, the captain invited his passengers to disembark on a convenient sandbank. Stretch your legs, why don't you, while you have the chance, is what he said: there's a long journey ahead.

'The Jews were so crammed into that little cockleshell they were glad to take advantage of the offer, perhaps even pleasantly surprised at such kindness from a Gentile. Except that when the tide turned and there was once more enough water under the keel to get moving, but before the Jews had time to climb on board again, the captain gave the order to weigh anchor and off they went, the ship and the sailors, leaving the Jews to drown as the water rose higher and higher and, at last, covered the sandbank completely. One of the crew said later that the Jewish fathers held their children high on their heads so that they would be the last to go. Funny: if it had been me out there with my child, and the water creeping up to my chin and my mouth and my eyes, I think I'd have held it under right away. Why prolong the agony?'

In the same level tone Miriam continued, 'Today it couldn't happen quite like that. Even if human nature is still capable of such behaviour, at least we've learnt to swim. But just the same, just in case someone should ever again take it into his head to turn the Jews of Angleby out on to a sandbank and sail merrily away, just in case—I want to be dead sure the man I marry is right there beside me, not waving goodbye from the shore.'

At that moment the floodlights went out. Reduced to the general level of night, the figures on their crosses became no more than the rest of the Market Place clutter.

Startled, the two drew together. Miriam gave a little 'Oh!' of concern. Jurnet laughed for the pleasure of finding her unexpectedly close. 'Wrath of the Lord!' he proclaimed.

'You!' protested Miriam, but not disengaging herself. 'They must be on a time switch.'

'Aren't we all? Time for bed, like I said.'

7

The telephone rang. Jurnet had the impression that it had been ringing for a long time. Even so, he made no move to reach out, lift the receiver off its hook.

The telephone went on and on. The cloud of bronze hair on the adjacent pillow, the one bare shoulder showing above the duvet, did not move. Little liar, the detective thought acidly, regarding hair and shoulder with love but not all that much liking. Worn out, was she, by the exertions of the night?

Oh yes, they had finally made it; gone to bed together, made love—if those were the right words to describe a hasty and vacuous greed it shamed him to remember. If that, he thought, the phone dinning in his ears, was what an evening of pop music did for you, come back, Ludwig van B., all is forgiven.

A body deliciously warm and buoyant pressed itself against him. From under the duvet a voice cooed, 'You aren't going to answer—oh, good!'

The options thus put into words, there was no alternative. Coppers always answered the phone, God rot that clever dick, Alexander Graham Bell.

There was no further sign of life from the bed as Jurnet dressed hurriedly, sluiced face and hands in the bathroom, grimacing with distaste at his reflection in the mirror, the chin rimmed with the dark stubble which every morning made him look more like something the Mafia had dragged in than a pillar of Angleby law and order.

No time to shave. The digital clock on the bedside table, one of Miriam's few so-called improvements, which he never glanced at without a pang of regret for the dear old wind-up alarm she had given to a CND jumble sale without even asking, jerked out 5.01 in its baleful green, and then 5.02 before he had comfortably accommodated himself to the earlier figure. With the old clock, time slid away unnoticed, not in a convulsive St Vitus' dance. God rot him too, the saintly jerk, along with AGB.

Outside, on the crumbling concrete of the forecourt, black plastic bags of rubbish put out for the dustman blocked the exit to the street. The detective hauled them aside, muttering only 'Bloody hell!' when one of them burst open, depositing a glissade of time-expired tea-bags over his trouser hems. He was in the car and reversing before he realized that the windscreen was frosted over, had to stop, fumble under the dash for a rag which was inevitably oily, and smear an approximation of visibility before getting on his way again.

As one who had long ago accustomed himself to the cosmic absurdity of violent death, none of this surprised Jurnet. The Superintendent awaiting him in the Market Place, combed and shaved, in cashmere coat and trousers whose creases were pure poetry, was no surprise either. In their early days of working together, the detective had deeply resented the effortless immaculacy of his superior officer, but no longer; recognizing that a higher authority than the Police determined who were nature's scruffs and who its swells.

Detective-Sergeant Ellers, arriving a moment later with his grotty old sheepskin car coat done up on the wrong buttons, redressed the balance, a little. In the first light the little Welshman's rosy chubbiness looked washed out. For that matter, the whole Market Place looked as if the departing night had taken with it more than its dark. Down among the stalls an occasional light, swinging in the wind, showed where some early bird was already at his daily pyramid building, heaping up the mounds of apples and cauliflowers, carrots and sprouts that, once the day cast off its early misery, would turn the market into a patchwork of colour, as pleasing to the eye as to the palate.

The Superintendent said without preliminaries, 'We'll

have to make do with what we have. There's no way we can get our screens up high enough, and I'm hanged if we're going to provide a spectacle for the populace.'

'Dr Colton—' Jurnet began.

'He's over there already. With that new fellow, Stanfield or something, the biologist. Not that there's much, if anything, either of them can do here beyond a formal assurance that we haven't got ourselves out of bed at this benighted hour without sufficient reason.' With the familiar touch of acerbity that made Jurnet's face stiffen with equally familiar dislike, 'We're not likely to do much better if we hang about.'

Whoever else had caught it, Jurnet reflected fleetingly, stepping with the others over the low wall on to the flower bed, it was curtains for the daffodils. The three of them, true, moved with practised care: but just wait till the scene-of-crime boys really hit their stride, going over every crumb of earth with a fine-tooth comb. Then—never mind the daffs—even the worms, gone down deep to get away from the frost, would wish they'd never been born.

On Angleby Market Place, in the cheerless light of dawn, a figure hung from the great central cross. Prepared as he was, Jurnet caught his breath, suppressed an exclamation for which, in the circumstances, there was no need to apologize. Admittedly, in his years in the Police, he had seen a fair number of men and women dead by violence. But it was, on the other hand, the first time he had attended a crucifixion.

8

'Like I told the officer on the desk, I brung over my first load from the van—onions it was, good old Ailsa Craig, you don't see all that lot about nowadays—and what do I find but them great feet sticking out under the skirting board like there was some bloody down-and-out bedded down there for the night.'

Nosey Thompsett took out a grubby handkerchief and blew a fanfare on the nose which was one of the sights of Angleby. By the time he had finished, that organ had lost some of its pallor and once more displayed, albeit in a delicate mauve rather than its normal clotted purple, the customary network of veins which striated it like a map of his native fens.

'Except,' its owner continued, stuffing the handkerchief into the pocket of an even grubbier windcheater, 'I knew all the time, really, no tramp in his right mind would be sleeping out in last night's weather barefoot and without so much as a bit of cardboard against the cold. And o' course, when I seen that ruddy great nail through the middle of the instep—'

The Superintendent prompted impatiently, 'Well?'

To Jurnet's not all that secret pleasure—it was part of the rum game, without winners or losers, he and the Superintendent played unremittingly—the market trader ignored both interruption and speaker and addressed himself to the Detective-Inspector exclusively.

'Believe me, Mr Jurnet, I know a creepin' Jesus when I see one, specially one that's been giving all of us here on the market the willies, hanging up there in the garden all week like the washing hung out to dry. First go off, I reckoned some of the lads been having a bit o' fun after closing time, ho ho ho, I don't think. Sense of humour's a

peculiar thing, I always say. But why me, for Christ' sake?'
The nose flared momentarily purple with affront. 'A whole
van to unload, Mr Jurnet, an' me there on purpose to
make an early start, never mind my fingers an' toes, to say
nothing of you know what, dropping off wi' the cold. But I
knew it weren't no good shifting the bloody thing somewhere else. You lot'd be bound to find out, you're so
clever, an' think I was mixed up in it, some way. So I left
it just as it were while I come up to the station to say what
I'd found—'

There was another pause. The handkerchief reappeared,
this time pressed into service to wipe lips that needed no
wiping; that were dry, and trembled a little.

'I come up them steps into the garden'—the tremor had
transmitted itself to the words spoken—'I didn't go anywhere near those fuckin' crosses—I'm chapel myself, I
don't go for graven images—I weren't even looking that
way. All I wanted was to get it reported an' done with. But
I did look, Mr Jurnet. I had to. Like someone said, "Over
here, Nosey," an' then took hold of my head an' twisted it
round. Even then, my first thought was, tha's funny! He
can't be in two places at once.

'An' then I looked again—'

Loy Tanner hung naked and dead on the centre cross in
the Market Place garden. On either side, the effigies of
Lijah Starling and Johnny Flowerdew still suffered their
emblematic agonies. But they had become meaningless—or
rather, Jurnet amended, obscene travesties, juxtaposed, as
they now were, to the real live death that hung between
them. The detective saw nothing contradictory about his
choice of adjectives. Violent death, in his book, did indeed
have a life of its own. It was a monster to be exposed and
disarmed, a monster and an obligation. An obligation put
upon him Ben Jurnet, personally. A settling of accounts
between a killer and a victim in no position to do the job
himself.

Not that he personally felt any more drawn to the Loy
Tanner who, the night before, had, against his conscious
will, enslaved, enchanted and enraged him. In the begin-

ning might be the beat, chum, but not in the end—oh, not in the end! No heart pulsated in that carcass tied to the cross by someone who, all too obviously, had been in too much of a hurry to make a proper job of it. It was a stranger who hung there, head flopped against one shoulder, lank hair over a face invisible save for a single eye which stared out at the burgeoning day with supreme incuriosity.

The Superintendent observed bad-temperedly, as if the sight of such sloppy workmanship offended him, 'The wonder is he ever stayed put in the first place. One side's all right, but the other! Those cords round the wrists and feet, and that belt fastened round upright and waist together—if anything of a wind had blown up during the night he'd have come down like Humpty Dumpty, bringing the cross with him. Picture cord, is it, or what? We'll see. My guess is the belt's the fellow's own.' With a disdain that, in other circumstances, would have made Jurnet's mouth twitch at the corners: 'It looks the kind of flashy rubbish a pop singer might wear.'

The detective, who had been studying with a kind of paralysed attention the thin line of pink-tinged ooze which, originating at the back of the dead man's head, had meandered a turgid way across throat and chest to deposit a terminal moraine just above the elaborate silver belt which had earned the Superintendent's disapproval, said, 'I never noticed him wearing it last night, though he could have had it on underneath his sweater, I suppose, and not showing.'

The other, as Jurnet had known he would, made no attempt to hide either his astonishment or the dark suspicions that went with it. 'Don't tell me *you* were at that concert!'

'Yes, sir.'

'Unplumbed depths,' commented the Superintendent with a dourness that for a moment made the other wonder if his superior officer weren't himself a Second Coming freak. 'From all I hear of the demand for tickets, I can only hope you didn't queue for yours in police time.'

'No, sir,' Jurnet returned neutrally, determined to provide the bastard with no further information, nor any explanation he wasn't entitled to. But then, immediately, because, bloody hell, there it was again, that inescapable compulsion to tell the bugger everything he ever wanted to know, more than he wanted to know: 'Somebody passed on a couple they weren't using.'

'Somebody must've wanted to get into your good books—' the tone was brazenly sceptical—'considering what they were fetching on the black market.'

'Not me, sir. My fiancée—'

'Hm!' The Superintendent said no more, Miriam being the one subject between them upon which it was silently understood that a strict communication blackout prevailed. Jurnet, for his part, squirmed in inward mortification. *Fiancée*—of all the wimpish words! Yet what could he have used instead? My life, my love, my live-in torment? He'd like to see the Superintendent's face if he had.

The Superintendent squinted up at the sky, daring it to be day before he was ready for it; then, turning to Jack Ellers, commanded peremptorily: 'Sergeant, let the men know they've got another two minutes, not a second longer, to get that body on its way to the mortuary, or we're going to find ourselves with an audience bigger than they had at the Middlemass last night. As to that cross he's hanging on, I don't care how hard the frost is, I'll give them another five minutes to get it out of the ground and on its way. Pinner must have taken enough pictures to fill an album. From here on we'll have to make do with those.'

'Yes, sir.' The little Welshman set off on his errand, happy to have something specific to do.

'And make sure those screens go up at once,' the Superintendent called after. 'Such as they are. Round Thompsett's stall as well. I'm assuming that by now that waxwork of Jesus is safely with Forensic, or if it isn't, I want to know why.' To Jurnet, with a friendliness as unexpected as it was welcome, and as chancy to put your trust in: 'I'll leave it to you, Ben, to pick out some PCs you reckon impervious to the charms of the grief-maddened maidens who, I suppose, will be converging on the spot in their millions once the news is known. We'll be needing crash barriers too.'

'Might be a good idea to get the other two crosses down right away as well. At least take away some of the drama.'

'Absolutely right!' But the Superintendent shook his head all the same. 'You know as well as I, Ben, the Police can't remove them just like that. Quite apart from the bishop excommunicating us with bell, book and candle, what that gorgon at Parks and Recreation might stir up by way of revenge I don't care to think. The damn things are supposed to stay up till Easter.'

'I didn't know. Still, a crucifixion without Christ—' Jurnet began reasonably.

'Even more delicate! Think of all the theologians who've been praying for that very thing! No—we'll have to pass this one to the Chief. Definitely a matter to be settled at the summit . . .'

In the garden above the Market Place, the screens had gone up at last, obscuring the effigies of Lijah Starling and Johnny Flowerdew from the waist down. At least the plaid jockstrap and the baby-blue shorts were no longer in evidence, Jurnet thought thankfully. The centre cross was down, and with it its burden of death. Over by the kerb, two men were shutting the rear doors of the mortuary van.

Absent, Loy Tanner was more than dead: null. Murdered, the last song sung, the pop star had been transformed into an intellectual exercise, a puzzle to be solved like it might be *The Times* crossword. No prizes offered for a correct solution, only a load of stick if you miffed it.

Carrion.

A brother.

For a moment, heavy with the weight of their thoughts, the two detectives stared into the awful emptiness between the two remaining crosses. Then they turned and made their way uphill, back to Headquarters: side by side, but not speaking.

9

'One or more, that's the question.' The Superintendent leaned forward in his chair, his carefully tended hands moving fretfully among the photographs strewn about his desk, picking up here one print, there another, for a brief, dissatisfied glare before going on to the next, and the next. 'Tanner looks light enough. All the same, no easy job to hold him in place while you get those cords tied and that belt cinched, all the time balanced on top of a ladder—'

'I'll go for one myself.' Jurnet, standing with Sergeant Ellers at the further side of the desk, spoke with conviction. 'Two would have made a neater job of it.'

'Do you think so?' The Superintendent was in one of his perverse moods—which Jurnet, making all due allowance, recognized as his superior's personal reaction to violent death just as his, Jurnet's, was anger. What the detective had never succeeded in discovering was the real target at which the perversity was directed—the murderer inconsiderate enough to leave no visiting card, or the subordinates too thick to recognize a clue even if it stuck them up the what's-it with a meat skewer.

Unless it was the corpse itself, the dumb bugger, knowing all, yet silent as the grave.

The Superintendent went on with the same air of insult, 'He, or they, had to get down that statue of Christ before they could string Tanner up in its place.'

'Nothing to it,' Jurnet proclaimed confidently. 'The hands and feet weren't really pierced. The nails were only for show. Each figure has rings at the back for hanging on to hooks which are fixed to both the horizontals and the verticals of the crosses. No more difficult than hanging up or taking down a curtain.'

'Where'd you get that idea?' The Superintendent went back to his irascible turning over of the police photographer's handiwork. 'I can't find anything here that shows—'

'Can't you, sir?' Jurnet's tone was a little too innocent. 'I must just have happened to notice it.'

'Ben's right,' Sergeant Ellers confirmed, without batting an eyelid. 'If you'd turned the Christ over at Nosey's stall you'd have seen the rings sticking out of the back.'

'If you say so.' Glowering, the Superintendent latched on to another of Pinner's shots. 'This one shows several blurred impressions where a ladder stood, or rather, was shifted about. Metal. Got one at home just like it.' Peering closely: 'Fairly deep, all of them, so probably made before the frost set in and nothing to do with us.' Jurnet and Ellers exchanged glances, the latter's full of suppressed mirth. 'For all we know, Mrs Parks and Recreation shins up there every day with a feather duster.'

Taking evasive action, the little Welshman inquired, 'Anything yet from Dr Colton?'

'Time you knew better than to ask! Just as light doesn't show up till it strikes something, so words don't exist for the good doctor until they're typed in triplicate, each copy on different coloured paper, for filing in three separate cubby-holes known only to himself and God.' Relenting: 'I did, however, after several abortive attempts to reach him by phone, elicit a return call, in which he finally admitted, if with considerable reluctance, that Tanner was indubitably dead, most probably as the result of several blows from a blunt instrument which was on the small side but fairly heavy. As to the time of death—as usual, he wants to have a word with the Meteorological Office, *Old Moore's Almanac* and the man in the moon before committing himself.'

Jack Ellers asked, 'Is he suggesting Tanner was actually killed right there in the Market Place?'

'I'm quite sure he's doing nothing of the kind. All the indications are that he was killed elsewhere.' The Superintendent sat back and his patrician features suddenly relaxed into a smile of great sweetness. At the sight Jurnet's spirits lightened almost as much as if the smile had been intended for him.

'What I like about Barney Colton,' the Superintendent

said with a confiding affection, 'what I honour the man for, is that, whatever the pressure, he will never compromise his integrity with facile guesses, not even to get an importunate superintendent off his back. Time of death is devilishly difficult to ascertain, and nothing's going to make Barney pretend it's an exact science when it isn't. For the moment, at least, we can usefully speculate only as to the time the body was placed on the cross.'

'It certainly wasn't there around eleven,' said Jurnet, well aware of what he was starting. 'There wasn't anybody then, except a few cats on the prowl. Apart from anything else, the floodlighting doesn't go off till 11.20. I can't see a murderer, however barmy, deliberately choosing to crucify his victim in the full glare of the floodlights. He'd be bound to wait until they went off.'

The Superintendent said coldly, 'From what you say, *you* appear to have been about in the Market Place, Inspector.'

'Yes, sir. My fiancée and I—' Jurnet's frown was occasioned less by being obliged once more to raise the curtain on what he did with himself in his own time than by the necessity of having to employ again that despised appellation—'my fiancée and I stopped off there on the way back from the concert. We didn't know about the crosses staying up till Easter, and she wanted to take a closer look at them. They were certainly all present and correct at that time.'

Deciding he might as well get everything relevant off his chest once and for all, the detective continued, 'She—my fiancée, that is—' he stammered a little, fancying, quite without foundation, the Superintendent's upper-crust face stiff with disdain—'she knows Tanner's mother. Miriam—' hanged if he was going to repeat the bloody word one more time!—'runs a knitwear-manufacturing business, and the woman is one of her outworkers. She'll need to be told.'

'So she will.' The Superintendent, unpredictable as ever, seemed suddenly to have recovered his good humour. 'Every one will need to be told, or, if not, will want our guts for garters.' His gaze wafted jovially from Jurnet to Sergeant Ellers and back again. 'What we have on our hands, God help us, is not just another murder. We have a media event, something that's going to sell record-breaking numbers of newspapers and keep television commentators in the style to which they are accustomed.' Eyes bright with irony, he announced, 'This is a solemn moment, gentlemen. We have become part of the great British right to know.'

Allowing a moment for the awfulness to sink in, the Superintendent resumed.

'There'll have to be press conferences, of course—'

'Dave Batterby—' Jurnet interposed desperately, naming the detective-inspector whose ill-concealed ambitions to rise in his profession were the source of much discreet amusement in Angleby CID—'Dave'd be the one for that.'

The Superintendent exclaimed, 'That's the first time, Ben, in all our years together, I've heard you actually *ask* for help! Wonders will never cease. But you disappoint me. Those romantic looks of yours on the box could do wonders for our corporate image. Still—'

'Right up Dave's street. He'd do fine.'

'By which you mean—' the Superintendent's eyes twinkled—'as you don't intend to tell him a damn thing anyway, he'll be in a perfect position to keep the press informed with all it needs to know! Ah well! At least it will enable me to assure the Chief, scout's honour, when he asks—as he's bound to—that Detective-Inspector Jurnet, this time round, is definitely one of a team, not a CID Lone Ranger galloping off into the sunset regardless.'

The phone rang, relieving Jurnet of the need either to concede or dispute an observation admittedly founded upon long experience. Control, asking for Mr Jurnet.

The detective took the receiver and listened, while the Superintendent drummed his fingers on his desk a little louder than was convenient.

Jurnet spoke into the mouthpiece, 'Get it picked up and brought in for examination right away. Set it up, will you, Mary? And tell Hinchley he's to stay where he is meantime, on the chance somebody turns up looking for it. Ta, love.' Handing back the instrument: 'The van—they've found it on the Chepe. From the look of it, it appears to have been parked there for some hours.'

'And what van is that?' inquired the Superintendent, making a noble effort to control his irritation.

'The one belonging to the group. A Datsun 1300. Jack and I happened to notice it yesterday in the Market Place. It's pretty hard to miss, actually. White, with a rainbow painted on it you can see a mile off. Soon as we got back here I put out a call, asking patrols to keep a look out. I'd already ascertained it wasn't parked back at the University, where you'd have expected it to be, overnight.'

The Superintendent stated in flat tones, 'There has to be something else special about it beside the rainbow.'

'Yes, sir. We'd both of us noticed yesterday that it had a ladder in it.'

'Ah!' The Superintendent sat silent for a moment, contemplating his beautifully manicured fingernails. Then he said, as if the conversation had never been interrupted, 'You realize it's the post-mortem bit that's going to grab the mesmerized attention of the world. Why should someone, having killed a man and put himself already into enough jeopardy, God knows, think it worth taking the additional risk inherent in fastening his victim's corpse to a cross in a public place?'

Sergeant Ellers ventured, 'Not all that much risk, sir, if you think about it. Nor, if you know Angleby, all that public either. I reckon the Himalayas must be a hive of activity compared to the town centre at night. At least the Himalayas have got their Abominable Snowman, which is more than you can say for us.'

'Death of a god,' murmured Jurnet, the only one of the three present to have been at the concert the night before. Even so, the instant he said it, he wished he hadn't, feeling daft and vulnerable.

As for the Superintendent, he got up from his chair, giving no indication that he had heard. He crossed to the window, and stood looking out and down: a symbolic action only, any view of the remaining crosses being cut off by the wing of City Hall which housed the Registry Office. When he turned back towards the room, the man's expression was one of grim humour.

'Can you imagine what they must have said, over at Jerusalem CID all those years ago, when they found out what had happened? Happened afterwards, that is. The empty tomb, and all that. How in heaven's name are you going to keep your statistics straight if the dead refuse to lie down? At least,' the Superintendent concluded, 'we must be grateful for small mercies. God or no god, this one's not going to rise on the third day, if I have to sit on him myself!'

10

The sun was shining when Jurnet and Sergeant Ellers parked their car in Gallipoli Street and turned the corner into Sebastopol Terrace, a kindly sun that graced the mean little houses—built of a raw brick that more than a hundred years of English weather had not succeeded in mellowing—with a spurious, period charm. Even so, the sunlight could not disguise the terminal dilapidation—the sagging gutters, boarded-up windows, the bits of mosaic missing from the lengths of path up to the front doors. A gap-toothed vacancy between a derelict Number 14 and a Number 22 propped up with a wooden buttress which looked itself on the verge of collapse seemed to have become the rubbish dump of the neighbourhood.

Only a number of estate agents' boards flaunted like banners along the ramshackle fences promised better things. 'This delightful bijou residence,' one of them had the cheek to offer, 'ripe for modernization.'

'Ripe!' Sergeant Ellers looked about him with narrowed eyes. 'Family trouble,' he pronounced, at the end of his inspection. 'Either that, or lacking in the top storey. Say what you like, no mum in her right mind with a famous pop-singer son would be hanging out in a dump like this if the two of them were on speaking terms. Why, it's the only bloody one in the whole Terrace left in occupation.'

'What suits some people doesn't suit others,' Jurnet returned with some heat. 'And you can leave Loy Tanner out of it. On what Miriam pays them they don't have to live here if they don't want to. You'll have to go a long way to find an employer who pays her outworkers more than she does—'

'Hold on!' the other cried. 'No insult intended to your

48

intended! Only, honestly, can *you* understand it? Would *you* choose Sebastopol Terrace if you had the choice?'

Carefully keeping the envy out of his voice, Jurnet said, 'Miriam says they're very happy here.'

The bright red door of Number 12 was ajar. As Jurnet gingerly wielded its brass knocker in the shape of a dolphin, a woman's voice, low-keyed and pleasant, called from inside: 'Come on in! Coffee's on the table!'

It seemed an unlikely welcome to bearers of ill tidings. The two detectives, one after the other, stepped out of the sunlight into the tiny hall, no more than a passage really.

This was a part of the job Jurnet could well have done without. He could have kicked himself for not, after all, bringing along a WPC to do the tea and sympathy bit, except that after what Miriam had told him about Mara Felsenstein it had seemed a kind of insult to proffer such phony comfort.

It was not so much that the grief of kith and kin, informed out of the blue that their nearest and dearest had been savagely done to death, upset him unduly. Somebody had to tell them, Jurnet accepted that. Rather, it was the overwhelming sense of his own inadequacy which always, at the opening of a murder investigation, undermined his confidence of ever bringing it to a successful conclusion.

At least, those who were thus incontinently bereaved mourned a real person. They had someone to remember. All Jurnet, the outsider, had to be going on with was a carcass, evil-smelling offal taking its revenge on the air it could no longer breathe by polluting it. Only when, by a laborious process of inquiry and elimination, he had eventually come himself to know the man or woman all the keening was in aid of, would he begin to understand the grieving; even—so close by then had the two of them become, the quick and the dead—to share it.

In the meantime, as he murmured the conventional phrases of condolence, he seemed to be talking about someone else.

There was no door to the front room which opened

immediately out of the passage, only a curtain of some dark-brown stuff, looped back. Within was a room lit by a window at either end, the rear one giving on to a narrow strip of garden where a substantial wash, a regular spring-cleaning, bedspreads, covers, curtains, flapped on a line as if to advertise that even in such unpromising surroundings a decent cleanliness could still flourish unimpaired.

Mrs Felsenstein, the houseproud housewife, Miriam's paragon, sat at what Jurnet assumed to be a knitting machine, one of a pair facing each other, though at first glance (perhaps it was the way the knitter's fingers moved, knowledgeably but with a loving concentration) they looked to the detective more like musical instruments: spinets possibly, or something else that stood upon spindly legs and, when played upon, emitted antique sounds that seemed to come from another planet.

As the detectives entered, Mr Felsenstein came in from a back room and took his place at the second machine where, its ribbed lower edge held straight by some small pieces of plastic hooked into the fabric, a substantial length of knitting hung down from what one might call the key-board, like music already played, waiting to be rolled up and put away. Not a spinet, Jurnet amended his earlier thought. More a pianola.

Sitting there facing each other, the silence broken only by a gentle hum which Jurnet realized was the sound made by the machines when they were working, the two, intent upon what they were doing, presented a picture of calm companionship which moved the detective to hope his task might be less disagreeable than he had anticipated. Those two could support each other.

Once the man stood up, and the detective had got a good look at him, he was less sure, so frail was the bent shape, twisted, with one shoulder higher than the other.

'Excuse us, please!' Mr Felsenstein exclaimed. 'Mara thought you were the milkman.'

Jurnet could not resist asking, 'Do you always invite your milkman in for coffee?'

'It is time for his break, is why. Before, he would go to the café, and we'd get no milk until he began work again, by which time, often, we were forgotten entirely, or, on a hot day, the milk had gone sour.' The man smiled, the bony contours of his face dissolving into a droll humour. 'So not kindness, you understand. We can take no credit for it. Expediency.'

Mrs Felsenstein slid the carriage of her knitting machine backwards and forwards two or three times along its bank of needles, her lips moving in a silent count. Satisfied she had reached a point where it was safe to break off, she looked up and said pleasantly, 'If the gentlemen will be good enough to tell us why they've called, Leo, perhaps we'll offer them a cup of coffee too, just to show we can on occasion be kind without ulterior motive.' Smiling at the two detectives: 'That is, if they don't mind it black.'

Not one of the hysterical sort at least, Jurnet thought thankfully, though he should have gathered as much from his conversation with Miriam the night before. Yet, at first sight, his expectations having been aroused, he was disappointed by the reality—a woman of average height and rather heavy build, dressed in a black sweater and patterned skirt, with shoulder-length brown hair tied back from a face which was in no way out of the ordinary, save for the eyes.

At a second glance, the eyes made up for everything else. Large and grey, they were the eyes of a child, disconcerting in their direct and uncomplicated gaze.

Apart from the knitting machines and the two kitchen chairs on which their operators sat, the room contained only a small couch, its loose-cover of a beige fabric faded but crisp and fresh, two more chairs to match the others, and a small table whose flaps had been let down. Plain brown curtains, unlined; no carpet, except for a hearthrug, but polished floorboards that filled the air with the smell of wax polish only slightly spiked with overtones of sulphur from the fire of smokeless fuel which flickered dispiritedly in the narrow grate.

Nothing to get into *Homes and Gardens*, that was for sure: but satisfying, in a way Jurnet could not easily account for. A home, not a collection of other people's ideas of what a home should be.

The woman sitting at the knitting machine was similarly her own and nobody else's. Mara Felsenstein, the detec-

tive decided, feeling at the same time a little dismayed by
the extravagance of the image, was—if her eyes were to
be believed, and if eyes like that could lie, nothing was to
be trusted—a woman of a startling purity of soul.

She did not disappoint him when he told her that her son
was dead, murdered. Leo Felsenstein groped blindly for
the couch, collapsed on to it with his head in his hands,
emitting a rusty noise that seemed to heave itself like
vomit up from the depths of his protesting body. His wife
sat deathly pale but silent, even managing a small smile
when Sergeant Ellers brought her some of the coffee from
the kitchen, and sipping obediently when the little
Welshman lifted the cup to her lips.

She did not sit long. She crossed to the couch with
unfaltering step and went down on her knees by her
husband, her full skirt spreading out over the floorboards.
She pulled away the hands and laid her face against his.

'Liebchen . . . Liebchen . . .' she murmured. 'It's all
right. We can bear it—' And, looking up at the two detectives, hovering full of goodwill but embarrassed by the
necessity of being there at all: 'When he was a boy, Leo
was in Auschwitz. He has had as much death as he can
manage.'

For a little, while they waited, she rocked the man in
her arms, until the horrible sound abated. Then she said,
without self-pity: 'Loy promised to come by this morning,
just for a quick look-in, before the group left. Just to say
cheerio.'

Jurnet said, 'I don't want to worry you now with
questions—'

'Oh, but you'll have to, won't you, sooner or later?' The
prospect did not appear to daunt her. 'You want to catch
whoever did it.'

'That is certainly our intention.'

The woman got up from the floor, sat down on the
couch beside her husband and took a mis-shapen hand
between her own two, strong, but red and roughened by
work.

'You're cold, my darling.' With a little laugh that seemed

such a token of intimacy between the two of them that Jurnet was pierced through with shyness simply to have overheard it: 'You were right as usual—I should have left the fire for you to do. All that mess and ash and coalite, and still hardly anything to show for it! Whatever will you say when you find out I've used up all your stock of papers just to get that miserable thing going?'

Leo Felsenstein responded shakily, 'One double sheet— how many times must I tell you?—torn into strips and crumpled up—' He broke off, pulled his hand from the woman's grasp and put it over his mouth. 'The boy! The boy!' he whimpered.

'The boy,' she agreed, recapturing the hand and kissing it on the palm with a tender delicacy. Looking up at Jurnet: 'You'll find him,' she pronounced. 'The murderer. You don't look a man to give up. But—' and to Jurnet's relief (there was such a thing as being too strong) the wonderful eyes, for the first time, spilled over with tears—'I can't see how I—how we—can help. We know nothing.'

Jurnet said gently, 'It often seems like that, when in fact there are things—important things—you may know without realizing that you know them. We'll talk about them later, when you feel able to. Letters your son may have written you, telephone calls. Things, however trivial, he may have said when he came to see you. Most of all, you know your son. We need to know him too.'

'We know nothing,' Mrs Felsenstein repeated, shaking her head. She had begun to tremble slightly. In the absence of the WPC, Sergeant Ellers, who knew the signs, looked about for something to drape round her shoulders; found a cardigan on one of the chairs and brought it over. The woman pushed it aside impatiently.

'Loy never wrote letters. Not to us, at any rate. And we're not on the phone. He popped in, just for a minute, Tuesday, the day he arrived in Angleby—the day before the concert—but he was in such a hurry Leo didn't see him at all. He'd gone to bed early, and Loy wouldn't let me disturb him. If I'd known there would never be another chance—' She suddenly sobbed aloud, a sharp, crackling sound, cut off abruptly.

'Forgive me—' Jurnet cleared his throat. There was a

limit to how long you could go on pretending a murder inquiry was a social call. 'I take it you and your son were on good terms?'

'Loy? Oh, yes!' Mrs Felsenstein was looking as if the unlovely noise she had just made had surprised her. 'It's only that the life he's led has taken him far away from us. What he wanted was to take us with him. Only—' she looked round the humble little room with love and pride —'we didn't choose to go. Did we, Leo?' Her husband, slumped in a seeming daze of exhaustion, said nothing. Mrs Felsenstein went on, stumbling a little over the words, 'I want you to know, Inspector, Loy was a loving and dutiful son. Always sending us money. We would send it back, of course—what did we need money for?—but in a little while he'd send it back again, as if he'd forgotten what we'd said. And then we'd have to send *that* back. It became a kind of game—'

'Weren't there letters with the money, at least?'

'It wasn't necessary. He knew we'd know where it came from.'

'You must have felt upset he couldn't spend a bit more time with you when, for once, he was actually back in Angleby.'

'A pop star's life isn't his own. We'd long ago accepted that. Besides, as I've told you, we *did* expect him, this morning. We quite understood that up to then he'd be much too busy with rehearsals, publicity appearances, and all the rest of it, to say nothing of the actual performance.'

'Was the arrangement about this morning made on the Tuesday evening then?' Jurnet felt obliged to persist.

The woman looked at the detective with a kind of mournful amusement. 'Do I gather I'm to have the honour of being your first suspect? His own mother! How terrible it must be to have the imagination of a policeman! But I mustn't play games with you—' the lovely eyes filled with fresh tears—'the road manager came round with a message. He said Loy would be looking in tomorrow—today, that is—before the group left town. He also brought two tickets for the concert, which we accepted, but later gave away to a friend, for her and her young man to use. It seemed a pity to waste them when they could give other

people pleasure. I wouldn't have said no to them anyway,
so as not to hurt Loy's feelings, but the truth is that pop
concerts aren't, as they say, our scene, not even when our
son is the lead singer.'

' "Our son",' Jurnet repeated stolidly. It seemed as
good a time as any for getting that little matter behind
him. 'I understand Mr Felsenstein is not Loy's natural
father?'

The woman looked at the detective, surprised, but in no
way put out.

'How clever you are, you police, to find out all about us
so fast!' After a moment's silence she added, her voice low,
'And have you also been clever enough to find out who the
natural father is, and what is his address and telephone
number?'

'We'd hoped you could help us there.' But Jurnet knew
already, from the way Mrs Felsestein had pronounced the
two words 'natural father', as if they were words in a
foreign language of whose meaning, without having a dictionary handy, she was uncertain, that the hope was ground-
less. 'Naturally we feel under an obligation to get in touch,
if only to let him know what has happened.'

'Naturally!' This time the irony was unmistakable. 'The
best help I can give you in that quarter, Inspector, is to let
you know that Loy's natural father—assuming he is still
alivè, as to which I have no idea—has no knowledge that
he ever fathered him. When we parted he did not even
know I was pregnant—I didn't know it myself—and I
never enlightened him.'

'I see.' Thankfully reverting to a former topic, Jurnet
asked, 'You mentioned the road manager. Dark chap with
short legs, would that be?'

'That's the one, poor man. Mr Scarlett. He also said that
Loy had told him to ask if there was anything, anything at
all, I wanted, and he'd see I got it, even if it was the
moon.'

'And what, if anything, did you ask for?'

'I told Mr Scarlett to tell him to get his hair cut.' She
cried a little at the recollection, whilst the two waited,
wondering when the real floodgates would open, cravenly
hoping it might be after their departure. 'Not that I ex-

pected him to take any notice—the moon would have
been likelier!—so I wasn't disappointed when I saw his
picture in the *Argus* and there he was, hair flopping over
his face same as usual!' The woman's eyes had become
brooding, fixed on the past. 'Even as a little boy, it was
the same. Reach for the scissors or the shampoo and he'd
vanish, anything to get out of having it done—'

Jurnet said, 'I'm afraid that I have to ask either you or
your husband to make a formal identification—'

'Not Leo!' she returned immediately. Then, 'Right away,
do you mean?'

'If you feel up to it, and you'd rather get it over—'

'Is he—is his face—?'

'Nothing like that.' Jurnet added, despising his own
hypocrisy, 'He looks very peaceful.'

'I'll get my coat.' Gently she disentangled her fingers
from those of her husband, and stood up.

Jack Ellers said, 'I'll keep Mr Felsenstein company till
you get back.'

'No!' Leo Felsenstein struggled to his feet, and stood
swaying. 'I'm coming with you!'

His wife answered with loving but dismissive kindness,
'No, my darling. Not this time. This time is my business,
my son. I bore him live and now I must see him dead, or I
shall never truly believe it has happened.' She kissed the
thin, trembling figure full on the lips with an unselfcon-
scious passion that made Jurnet draw in his breath sharply.
'Besides, what will the milkman say if he doesn't get his
coffee?'

11

In daylight, the foyer of the Middlemass Auditorium, lit from above by vast areas of glass which let in the frigid skyscape of an East Anglian March day, had quite lost its air of mystery. Warm as it was within doors, Sir Cedric Middlemass's gods and goddesses had a pinched and diminished look. For all their brash coloration they stood, in that English light, revealed as what they were—refugees admitted on sufferance to massage the vanity of their self-proclaimed cultural betters. Winding his way between them to the little group forlornly awaiting his arrival, the detective felt closer to being a Jew than he had ever felt before.

The three people who awaited him stood up as he approached, and drew together defensively.

'Is that the policeman you phoned for?' demanded a voice which came from none of them. From behind a tumescent hunk of tree topped with a head-dress of parrot feathers emerged a grey-haired man with metal-rimmed half-spectacles and a bad temper. He was followed by the man Jurnet had noticed onstage the night before telling the technicians how to do their job, the man with his vanished youth squeezed into clothes a size too small. Today he had exchanged his jackets and slacks for jeans and a denim blouson which, unbuttoned, disguised his waxing paunch with more success than he had any right to hope for.

Despite this sartorial coup, the man didn't appear to feel good. He stood glowering at Jurnet and the grey-haired man impartially.

'Detective-Inspector Jurnet, Angleby CID.' Jurnet announced himself in the tones of clipped reassurance televi-

57

sion had taught the public to expect of its guardians of the
law. Phonies always brought out the phony in himself.
'Did you say "telephoned", sir?'

The grey-haired man returned waspishly, 'We certainly
didn't send a carrier pigeon!' Peering over his glasses with
eyes narrowed: 'I suppose you have a warrant card?'

Jurnet produced the evidence, then said pleasantly, 'Matter of fact, sir, I'm here on another matter altogether, one
of some importance. Still, if there's any urgency, perhaps
you could let me know briefly what the trouble is. No
doubt another officer will be along directly in response to
your call—'

'In other words, tell it twice over! Typical! What makes
you think, Inspector, that this, too, is not a matter of some
importance?' The grey-haired man directed a look of loath-
ing at his denimed colleague. Effecting the introductions
without grace: 'I am Professor Whinglass, head of the
Department of Archaeology. And this, as you may or may
not be aware, according to whether you do or do not
watch the quizzes and chat shows which abound on
television—' he made them sound like some new pond
weed which had got out of hand—'is Professor Culliver,
who occupies the Chair of Contemporary Institutions in
this University.'

There was no mistaking the contempt in the voice, or so
the detective would have thought. Professor Culliver, however, appeared to mistake it completely. His face cleared,
assumed a blend of self-satisfaction and mock-modesty which
approximated to charm as near as made no matter.

'Simon Culliver,' he corrected, in a voice that was carefully young, like his clothes. 'And whatever Lionel here
may tell you, I want to go on record at once as saying that
I utterly refuse to accept that any of the marvellous kids
who were at the concert last night were responsible. Kids who
are turned on by Second Coming simply aren't like that.'

'Like what, sir?'

Professor Whinglass turned away without looking back
to check that the others were following. He led the way
between the breasts and the buttocks to a plinth faced
with knapped flints which stood in a curved niche a little
apart from the rest of the Middlemass Collection.

'Like the bugger who did this,' said the Professor of Contemporary Institutions.

The figure on the plinth was no more than eighteen inches high, a woman in the last stages of pregnancy, the belly enormous, the udder-like breasts hanging to below the navel. Thick legs ended in stumps that paddled in the crude basin which made up the base of the statuette. The features, barely indicated, were flat and expressionless, save for a tiny mouth, stoic and implacable. Hair crimped into unlikely waves fell down the broad, strong back.

Jurnet took in the statue at once; took it in whole even though, in actual fact, its head lay on the floor amid a mess of flaked chalk, whilst one breast reposed in the basin looking like a sloppily put together pork sausage. Shattered as it was, it was indestructible.

Professor Whinglass said, as if mouthing a curse, 'Out of all that ineffable junk they had to pick on this.'

'What is it, exactly?'

'We call it the Hob's Hole Venus, after the place where it was found. Hob's Hole is one of the many open-cast flint workings dating from Neolithic times to be found in the Norfolk Breckland, between Brandon and Swaffham. You've probably heard of Grimes' Graves, where no less than 366 separate pits have been located. Hob's Hole is just the one excavation, but approximately of the same period, around 2100 BC.' Directing at the violated torso a look of desolation which for a moment transformed his dyspeptic countenance, the Professor continued, 'We take it to be a votary figure to which those early miners brought offerings to ensure their safety in the tunnels and caves gouged out of the chalk. It is, of course, far from being the only figure of this kind to come to light, but in quality it is quite unique. None of the others comes within miles of it either conceptually or, in the context of the time, in audacity of execution. In its beauty it is in a class by itself.'

'Beauty! Cripes!' Simon Culliver opened his eyes youthfully wide. 'Look, Lionel—I couldn't be more sorry it's been damaged—ancient artefact, and all that. But beauty! It's bloody hideous!'

'If you say so.' It was obvious that the Professor of Archaeology couldn't have cared less what were the opin-

ions of the Professor of Contemporary Institutions. Jurnet
he eyed with a kindlier air. The detective's reaction to the
statue had not been lost on him.

'Can it be mended?' Jurnet asked.

'Something can undoubtedly be done, and will: though
it is galling beyond words that an object which has survived unharmed for four thousand years should be mutilated on the mindless whim of some retarded adolescent.'

Professor Culliver insisted, 'I'll say it once more. The
concert had nothing to do with it!' To Jurnet, turning on
the boyishness as far as it would go: 'I'm the one he's
really getting at, Officer, because it was my idea to bring
Second Coming to the Middlemass in the first place. Dear
old Lionel—he thinks nothing's gone right with the world
since we made the dreadful mistake of changing over from
BC to AD.'

The severed head lay on the floor turned towards the
detective. *Beautiful?* It depended what you meant by
beauty. Ravishing, if you like. Ravenous. The size of that
belly, it could have been her old man in there along with
the baby, swallowed whole once the poor sucker had
served his turn. Aloud, he said, 'I must say it surprises me
not to find such a unique object locked up in a glass case.'

'Or here at all,' Professor Whinglass growled. 'I couldn't
agree more. The man who found her—an amateur but a
person of wide knowledge—very properly turned her
over to the Museum who, most magnanimously, decided
it should go to the archaeological collection we're in process
of setting up here at the University. You can imagine
how gratified we were to be promised a piece of international importance. Only unfortunately Sir Cedric Middlemass
saw it as well, and he, God help us, thought it would fit in
splendidly with his own graven images. And, in this University, when Sir Cedric says jump, we all jump. If it had
been the Venus de Milo instead of the one of Hob's Hole,
and he'd fancied her in a bikini and grass skirt, a bikini
and grass skirt it would have been.'

'That shouldn't have affected giving the statue some
physical protection.'

'Sir Cedric,' the other explained drily, 'lays particular
stress on what he calls the tactile values, a credo which he

appears to derive from a study of the shelves of his super-
markets. Though I imagine he might change his mind if
the customers started toppling his stacks of instant coffee
or rice crispies.'

'I'm sure he would, sir,' agreed Jurnet, who was beginning to feel that a little academic bitchery went a long
way. He greeted with relief the approach of Detective-
Inspector Sidney Hale, long-faced and melancholy, his
face, as ever, that of a man saddened by the world's ways,
but never surprised by them.

Well, almost never. Even Sad Sid looked a little bemused by the Middlemass Collection.

Eager to get away, though in no way sorry to have kept
his real clients waiting—when it came to interviewing
people who, you never knew, might wind up as suspects
in a murder investigation, a little angst never did anybody
any harm, except those with something to hide—Jurnet
made the introductions and put Sid in the picture in a
verbal shorthand which, to their ill-disguised annoyance
when it came to the point, left the two academics with
little to add.

'*Simon* Culliver,' the Professor of Contemporary Institutions was insisting winsomely, as the detective turned
away.

The three who had been left waiting, Jurnet was quite
pleased to note, were looking angry. Anger was a more
amenable emotion than grief, part of the normal human
in-flight baggage. Men and women spent the best part of
their lives het up about something or other. Grief, on the
other hand, took study, even talent. A ritual to be celebrated with a due regard to tradition and propriety. Like
all skills, you couldn't expect to get it right first time.

'Sorry to have had to mess you about—' he began.

'Messed *us* about?' Queenie King protested shrilly. Her
green quiff, unlacquered, hung down over her childish
forehead, her pointed little face was stiff with malice.
'What about the way you geezers messed up our caravans,
then? Everything turned arse over tip—'

Jurnet, who had been present at the search and distinctly turned off by the slatternliness of the Dormobile which, it appeared, was the General Assistant's home from home, nevertheless returned placatingly, if with tongue pleasurably in cheek, 'I'm sure you'll find everything put back exactly the way it was. We're very grateful to you—to you all—for your co-operation.'

'Fat lot of choice we had!' the girl retorted, thrusting away the hand with which Guido Scarlett had touched her arm. The man's expression of loving commitment did not waver. 'If Loy was here, you'd never dare!' She stopped abruptly, put a skinny hand to her mouth. 'Oh Christ!' she wailed.

Johnny Flowerdew's anger was more complicated. His clown's face twisted into planes of impatient derision, he rested his lean length against the stubby flanks of a Mayan fertility god, and demanded, 'How long before we can get moving? I hope you peelers understand we've a gig in Nottingham tonight, every ticket sold out weeks ago.' The voice was carriage trade. Definitely not another working-class boy breaking into the big time on the strength of four guitar chords and a double-jointed pelvis. 'The boys drove up there with all the gear directly after the show. They'll be wondering if we haven't had an accident and are lying drenched in our gore somewhere along the A52.'

'You'll have to get on to them, won't you, and explain just what kind of accident you *have* had—that is, if they haven't heard already, over the radio, or on TV. I'm afraid, Mr Flowerdew, you're going to have to put up with our company a while longer. There are questions that have to be asked, and we shall require you all down at Headquarters to answer them. As I know you're all at least as anxious as we are to apprehend Mr Tanner's killer, I'm sure we can rely on your full co-operation. In any event—' Jurnet cast his eyes over the young man deliberately, a long, speculative gaze—'can you and Mr Starling seriously be planning to put on a show, just the two of you?'

'You mean, without Loy we're not worth the price of admission?' The other's face broke into a smile of unexpected appeal. 'Flattering, I must say! If you'd ever heard Lijah drumming you'd know he could fill the Albert Hall on his own and still have half the population of the UK milling around outside screaming to be let in. All I do, admittedly with a little assistance from Moses, King David, and a few other ideas men from the same agency, is write the numbers. I'm dispensable,' the young man said likeably. 'No illusions. It's just that I thought you ought to know it's going to cost you a packet if we have to cancel. If I know Lenny, he'll sue the police for every penny they've got.' Johnny Flowerdew finished, po-faced, 'Just thought you'd want to be put in the picture.'

'Ta very much. Do I know this Lenny? Your solicitor, is he?'

'Christ! There's actually life on earth that hasn't heard of our Lenny! I don't believe it!'

Guido Scarlett interposed in the angry voice which was his normal mode of speech, 'Stop arsing about, Johnny, will ya! He'll have us here all day!'

Jurnet nodded bland agreement. 'Longer, I shouldn't be surprised.'

'What I tell you?' The man came forward, rolling on the pitiable legs at which, Jurnet noted, the girl stared without pity. 'Lenny Bale. Our manager. Puts the show on the road an' takes it apart again. Don't know why he ain't here 'cept he had to go up to London yesterday sudden an' must have got back late. Too late for the show, anyhow. First time he hasn't showed at one of our gigs since he had his tonsils out, three, four year ago. Having a bit of a lie-in, I shouldn't wonder, and hasn't turned on the news.' The roadie's dark face turned suddenly sallow and exhausted. 'Loy gone!' he whispered hoarsely. 'I still can't believe it!'

Johnny Flowerdew said, 'You'll believe it tonight, Guido baby, when a whole twenty-four hours have gone by without anybody once calling you a frigging dwarf, a bandy runt, or a misconceived abortion, to name but a few—'

'You—!' The other lunged forward, not, as was to be expected, fast enough for the guitarist, who moved aside with no appearance of haste. Scarlett's fist lammed into the belly of the Mayan god who rocked slightly on his pedestal but seemed otherwise unmoved. A trickle of blood from the roadie's abraded knuckles settled into the statue's sandstone navel, where it appeared quite at home. 'Keep your filthy mouth shut!'

'Not *my* mouth, man. I was only quoting.'

'I can see we shall have plenty to talk about,' the detective observed, addressing his remark to all three impartially. 'Where's he staying, then, this Lenny what's-his-name?'

'The Virgin—' naming Angleby's most prestigious hotel, called after Queen Elizabeth I who had slept there on three separate occasions—with whom, if anyone, nosey parkers had still not given up trying to discover. The roadie burst out, 'He's the one supposed to be looking after us! What's he doing, for Christ' sake, lying there dead to the world, an' Loy crucified like he was the Son of God?'

'*I am my beloved's, and my beloved is mine*—' Lijah Starling came into the Middlemass foyer carolling. His voice seemed literally to change the nature of the light coming through the great skylights, infusing the grey with a Caribbean glow. Unless it was just a coincidence and the sun was coming out anyway.

The detective could not remember ever seeing a man, of whatever colour, so handsome, so well-formed, and so—not unaware, for that would have been to label him simple-minded and the man was plainly no fool—but so dismissive of his natural advantages. Not one for pretence either, by the look of it. No anger, real or assumed. Positively no lamentations for a mate bizarrely done to death. None, even, of the conventional postures of regret one might well, in the circumstances, have thought it politic to display in the presence of a police officer.

Unless it was that Lijah Starling had chosen his own, unique way of celebrating the death of Loy Tanner.

At the sight of him Queenie King screeched and covered her face with her hands. Guido Scarlett cried out, 'Jesus!' Johnny Flowerdew, eyes shining, came forward and grasped the drummer by both hands. Drew him to where Jurnet stood silent, wondering.

'What d'you think of that, then?' Johnny Flowerdew demanded proudly, almost as if he had had a hand in it. 'What d'you think of that?'

Lijah Starling himself said nothing. Waited, smiling.

His hair! Gone were the clattering braids, shorn off close

to the skull with more enthusiasm than art. In places the skull was all but bare, the skin several shades lighter than the skin of the man's face. In others, sawn-off squiggles stood straight out from the head like a hybrid tea pruned rashly back to its last bud. For the rest, a springy frizz was divided by a criss-cross of canals where the hair had been drawn tight for plaiting.

Absurdly, Jurnet's first thought was that the man must be missing those jolly beads click-clacking companionably; and as if he had read the detective's mind, the black man stretched his neck, ran a hand luxuriously from nape to forehead, and announced with a smile of relief, 'Man, that bloody racket was sending me round the bend!'

The guitarist asked, as if it were a matter of importance, 'You didn't throw the hair away, Lij? You could have had it made into a necklace.'

'Or a wreath,' Lijah Starling said. 'In memory of our dear departed brother. What I did, man, I made a fire. Down by the river, under the trees. A funeral pyre. Very solemn. Very sacred. And I burnt them, one by one.' He paused and corrected himself. 'All except one, that is. One of the gardeners nearly had a fit when he saw me scorching his pretty grass, so I gave him one, to show I was sorry. At first he just got madder, but when I pointed out that one of Lijah Starling's braids would fetch good money, he let me be, except to ask could I make it a couple, chummy, while I was about it!'

'Old Caribbean custom?' Jurnet enquired carefully.

The noble structure of cheekbones and mouth dissolved in gargantuan laughter. 'Old Caribbean bullshit!'

'Then why?'

'Because Loy's dead—why else? Snuffed it, copped it, gone to meet his Maker. Hosanna in the highest and the lowest! Because at last I'm free, man. I'm free!'

12

Jurnet did not think much of hotels. In his book they were not real places, their public spaces full of a spurious luxury, their private ones of a spurious living. The very air that pervaded those human pigeon lofts seemed to him ersatz, specifically designed to deprive the brain of oxygen and thereby encourage the fantasy that life itself was meant to be dispensed in predetermined packages like the little metallic containers of UHT milk on the tea/coffee-making trays, the parcelled-up marmalades and foil-wrapped butter pats on the breakfast tables: hell to open, and once you'd finally managed it, not worth the trouble anyway.

The receptionist at the Virgin desk, her regrets doled out with similarly meticulous portion control, said that Mr Bale had left instructions he was on no account to be disturbed. When the detective produced his card, she compressed her glossy lips into an expression of well-bred distaste, pressed a button under the desk with the finality of one unleashing the nuclear holocaust, and, washing her hands of the consequences, returned to filling a display stand with postcard views of an Angleby that looked no more real than the hotel itself.

The manager, who, as it happened, remembered gratefully the discreet way in which Detective-Inspector Jurnet had engineered the removal of the earthly left-overs of a suicide pact from—the nerve of some people!—the very four-poster which the Virgin Queen herself had once graced with her presence (£15 supplement, excluding VAT) made no further difficulties. Jurnet stepped out of the lift on the third floor to find a chambermaid with a pass key waiting for him.

Outside room 317 a pile of the day's papers lay uncollected.

'Just unlock it, please. Don't knock.'

Jurnet waited until the woman, Portuguese and incurious as to anything that might happen so far from home, had retreated back down the corridor. Then he turned the handle and went in.

The room was dark with the darkness of four-star hotel curtains, lined and light-excluding. The detective found a light switch, switched it on, and made for the window.

He made no attempt at quiet: dumped the papers on the bed en route, purposely rattled the lid of the electric kettle. The shape hummocked under the bedclothes did not stir. Surprisingly, it was the whisper of expensive curtains sliding along their rails which brought Lenny Bale back to the land of the living. The man sat up in bed, squinted painfully at the tall figure silhouetted against the light, and demanded thickly, 'Who the hell are you?'

Jurnet said, dispensing with preliminaries, 'Detective-Inspector Jurnet, Angleby CID. I felt sure that, as his manager, you'd want to be told at the earliest possible moment about Mr Loy Tanner being dead. Murdered.'

The man in the bed stared, shook his head, scrubbed at the thick brown hair which, expensively layered, kept its shape even after a night in bed.

'I'm dreaming this.'

'Unfortunately not, sir. Mr Tanner was killed late last night or in the early hours of this morning.'

'*I'm dreaming this!*' This time the words came out in a shout, the very volume of noise, it appeared, finally convincing the shouter that he was indeed awake. He flung back the covers and swung himself out of bed, a small man, naked and well-made, the body looking too young for the hung-over face which topped it. Jurnet noted without surprise the purple puncture marks on the whippy, muscular arms, and the scars of old ulcerations.

'Loy, you bastard,' Lenny Bale demanded, looking up at the ceiling, 'how could you do this to me?'

'I haven't made myself clear—'

'I heard you!' The other was striding up and down the room now, less grieving than aggrieved. 'Loy's dead.'

'Murder. Not suicide.'

'Murder, not suicide!' the other mimicked derisively.

'As if Loy of all people would be dead if he didn't choose
to be!'

The man came to a stop in front of the dressing-table
mirror; approached the glass as if he had glimpsed therein
something, someone, seen for the first time. For a little he
studied the image, his face expressionless. Then, before
Jurnet could forestall him, he picked up an onyx ashtray
and flung it at his reflection.

Just in time, Jurnet threw up an arm, felt something
wet and warm sliding towards his wrist.

Lenny Bale, himself miraculously untouched among the
sword-sharp splinters, turned away from the shattered
glass and inquired, with a childlike wonder that anyone
could ever have imagined otherwise, 'How could a god
like Loy ever have loved a bag of shit like that?'

The Superintendent stood at his open window, wrinkling
his patrician nose. He complained sourly, 'It smells like a
funeral parlour!'

No one disputed the statement, though, to Jurnet at
least, what wafted into Police Headquarters was no more
than the usual daytime air of Angleby Market Place, an
olfactory cocktail based on cabbages mainly, spiked with
the zest of orange peel past its prime and the fragrance of
the vinegar sloshed so generously over the tiny plates of
seafood set out on the cockle stalls. For a moment, until
sternly reminded by higher centres of his being that his
days of eating shellfish were gone for ever, the detective's
mouth watered—he had, after all, eaten nothing since that
early rising—with longing for a taste of those delicate
morsels forbidden by the Mosaic law. To his way of thinking, cockles never tasted better than when consumed in
the open air, amid the shouting and banter of the Market
Place; the inborn scepticism of Norfolk voices curving up
and over towards the end of every sentence as if in wry
acknowledgement that, properly understood, there were
no such things as statements, only question marks, and
anyone daft enough to expect answers had it coming to
him, bor.

Not that it was like that today. The quiet of the Market

Place had been almost palpable: business poor, people
talking in low voices, even the twittering budgies mum.
Only the flower sellers, albeit a whit shamefacedly, could
not disguise a certain satisfaction—understandable when
even the roses of the day, if not the week, before, their
stems flopping despite all that tight-wrapped polythene
could do to arrest the decline, were going at a premium,
so far did the demand outstrip supply.

Where they were going was no mystery. Making his
way uphill, back to Headquarters, Jurnet had seen the
great tumulus of flowers long before he actually reached
the garden where the crosses had stood. The detective was
relieved to see that the other two crosses and their atten-
dant effigies had been taken away.

Calvary was never like that. Iris, roses, daffodils, tulips,
piled up as if there were a grave beneath—as indeed there
was, if one counted the daffodils; and an unending line of
boys and girls with reddened eyes, a few weeping noisily,
most of them shocked and silent, waiting to add their
tribute to the rest. Even the photographers, darting about
like water bugs on the skin of a pond, could not entirely
devalue the real tears, the real sense of loss.

As Jurnet watched, an older woman, obese and un-
gainly, came forward, purplish channels irrigating the
make-up which plastered her nose and cheeks. Mrs Lark,
Chair of the Parks and Recreation Committee, tenderly
placed a single dark red rose on top of the fragrant heap
and went away, back towards the City Hall, a pink tissue
long past its prime held to her trembling lips.

Who the hell *was* this Loy Tanner, so greatly mourned,
and so very, very dead?

Back in his seat behind the wide desk which put a
proper distance between the star and the chorus line, the
Superintendent fidgeted with the papers in front of him,
then flung out off-handedly, 'Preliminary report on that
van of yours, Ben. Enough prints, inside and out, to send
our lovely new computer into hysterics. Not a single one
clear enough to be of any use. Nothing to suggest the
vehicle was used to transport a body. Further examination, of course, may reveal something of value.' He did not
sound as if he would put any money on it.

Jurnet said, 'Early days.'

The Superintendent was in no mood to be comforted. 'No days are early where murder has been done.' He scrabbled among his papers once more and selected one with scorn. 'It appears that the University, with a faith in human nature granted only to academics and the mentally subnormal, took on, as a temporary guard on the performers' caravans, a pensioned-off old retainer with—can you believe it?—an unpredictable sphincter muscle. In one of his rare surfacings from the jakes, this Argus-eyed Cerberus states that, some twenty or thirty minutes after the end of the concert, he saw Tanner leave the girl King's caravan and go out of the paddock by the gate which leads to the standing normally used by vans bringing supplies to the University. A few moments later he heard a vehicle start up, and a scrunch of tyres on gravel.' There was a pause before the Superintendent ended, 'Assuming it was Tanner in the van, that would have meant he left by the back way, the tradesmen's entrance. The way round to the front had been blocked off earlier in the evening for fear of gate-crashers.'

Sid Hale, close to cheerfulness at finding things turning out as badly as he invariably expected, enquired hopefully, 'And I suppose there was nobody on the back entrance either?'

'Actually, there's a lodge with a resident keeper whose job it is to monitor all comings and going in that direction. Except that yesterday—what ills infest the groves of Academe!—it seems the poor fellow had an ingrowing toenail and had retired to his bathroom for a soothing soak of the same. He says—' rooting for the relevant note with the sick pleasure of de-scabbing a wound—'that he may have heard a vehicle leaving the University grounds, but then again, he may not. When his bath taps are turned full on, hot and cold together, they sound so uncommonly like a motor vehicle it'd be anybody's guess to know if it was one or if it wasn't.'

Sergeant Ellers, taking evasive action, volunteered, 'The Chepe, sir. Where the van was found parked. It's bang opposite the Virgin. Their own car park's such a hassle to get in and out of, especially when you've had a drink or

two, a lot of people going into the hotel leave their cars on
the Chepe instead. And the Virgin's where Mr Bale's
staying, isn't it?'

'So it is, Jack. So it is.'

'You have fight?' the Portuguese chambermaid had demanded, with, for the first time, a light of interest in her
eye. She had entered the room with her pass key, without
knocking. 'I hear smash. I come see if is fight.' She surveyed the broken mirror with disappointment, the hairless
nakedness of Lenny Bale with indifference. 'You no have
fight?' she asked, the animation fading from her face.

'Sorry not to oblige,' Jurnet responded. 'Seven years'
bad luck, that's all. Have it put on Mr Bale's bill, and fetch
me a Band-aid, there's a good girl.' The detective held out
a gashed forearm, blood trickling between his fingers.

'Is nothing,' the chambermaid pronounced, peering: but
her eyes had brightened again. She lifted the hem of her
white apron and unconcernedly tore off a wide strip along
one side. With her strong brown fingers she bandaged the
wound with a deftness Jurnet found altogether admirable,
and said so.

'In Spain one time I live three years with matador. Not
very good matador.'

Lenny Bale complained peevishly, 'I can't stand blood.'
He got back into bed and pulled the covers over his head.
He began to cry, his body shaking, the brass bedstead
tinkling prettily.

The chambermaid left the room and returned a moment
later with a dustpan and brush.

Jurnet said, 'Take my advice, leave it for the blokes
who'll have to come and fit a new one. I'm sure you can fix
Mr Bale up with another room instead.'

'Three doors down is nobody in.'

'Then why don't you move Mr Bale's things in there? I'll
make it OK with the manager.'

Obediently, without asking questions, the woman put
her implements aside, opened the suitcase which stood on
the luggage stand, and with stolid but sure-fingered effi-

ciency packed it with the underpants and shirts from the
drawers, the expensive toiletries out of the bathroom.

'You see I put,' she admonished the detective, picking
up an ornate signet ring, several gold chains, and a watch
that looked expensive enough to buy all the time in the
world, and dropping them into a side pocket of the Vuitton
suitcase.

'I see you put,' Jurnet confirmed with a smile. 'I will
also, when we arrive three doors down, see that you
unput.'

The woman opened the door of the clothes closet, removed the shoes at the bottom and stowed them away,
then took out the jackets and slacks which hung above.
The clothes over her arm, she paused in passing the bed.
The crying, muffled by the bedclothes, sounded not entirely believable.

'*Qué bandalho!*' she pronounced disdainfully.

Jurnet yanked off the blankets, not unkindly. 'Time to
go, Buster!'

Lenny Bale came quietly. The detective draped his
unresisting form in one of the blankets, and led him out
into the corridor. Waiting to be told which way to go, the
man let the covering slip to the floor, making no move to
retrieve it. An American lady of mature years who happened to be passing, ran an experienced eye over what
was on offer and exclaimed 'Cute!' before continuing unruffled on her way.

In the new room Bale made straight for the bed as if
bent on resuming the threnody where it had been rudely
cut off in mid-flow. Jurnet, one hand clamped on a scarred
arm, called across to the chambermaid, busy settling the
man's clothes into their new home, 'Got a dressing gown
among that lot, señorita? Ah!'—accepting a feather-light
cashmere gown, and forcing unwilling arms into the
sleeves—'just the job. Ta! Now—' to Bale, brisk and
businesslike—'no more wringing of hands and beating of
breasts. Let's hear all about it.'

Lenny Bale slumped into a satin-upholstered armchair.
'You came to tell *me*. I don't know a bloody thing.'

'That's what they all say.' Jurnet, changing over to his
rural routine, returned heartily. 'Till they get going. Then

it's all you can do to get them to belt up, there's so much they want to get off their chests. For a start, did you see Loy last night?'

'I did not! I had to spend the whole day in London—and I mean the whole bloody twenty-four hours. Couldn't have been four in the morning when I started out—'

'But you'd only just arrived in Angleby! Hardly seems worth the trouble of coming in the first place—'

'Wasn't to know, was I? Guy from LA passing through unexpectedly. Big wheel in video, biggest on the coast. Phoned the office from Heathrow and they put him on to me here. Had a proposition. Lot of money involved—' Lenny Bale tightened his dressing-gown about him and knotted the girdle. It was obvious that the mere mention of money was a great energizer—almost, one might say with, in the circumstances, a particular aptness, a shot in the arm. 'I couldn't let a chance like that slip.'

'The group must have been a bit put out.'

The manager of Second Coming raised his head in unaffected astonishment. 'Those punks.? If it weren't for me, they'd still be hanging about on street corners, trying to cadge a joint.'

'I take the point. All the same, I suppose you did apprise them of your change of plan?'

'I phoned Guido, if that's what you mean. I'd already had a day to iron out any snags. Anyway, I told him I'd be back by evening—'

'But, in the event, you didn't make it?'

'I made the mistake of driving. I should have left the car in town and come back by train. By the time I got in I reckoned the concert must be about half through, but I was too tuckered out even to ring and ask how things were going. I took a couple of pills and went to bed.'

'Hope your trip to London wasn't wasted.'

'Let's say, the seed was sown.' A tinge of grey had crept into the expensively suntanned complexion. 'If that's the lot, Officer, or even if it isn't, I've got to get some more sleep—'

'I shall need the name and address of the guy from LA.'

'My office will know. The name's Brown. Only you won't find him home. He was on his way to Hong Kong.'

'Came a long way round, didn't he?'

'Not if he wanted to see *me*. Now, if you'd kindly get the hell out of here—'

'What about the others?' the detective countered, with a touch of fatherly reproof. 'They're milling about, out there at the University, like sheep without their shepherd.'

'Shit to that, and mind your own business.'

'Oh, but I am,' Jurnet objected, still doing the artless bit. 'My business is to find out who killed Loy Tanner.'

A sudden sob shook the slight frame. 'Fat lot of good that'll do him.'

'None at all. But hopefully it won't do any to the person or persons who killed him either.'

'I want to go to bed!' Lenny Bale put his fists in his eyes like a thwarted child. 'I don't want to think about it!'

'Unfortunately, sir, it'll still be there when you wake up. That's the thing about death, it only gets deader.' The detective waited a little. Then: 'One other thing you might be able to throw some light on. That white van of yours, the one with the rainbow on it. It was found this morning parked on the Chepe. Could well have been there all night.'

'The Chepe?'

'Name we have for that open space across from the hotel. Acts as a kind of overflow car-park for the Virgin. What I was wondering was whether Loy might not have come by after the concert for some reason.'

Lenny Bale received the suggestion with no apparent unease.

'For none I can think of. If he did, it wasn't to see me.'

'To find out how your business deal had gone, I thought—'

'If you think I'd ever discuss a business deal with Loy, you don't know me—and you certainly don't know *him*.'

Jurnet protested mildly, 'I'm doing my best.'

'What I always say to them, it's a matter of trust. Either you accept without question that I'm doing my best for you, or you get out—right? Did you know—' the man demanded—'that Lijah Starling owns half a dozen streets in Brixton, to say nothing of a flat in Eaton Square and a villa outside Golfe Juan? All my doing, and he knows it. Johnny now, he's county, so he's gone into land. Thanks to me, he's got a couple of sporting estates in North Norfolk with more pheasants than you could count in a lifetime. Neither of them would ever dream of handing over a penny without I say so. Trust, you see. Complete trust.'

'And Loy?'

The other shrugged. 'Two-room dump back of King's Cross, and a beach hut at Havenlea, rented by the season.'

'How's that? What did the lad do with his money?'

'Don't ask *me*! Numbered account in Switzerland, for all I know, or krugerrands under the bed. Fair enough.' Bale's face, which had for a moment crumpled itself into furrows of childish spite, reassumed its aspect of incredulous grief. 'His money, to do what he liked with—'

'Wonder who'll come into it now he's gone.'

'Guido said something about an old ma—'

'You've never met the lady yourself, then?'

The other shook his head. 'Not a chance. With Loy, everything was a secret. Ask him about his mother, he'd have sworn it was a virgin birth.' With a sharp upward look from under the thick eyebrows: 'Did you know he couldn't bear to be touched physically? Touch his hand by accident and he'd jump like he'd been stung.' The man brooded upon this last for a moment, then finished, 'I'll take a bet that's why he chose the guitar—a good excuse to put a hunk of wood between himself and anybody trying to get close.' Voice breaking: 'Don't you find that terribly sad, when the world's so full of people longing to get close?'

Lenny Bale sat down on the bed. 'I really am very tired.'

Jurnet looked at him carefully. Then: 'Sleep,' he said, pulling back the bedclothes.

The detective went out of the room, disconcerted to find the Portuguese chambermaid following behind. He had quite forgotten her presence, so still had she stayed, quiet as a mouse.

Outside in the corridor he closed the door gently, and turned to her. 'Hope you're not going to get into trouble over that apron on my account.'

'Sod that apron,' the chambermaid said surprisingly.

She looked up searchingly into the detective's face. 'Who this Loy?' she demanded.

'Who indeed?'

Jurnet went down to the ground floor, choosing the stairs in preference to the lift. He needed a short interval for thought. The Georgian staircase, swooping in graceful arcs from floor to floor, suited his purpose admirably.

Arrived once more at the desk, he spoke to the receptionist's back. 'Anywhere here I can make a phone call?'

The receptionist turned reluctantly. Her carefully constructed face was a shambles. Out of the ruins a young girl peered out upon a world in desolation.

'I just heard it on the radio. Have you heard the news? They've murdered him, the swine!'

Jurnet answered, 'I did hear something about it.'

13

Jurnet found Johnny Flowerdew the hardest one to explain, to himself as well as his colleagues, as they foregathered in the Superintendent's room. The Superintendent himself had not disguised his derision.

'*Hereditary enemies!* The fellow's been having you on. Unless it's a publicity gimmick he's trying to manipulate us into giving currency to?'

'I don't think so,' Jurnet persisted, in his mind's eye a vision of that knowing face, the dark smudges of suffering under the eyes. 'Hereditary's what he said—but after he'd told me how it was, I couldn't help thinking maybe *heraldic* expressed it better. Like those knights in armour in old tapestries, forever threatening the blokes opposite with their lances, but nobody actually hurting anybody.'

'A game, is that what you're saying?' The Superintendent sounded mollified. Robert Tanner, the great Norfolk rebel, had been one of his childhood heroes, and the historical conceit pleased him. 'Just so long as you're not asking us to believe that Tanner's Rebellion is still alive and kicking 450 years after the event!'

Except that Johnny Flowerdew had asserted exactly that.

The young man had straightened his back against the dubious ergonomics of the plastic chair, issue No. 3760/259/M/ black, eyes narrowed as he peered past Jurnet and the dull green walls, and the snazzy blinds with vertical slats which proclaimed to all and sundry that, whatever some might think, Angleby police had made it to the twentieth century. The eyes, light blue and set in the head with a disconcerting shallowness, looked all the way back to a time when a boy king had sat on the throne of

Tudor England, and in Norfolk the common people were
being pushed out by sheep.

'It all began as a local, a family, quarrel, really. The
Flowerdews and the Tanners were neighbours, connected
by a whole network of marriages and shared business
interests. But—' courteously—'you know all about that.'

'Don't be too sure! Tell me.'

'What a time it was!' Johnny Flowerdew spoke as if he
had been there. 'A farming revolution was taking place,
just like today. And just like today there were money
mountains waiting to be picked up, fortunes to be made
by the wide boys who weren't queasy about turning peasants out to starve and fencing in the common lands where
they'd been pasturing their cows since the year dot. Still,
as my revered ancestor John Flowerdew undoubtedly said,
more than once: there's always a price to be paid for
progress, so long as you make sure you aren't the patsy
who has to pay it.

'Every now and again, men driven desperate by hunger
would go out and pull down the odd hedge or two, for all
the good that did. Well, one day some of these hedge-
levellers paid a call on John Flowerdew who, being the
bloke he was, bought them off by paying them to go and
pull down a hedge belonging to his old pal, Robert Tanner, instead.

' "Old enemy's" what I mean, of course. For reasons I
don't have to go into, those two had had their knives into
each other for years. But it's a funny thing—' Carried away
by the force of his own narration the young man jumped
up, came over to the desk and bent towards the detective
until each could feel the other's breath on his face. 'Up to
that moment Robert Tanner had been in on the land-
enclosing racket as much as any other wheeler-dealer.
Then, suddenly—whether it was the sight of those poor
tykes, the bones showing through their skin, or simply a
pigheaded determination to get his own back on that twister
Flowerdew—it doesn't do, does it, to assume that heroes
invariably act from the highest motives?—from that day
forward he's a changed man, throwing in his lot with the
peasants, and risking everything as the captain of an army
of 30,000 men in armed revolt—'

'And,' interposed Jurnet, who had never had much use for heroes, win or lose, 'ending up dangling from the ramparts of Angleby Castle, to say nothing of leading to a bloody death thousands of simple men who trusted him.'

'That's the amazing thing. Robert Tanner was nobody's fool. He must have known from the beginning he hadn't a hope in hell. John Flowerdew must have split his breeches laughing when he saw him hanging up there, the crows pecking out his eyes.' Johnny Flowerdew laughed in his turn. 'Funny, isn't it, the way time twists everything arsyversy? A paradox, 'pon my soul! There they are, those villainous Flowerdews back in the reign of Edward VI, taking the bread out of the mouths of the poor by planting the very hedges which today's ecologicals throw themselves in front of bulldozers to preserve. So who's to say who's good and who's bad? But when I pointed out as much to Loy, was he wild!'

'Don't tell me either of you took it seriously?'

The other stayed quiet for a moment. Then he said, 'I didn't. Not at first, at any rate. When the two of us first met—it was in some lousy pub in Havenlea—and found out what each other's name was, I just thought, Flowerdew and Tanner, that's a coincidence. But Loy, he took it in deadly earnest, right from the start. Being a Tanner meant a lot to him. It was our karma, was what he said—Tanner and Flowerdew, two opposing poles, light and dark, good and evil, programmed by fate to be at each other's throats through all eternity—' Johnny Flowerdew suddenly covered his face with a long, white hand. When he took it away, his eyes were still dry, but stricken.

Jurnet said, 'You never believed all that guff?'

'I did and I didn't. I don't and I do.' Desperately: 'He devised roles for us to play, don't you understand? For me and for Lijah, for Lenny, Guido, even that pinhead, Queenie. We might not have cared for his type-casting, but there we were, each with his own part no one could take away from us, ever. Now—' the voice, dry like the eyes, held something akin to terror—'we shall have to find out who we are, all over again.'

* * *

Jurnet had said, 'I need to know what you did after the concert.'

Johnny Flowerdew answered tiredly, 'I didn't do anything. I went back to the caravan, made myself some cocoa, and went to bed.'

'Let's take that a bit slower, do you mind? You returned to the caravan, you say, the one you share with Mr Starling, right? Was Mr Starling with you? And what about Loy?'

The other shook his head.

'No one ever knew where to find Loy after a gig. It was one of the unwritten rules—leave the boy wonder alone till he's once again fit for civilized society. Way we all feel after a show as a matter of fact—though me, I go for a mug of hot cocoa. Short of a complete blood change, best thing I know to bring down the adrenalin level and get the beat out of your system till next time. As for Lijah, he's always the last one off the stage, letting down his own tension as he lets down his drums. Last night he and Guido came in just as the cocoa was boiling up. I told Guido there was plenty for three, but he didn't fancy any. He helped Lijah stow the drums under the seat, then he said good-night and went off.'

'Back to his own van, I suppose?'

Johnny Flowerdew responded irritably, 'I suppose. Am I my roadie's keeper? Hold on, though.' A moment's hesitation; then, on a note of apology: 'That's not quite right. Lijah didn't want any cocoa either, and there was this bloke the University had laid on as a bodyguard, ninety if he was a day, out there in the freezing cold. Don't jump to any false conclusions.' The young man stared poker-faced at his interlocutor. 'I am not a caring person. I am, if anything, insensitive and bone-selfish. It was simply that I couldn't stand pouring all that good cocoa down the sink. So I went outside and asked the poor old geezer if he could use a cup.'

'Any trouble locating him?'

'None at all. They've rigged up a couple of floods for us out there, and he was standing bang under one of them, as if he hoped it gave out a bit of warmth as well as light.'

'He must've been glad of the cocoa.'

'As it happens, he said he had a bad stomach and daren't touch it. In fact, he looked so mangy I told him to call it a day, bugger off home. Which he did.'

'Wasn't he supposed to stay on duty till midnight?'

'Oh, was he? Sorry I mentioned it, then. I wouldn't want to get him into trouble.'

'Not to worry. He was only taken on for while you were here.'

'Where did they dig him up? Night like that, I doubt he'd have lasted out till twelve.'

Jurnet smiled. 'Not a caring person, eh? And, to get back to cases, what's it got to do with Mr Scarlett? You saw something—'

The other nodded reluctantly.

'Guido. He was standing outside Queenie's Dormobile. There was a sound of voices coming from inside—too far off to make out whose, so don't ask—and he seemed to be listening. He could have seen me and the old fella easily if he'd happened to look our way. Next thing I knew, he was lumbering off into the dark between the Dormobile and Loy's van. Could have gone to pee for all I know. Too cold for curiosity. I got myself back into the caravan quick as I could. Lijah was already snoring his head off.'

'Could it possibly have been Loy in Queenie's caravan?'

'You'll have to ask her, won't you?' Johnny Flowerdew shrugged. 'Shouldn't think so, though. Sixty seconds of our Queenie's artless prattle was enough to send Loy howling out into the wilderness.' The young man let a little time pass before throwing off nonchalantly, 'I *did* happen to see that ineffable pa of hers backstage before the show. With one of his little playmates, as usual.'

Never one to stand on his dignity, Jurnet waited a moment, then grinned and said, 'You *are* going to tell me, aren't you?'

Demurely: 'I thought policemen knew everything.'

'So we do, usually, by the time we've finished with the rack, the iron maiden, and the Chinese water torture. So tell me about Queenie's pa.'

The Superintendent said with some asperity, 'That phone

call of yours from the Virgin—did we really have to send Dave hotfoot up to London on the strength of it? I know he's only too glad to seize any chance of checking up that the Yard's still there, pending the glorious day he makes his triumphal entry as Chief Commissioner, the trumpets sounding. But do we have to feed the romantic fantasies of every DI on Angleby CID? Jack here would have done just as well.'

The little Welshman nodded vigorous agreement. 'I shouldn't mind being Chief Commissioner either!'

'Dave does have some useful contacts there,' Jurnet returned placatingly, 'and as he'll have to clear it first, he seemed the obvious choice. Beside, I need Jack to chat up the Virgin staff—the late shift that came on this afternoon. Did any of them see Tanner in the hotel last night? From what I've seen of them, ninety per cent at least aren't English, and—' with an affectionate smile in his friend's direction—'being a bloody foreigner himself he'll understand better than Dave how to get on terms with them.'

'That's all very well,' the Superintendent countered fretfully. 'Except that the bloodhounds have been baying for an evening TV announcement, and there isn't a hope Dave'll be back in time.'

'Incidentally, how was he on the morning show?'

The two little curves at either side of the Superintendent's mouth expanded briefly, as he answered, 'Good enough to eat.'

14

Lijah Starling had kept on his hat, a sharp number in white straw with a polka-dotted ribbon: an Easter bonnet which—if it hardly went with the rest of his toilette— concealed the massacre of his hair very adequately.

It was the only thing about him that looked happy. His dark suit and overcoat, conservative in cut, looked in mourning; the dark skin sallow and sad. Hard to visualize the magnificent body buried beneath those undertaker's weeds.

Affecting surprise, Jurnet said, 'And I thought you were over the moon to be free at last.'

'Freedom,' the other returned listlessly, 'is an over-rated state of being.' This time, the detective's surprise was unfeigned. Except for a slight North Country timbre, the man spoke standard English. Gone the velvet consonants, the liquid vowels of the West Indies. Gone, too, as he crossed the room to the seat Jurnet indicated, the lazy, hip-swinging walk that seemed a ballet danced to music just out of earshot. 'Unless there's more than one kind, and I was too much of a bloody fool to recognize the difference.'

'You'll have to spell that out for me in words of one syllable.'

The noble figure slumped: slouched with his hands on his knees, the palms upturned as if deliberately to show off their pink undersides.

Lijah Starling said, 'He turned me into a black, that's what he did.' Reversing the hands so that the dark backs were again uppermost: 'OK, God got there ahead of him, but Loy did it all over again, and this time made a proper

83

job of it—turned me, in the country where I was born, into an alien, an object of guilt and suspicion.'

The man leaned forward, anxious to make himself clear. 'Oh, I'm under no illusion, Inspector. I know I'm not really a white man who has somehow found himself stuffed into a black man's hide: but I'm no Little Black Sambo either. My father's a doctor, my mother's one of the best-known textile designers in the UK. They are people by virtue of their gifts and personalities, not their colour. I grew up in Harrogate—Harrogate! How English can you get?—and I got a good second in Natural Sciences at Cambridge.' The man levered himself out of the chair, his size and power making the room even smaller. 'OK, there were times, even in Harrogate, when they called you a bleeding wog—nobody needed to tell me the world wasn't a Garden of Eden—but it wasn't a white racist hell either—' He broke off abruptly.

'Nobody told you to go along with it.'

'Oh yes, they did! The drums!' With a grin of disarming candour: 'Do I see you thinking, once a wog, always a wog?' Lijah Starling carried on, even as Jurnet shook his head in disclaimer. 'The thing is, I carry my particular jungle inside me, not on show for all the world to see. The drums! I feel them with every heartbeat, in every flutter of my pulse. And when we first got together, Loy and Johnny and I, and set up Second Coming, I knew we had to stay together, whatever the price, even if it was the death of us. We were great, the greatest.'

Jurnet said, 'I know. I was there last night.'

'You were?' The other showed his surprise. 'In that case I don't have to explain, do I, why I let Loy turn me into that ethnic vaudeville act? I'd tell myself, never mind, when the time comes we can't make great music together any more, that'll be the time to make up for the degrading razzamatazz. I'll kill the bastard. It was as simple as that.'

'And was it?'

'What do you mean?' For a second the drummer seemed knocked off course, dazed with his own eloquence. Jurnet found himself wondering if the man had taken a little something to fortify himself for the interview—some speed, perhaps, or a snort of cocaine?

Or had he prepared himself in another way: sat quietly in his caravan, drumsticks moving questingly among the drums clustered like children about his knees, memorizing what they had to say to him? Jurnet said, 'I meant, did you kill Loy Tanner?'

'Don't talk balls! You say you heard us last night. Then you must know we still had a long way to go together.'

'Yet at the same time you hated him.'

'We all did,' Lijah Starling agreed, as if it were the most natural thing in the world. 'Just as we all loved him, the bastard.'

His voice suddenly sharp and unfriendly, Jurnet demanded, 'Love him how? Sexually?' The other sighed. 'Love. Does it come with different centres, like chocolates? Hard or soft, sexual or spiritual, take your pick?'

'Assorted, for all I care. You know damn well if you ever went to bed with your late partner.'

'Oh that!' The man actually laughed. 'Hasn't anyone told you yet about how Loy never let anybody touch him, if he could help it?'

'Mr Bale said something—'

'Mr Bale's gay, I'm straight, what Johnny is not even Johnny knows. Yet we'd all have come running like dogs after a bitch if Loy'd so much as crooked his little finger. Guido would have left his Queenie without looking back, and as for Queenie—! Does that answer your question?'

Lijah Starling leaned forward confidingly.

'You want to know how we all loved Loy? I'll tell you. Hopelessly.'

Jack Ellers asked brightly, 'Are we any nearer to fixing the time, then?'

The Superintendent studied some pages of typescript spread out in front of him. Judging by the expression on his face, the examination gave him no pleasure.

'Simple!' he answered, looking up at the end of it. 'You take the time Tanner was last seen alive, and the time Nosey Thompsett found him. We can then state with absolute certainty that the murdered man met his death

some time between the two. The advances of forensic
science leave one gasping.'

Jurnet said soothingly, 'At least Dr Colton hasn't kept us
long.'

'Not a report, Ben. A sop to keep me quiet.' Glaring at
the uppermost page: ' *"Post-mortem abrasions which could
have been caused by bumping about on the floor of a
vehicle. Star-shaped wound—blood—bone chips—extru-
sion of brain"*— ye gods! If that was all we required of a
PM we could do it ourselves.' Addressing himself afresh to
the police surgeon's memo: ' *"Weapon in doubt—small,
heavy, some indentations on edge, not clear whether fortuitous or man-made. Possibly beach pebble, smoothed by
wave action—perhaps paperweight or similar—"* '

The Superintendent snorted.

'Small, heavy, some indentations on edge—sounds more
like one of the canteen's steak-and-kidneys!'

The duty sergeant had phoned through to say that the
young lady at the reception desk had a letter with her
which she insisted upon delivering in person into the
hands of Detective-Inspector Benjamin Jurnet, and no
other. The duty sergeant had not felt called upon to report
the young lady's exact words, which were, 'I want that
dark, dishy one who looks like he just stepped on a mess
of dogshit.'

The young PC who had escorted Queenie King up from
the ground floor to the cubby-hole opening out of the
incident room had eyed the girl with an envious admiration which had at first astonished Jurnet, and then touched
the springs of his compassion. To a youngster in uniform,
with a short back and sides, how liberatingly anarchic
must seem green hair and clothes that looked as if they
had been posthumously exhumed from the builder's skip
where they had crawled away to die. Maybe all that was
needed to give the police a new lease of life was permission to wear a single earring dangling above the impecca-
ble crispness of the official shirt.

Ignoring an invitation to sit down, Queenie stuck the
envelope under the detective's nose, and warned belliger-

ently, 'If I don't get a receipt, you don't bleeding get it in the first place!'

'I'll have to open it to see what I'm giving a receipt for.'

'Go on, then! It's not stuck down.' Unable to stay quiet while Jurnet extracted the single sheet from the envelope, the girl burst out with an air of childish pride at what she had found herself capable of, 'Thirty guineas it cost me, true as I'm standing here. Hope yer hands are clean!'

Jurnet read the brief paragraph, wondering what its signatory, the best-known gynaecologist in Angleby, had privately thought of the application made to him, to say nothing of the applicant. There couldn't be all that many girls looking the way Queenie looked, to whom it would have occurred to seek medical confirmation that they were *virgo intacta*, let alone who would have been in any condition to procure it.

The girl scanned the detective's face, watching eagerly for signs of a reaction commensurate with such an expenditure of wealth for such a cause: and he did his best not to disappoint her.

'Well, well!' he exclaimed, endeavouring, without much success, to look both flabbergasted and congratulatory. But it seemed to be enough.

The girl reddened with pleasure, smiled quite charmingly. She sat down, crossed her legs, and rested an elbow comfortably on Jurnet's desk.

'One girl travelling round with a bunch of fellows—' she chattered away happily. 'I knew what you'd be thinking, you lot—you don't have to open your mouths, I can read you like a book! Must be a scrubber, it stands to reason— that was it, wasn't it? Not that I blame you. How many girls you meet, my age, still haven't had it off, not even once, let alone got a certificate to prove it?'

'You're the first one I've met,' Jurnet answered truthfully. 'And when we've finished talking, I'm going to get a copy made for our files, so you can keep the original and put it away carefully in a safe place.' The detective had not the heart to point out that such a piece of paper was, like a cheap day return to the seaside, valid only on the day of issue.

'I want yer to know,' the girl said, and something about

the sweet absurdity of her youth caught at the detective's throat, 'that, one way of looking at it, I don't deserve that certificate, whatever it cost me. Because if Loy had ever asked to screw me, the way I felt about him, I'd have let him without thinking twice about it. Even if he hurt me something shocking. Even if he did things—' the girl frowned, the childish forehead arranging itself in prominent ridges—'horrible things you can't hardly bear to think about—'

Jurnet said, 'You got a funny idea what it means for a man and a woman to get together in that way. Nobody hurts anybody.'

'Oh ah?' The small pointed face had become sullen and withdrawn. Queenie King said, 'You want to have a word with my pa.'

15

Sergeant Ellers said cheerio, got into his car and went off to quizz his fellow-foreigners at the Virgin. Jurnet drove home.

Nothing had changed since the morning, save that the frost had yielded to a greasy thaw. The bags of rubbish were still there waiting for Godot. The lean black cat who haunted the premises sat on the low wall which divided the forecourt from the street, and watched unblinkingly as the detective locked the car, got out his doorkey, and went inside.

Suddenly, hunger overwhelmed him, making even the familiar *bouquet* of slow-simmered underwear which pervaded the stairwell smell appetizing. There must be, he thought, willing it to be so, a can of beans left in the cupboard to stave off the pangs and give him strength to make it to the Chinese takeaway or the chippie. Unless, of course, Miriam was back, in which case he would take her out for a slap-up meal. Mario's, the Nelson, that new place in Shire Street where everybody said the food was out of this world—Jurnet was still reviewing the mouth-watering choices when he arrived at his front door, and collided with Miriam coming out of it.

Which would have been no great matter, if only she hadn't been carrying her suitcase.

Miriam said, 'After the way you lit out of here this morning, I knew you had to be in on it. But I phoned Headquarters and spoke to the duty sergeant, just to make sure.'

For what it was worth, Jurnet asked, 'Make sure of what?'

89

She did not condescend to explain further. The beautiful eyes were shadowed. She's been crying, Jurnet thought —as much, that is, as he could think of anything for the hunger that was consuming his vitals.

It did not seem a good moment for asking if there were any beans in the cupboard.

'I'm a bit tired,' he pleaded. 'Can't we talk about it inside?'

'Nothing to talk about. I phoned for a cab.' She pulled her white coat about her. 'When I told you last time I couldn't stand it one more time, I meant it.' She picked up her case and would have moved towards the stairhead if he had not barred her way. 'Please! The man will be here in a minute!'

'Are you saying you don't want Loy Tanner's murderer apprehended?'

'Apprehended! What a police word!'

'Why not? I'm a policeman, and that's what policemen do to murderers when they get the chance. Or would you rather whoever did for Tanner got off scot-free?'

'Don't be silly!' Miriam cried. 'Only why do you have to be the one to do it?'

'Because it's my job.' Too tired for argument, he said, 'I love you.'

'You don't, you know!' She burst out in tearful anger. 'Or not half so much as you love death. Someone you wouldn't spare the time of day for when he's alive, dead, you're obsessed! He's never out of your thoughts for a second, day or night. You come to bed and there's this corpse with his skull bashed in or his stomach hanging out or whatever, lying there between us.'

'Sorry about that.' Jurnet mumbled something about justice.

The other picked up the word as if she had been proffered an insult.

'Who are you to put the world straight?'

Up the stairs, trailing a delicate aroma of gin-and-it and Yardley's Lavender to mingle with the simmering under-wear, came Mrs Petherton, the widow lady who lived

across the landing, home from her Happy Hour at the
Hacienda Wine Bar. For the duration of the Happy Hour
all drinks at the bar were 25p off: which, as Mrs Petherton
often assured Jurnet with a widow's anxious regard for
economy, meant that the more you spent the more you
saved.

She had, it seemed, making the landing with a surprised
pleasure to find it actually under her trim but uncertain
little feet, been economizing even more strictly than was
her wont. Drowning her grief.

'That lovely Loy,' she mourned, and sang a few bars in
her gentle, gin-hazed voice. ' "*I am my beloved's, and my
beloved is mine*". Taking a holiday?' she went on without
pause, catching sight of the suitcase. 'That's nice.'

Jurnet and Miriam watched as she fumbled in the depths
of a large tapestry handbag and, unearthing her doorkey,
made an ineffectual pass with it in the general direction of
her door. The key clattered on to the lino.

Jurnet picked it up and unlocked the door for her.

Mrs Petherton thanked him prettily. She was a daintily
made little woman who must once have done everything
prettily. Even with her blue eyes faded, her ash-blonde
hair dull as dead leaves, she still retained something of the
air of a Dresden shepherdess, if one long past the days of
wine and roses—the tip of a tiny pointed slipper missing, a
couple of fingers glued amateurishly back in place, a rose-
bud mouth that had outlived kisses.

Mrs Petherton took the key and let it fall again. This
time Jurnet picked it up and dropped it into the tapestry
bag.

'The cussedness of illaminate objects,' Mrs Petherton
said brightly. She went into her flat and closed the door,
only to reopen it a moment later, poking her head out
perkily.

'Illaminate objects! What could I have been thinking of?
What I meant, of course, was enamelate. Why I said
illaminate I can't imagine.'

Jurnet carried Miriam's suitcase down the stairs for her. It
was heavy, signifying no token departure. A removal, back

to her own flat in a chic conversion of one of the old warehouses down by the river.

On the first floor landing where, to judge by the smell, Miss Whistler, the late-blooming spinster, was cooking fish fingers with gin-seng and rhino horn, he put the case down, as if to gather strength for the final flight.

Miriam said in a diminished voice, 'You know what the trouble is, Ben? I'm not good enough for you.' Putting up a hand to ward off interruption: 'You know it's true. I lack all sense of public service. I know somebody has to catch murderers. I just can't stand it being you. I'm selfish and unkind—'

'You know me—' Jurnet wondered if it were as much of a joke as his lightness of tone intended to suggest—'a masochist. Made to be a doormat. And you're another. You should have found yourself a lovely young chartered accountant years ago—numbers don't bleed—before ever you took up with the likes of me.'

'All I do is make you unhappy. You just like me in bed.'

'In bed and out. I'll write you out a list, if you like, beginning with your courage which sustains me, your honesty which delights me, your beauty which—' He broke off, the passion in his voice taking even himself by surprise. He put a foot on the topmost stair. 'I'll go down and tell that cabbie to bugger off.'

'No!'

She picked up the case herself and ran downstairs and out of the front door. The cabbie, ill-pleased at having been kept waiting, took it from her and rearranged his face when he saw what a smasher he'd drawn as a fare. Miriam's presence brought the forecourt alive, her white coat richly shadowed, her magnificent hair blazing beneath the orange street light. The woman clothed with the sun.

It was cold again, getting colder. The two, moving their feet a little to keep warm, said nothing while the cabbie stowed the case in the boot: did not kiss, nor touch. When the man came back to the front of his vehicle, Miriam got into the rear, gave him the address with an exaggerated articulation, as if it were a direction to foreign parts, as indeed it was.

The cabbie swung the cab round in a circle that cleared

the low brick wall with an inch to spare. The black cat, still perched there, did not move so much as a whisker, its eyes shining green in the cab's headlamps. Jurnet did not move either.

When the cab had gone, he turned back to his home, past the rubbish bags whose number seemed to have increased with the dark. To his surprise, when he reached the entrance to the block of flats, the cat was there before him.

There were no baked beans in the kitchen cupboard; only a tin of sardines whose escaping fragrance, as Jurnet turned the key to open it, filled the hungry detective with a desire that was almost sexual. Quickly, before he could weaken, he turned the compacted mass into a bowl, and set it on the floor for the cat to polish off with a speed and elegance that, but for the evidence of the discarded tin and the residual perfume tormenting Jurnet's starving senses, would have made the detective wonder whether it had ever been there at all.

Seeking the only comfort available, Jurnet put out a hand to stroke the cat. Dead to all sense of gratitude, the creature moved away before he could make contact with the black fur still diamonded with frost and dew. Like Loy Tanner, the detective thought dismally: hating to be touched.

Unable to face the thought of the long evening and the longer night alone, he went early to bed in hope of thereby shortening them; leaving the window open so that the cat could push off whenever it had a mind to, and taking a self-pitying satisfaction in the piercing chill which tumbled over the sill as he pushed open the casement and fastened the latch on the second hole.

The bed at least, he had hoped, would provide some kind of solace, the bedclothes retaining for a little some intimate essence of his lost love. But no: with unaccustomed housewifeliness Miriam had changed the pillow cases, the sheet and the duvet cover. Only the cold from the open window was there to greet him with a dank embrace.

The cold and Loy Tanner, the latest body between.

Jurnet moved well over to his own side of the bed to

leave that invisible, omnipresent bedfellow plenty of room. Anything rather than frighten it away altogether. Even a cadaver under the duvet was better than nothing, nobody.

In the freezing dark the detective found it hard to put two consecutive thoughts together. The wound in his arm, which he had left bandaged, itched like mad. See Queenie King's pa, he made a mental memo. Just as well Miriam had moved out. That white coat of hers wouldn't have stayed white for long in that place. Had he in fact, as he had promised the Portuguese chambermaid, spoken to the manager at the Virgin about the shattered mirror? Remember to let Rabbi Schnellman know the lessons would have to be called off for the time being.

Would he, Benjamin Jurnet, ever make it to becoming a Jew, whatever that might be? Sometimes it seemed to him Jews themselves weren't over-sure.

Jurnet tossed on his bed, and said aloud to the God of Moses, 'Stop mucking me about, for Christ's sake.'

It was twenty past two by the awful digital clock when Dave Batterby rang, going on for so long about the unreliability of British Rail that Jurnet knew without being told he'd balled it up: hadn't got in London what he'd gone there for.

Out of a fellow-feeling for losers Jurnet allowed him to put off the moment of truth by inquiring what the other had done to fill his evening; and was presently rewarded—if that was the word—by hearing the old note of self-congratulation seep back into the man's voice like olive oil into French dressing.

'Had dinner with a couple of chaps from the Yard—surprising how much you can learn from people at the heart of things . . . Wonderful little restaurant—need an introduction before they'll book you a table, but if ever you're interested, let me know and I'll put a word in, in the right quarter . . .' Only when the colleague launched himself into a course by course description of the menu did Jurnet feel it was time to call a halt.

'So how did it go?'

By now, bolstered in his self-esteem, Dave Batterby did

not seem to think it had gone as badly as all that. Not his fault some old crone old enough to be his great-grandmother had been prepared to lie her head off for Lenny Bale. 'They're like that,' he expanded, for Jurnet's benefit. 'Queers. If it's got to be a woman, it has to be somebody who reminds them of Mummy.'

'And Lenny Bale keeps one of them on hand in his office?'

'One! A coven! Address in Savile Row, very nice entrance, you think you're going to find someone on reception with legs and a bit of class. And instead there's this collection of old bags with faces like billy goats, knitting.'

'Knitting?'

'That's right.' The voice moved up half an octave. 'Squares. Blankets for starving Dinkas, king-size because they're all at least eight feet tall and any smaller won't cover their you-know-whats. Needed so urgently, the one who said she was the telephone operator told me, she hadn't had time to keep the phone log up to date.'

'Did she at least remember the call from Heathrow?'

'Too well. It was what first put me on my guard. A Mr Brown from California. With an American accent, surprise, surprise. But as to the gentleman's address, she couldn't help me.'

'Did she say if Bale was in the office Wednesday?'

'In and out, she said. In a tearing hurry because he wanted to get back to Angleby for the concert. Lies, every last word,' Dave Batterby pronounced confidently. 'I could swear to it, so long as it wasn't in court. Proof's another matter.'

'You think she'll stick to her story?'

'They all will. Lenny's their golden boy. They think the sun shines out of his arse.'

Jurnet's naked arm, holding the receiver, had begun to feel numb with cold. 'Never mind,' he said. 'It was worth a try. And Savile Row, eh? You could have treated yourself to a tie, at least.'

'Matter of fact, I did,' Batterby admitted. He prided himself on being a sharp dresser. 'Raw silk with a thin red line. Quite something.'

'Then it's not all loss.'

*   *   *

Whilst he was still debating with himself whether to get out of bed and shut the window, Jurnet fell asleep: uneasily, for the outside cold had possessed the room, and the duvet—another of Miriam's bloody innovations—was, in the detective's opinion, no substitute for blankets and still more blankets, topped by a quilt and, for good measure, one's winter overcoat to keep the whole glorious edifice from sliding to the floor. Foolishly, too, he hadn't bothered with pyjamas, never used them with Miriam there, couldn't remember whether he still owned any. Between sleeping and waking, he made a mental note to get himself a couple of thermal nightshirts proper to his years, now that he had no lovely lover to warm his bed.

One thing to be said for murder. You didn't die alone.

Jurnet fell asleep again, and again awoke. Someone, something, was in bed with him. *Miriam had come back!*

As he stretched out a hand in incredulous joy, a velvety pelt brushed against his cheek. The cat gave a small mew and settled itself into the angle between the detective's shoulder and neck.

For a long time Jurnet stayed still, afraid to move. The smell of sardine, breathed rhythmically into his left ear, was not unpleasant. Gradually the man relaxed, dared to put a hand on the gently rising and falling body. At the touch, the cat gave a little twitch, whether of pleasure or irritation it was impossible to tell, but did not otherwise shift its position.

Jurnet slept, greatly comforted. When he awoke in the morning, the cat was gone.

16

'HAVENLEA IS HEAVENLY' proclaimed the poster flapping on
its hoarding at the entrance to the pier. Beneath the
outsize lettering, her suntan bleached by the past winter's
gales, a long-legged girl in a scarlet bikini bared her gums
at passers-by in a wide, wide smile, the effect only a little
diminished by the fact that somebody had blacked out
several of her teeth and decorated her dewy upper lip
with a fine handlebar moustache. As Jurnet and Sergeant
Ellers emerged from the shelter of the car-park, the wind
came at them with the roar of a maddened elephant.
Failing to topple the rash mortals who presumed to walk
the sea-front of Havenlea in March, it took out its wrath
on the poster girl. With a rip and a swoop a well-stacked
bosom took off for the Arctic, or perhaps the Antarctic,
Circle, the wind seeming to encompass both Poles simultaneously. Two storm-tossed gulls, legs dangling, shied
away screeching.

The little Welshman sang, the wind wrenching away
every note before it was out of his mouth: ' *"I do love to be
beside the seaside!"* '

'When I was a kid,' said Jurnet, making himself heard
above the tempest, 'we used to come here for the day, and
I'd sit on the beach with my bucket and spade trying to
dig down to Australia. Just when I seemed to be getting
somewhere, suddenly, there was that bloody sea seeping
into the bottom of the hole. Put me off the briny for good
and all.'

'Today's not going to change your mind.' Beyond the
arid expanse of beach the North Sea heaved as though it
might throw up any minute. 'Can you imagine, a few miles

over the horizon, there are blokes actually living out there day after day? Earn a fortune on those rigs, so they say— must deserve every penny of it. No wonder they take the place apart when they come on shore leave.'

Crouched against the stinging air, Jurnet lifted his head tortoise-wise, and let his disenchanted gaze roam along the sea-front, the boarding houses whited sepulchres in need of a repaint, the ice-cream stalls battened down as if against an impending visitation of Hell's Angels.

'I had a job on the rigs, I'd stay out there with a good book if this was the best I had to come home to.'

'Don't be taken in by appearances, boyo. This is the heavenly face of Havenlea. Behind the quays is where it's all at, the original Sin City of East Anglia. Every night, candles in the front rooms and women hanging out of the windows with everything hanging out—'

'I know all about that. They say that when old hookers die, they go to Havenlea. Ever seen one of 'em by daylight?' After a moment he added, 'Come to think of it, we just did.'

The woman who had opened the door to them at the trim little house with its front garden paved with pebbles from the shore, in the midst of which a model windmill gyrated manically, had her hair in curlers, her left leg in plaster, and her nose caged like a sugar mouse in an ingenious construction of gauze and sticking plaster. At sight of the two detectives' ID cards she burst out with, 'How many times I got to tell you lot I fell down the stairs before you believe it? I got to do it all over again to prove it to you?'

When Jack Ellers replied placatingly that all they wanted was a word with Mr King actually, her wrath waxed unabated.

'And how many times I got to tell you Punchy weren't even home at the time? Children's party, over Martham way. Give you the bloody address, if you want.'

'Mrs King—' Jurnet tried his luck with no more success than his subordinate. The woman rounded on him.

'Where'd you get that Mrs King from? Social Security put you up to it, did they, bleeding nosey parkers? They do it just once more, I'm going to complain to Helsinki. *Miss* Adelina Rice, if you must know. And, for the umpteenth time, Punchy and I are *not*, repeat not, cohabiting.' With a wink and a sudden, startling change to a bawdy bonhomie: 'Lost the habit, as you might say, poor old sod!'

Swift to take advantage of the unexpected change of climate, Jurnet asked, 'Any idea when Mr King will be back?'

'Why you asking? In trouble, is he?'

'No trouble at all. His daughter Queenie gave me the address—'

'Oh—her? Lady Punk de Punk. What's she gone and done this time?'

'Nothing that I know of. Just a routine inquiry.'

'I know your routine inquiries,' Miss Adelina Rice snorted. 'End up in front of a routine beak with a routine fine and a routine warning not to do it again, leastways not in daylight. On the game, is she?'

'Nothing like that.'

'Pity,' said Miss Rice. 'Do her a power of good.'

'You don't happen to know where Mr King might be?'

With another of her disconcerting swings of mood, the woman snapped back, 'Not where the old bugger *might* be, copper. Where he bloody well is. On the beach, where else, having it off with one of his fucking dolls!'

Jurnet had taken to Miss Jerome, the social worker, on sight: the neat, uncluttered form, the serene but penetrating regard.

'Queenie says I'm to tell you anything about her you want to know.' The young woman smiled, and pushed a hand through her short, dark hair. 'Not that I know all about her, any more than I do about any other client. It's simply that she was one of my first, so of course I remember her case well, especially the mistakes I made.'

'Tell me.'

The woman touched a file which lay in front of her, but did not actually refer to it.

'Her mother was already dead when I came in on it. She died when Queenie was five. She was nine years old and living with her Auntie May when I first came on the scene because the child had run away, run back home for the third time.'

'What was the trouble?'

'That *was* the trouble, in a way. That there wasn't any. The aunt was a warm, loving woman, only too happy to provide a home for her sister's child. The house was bright and inviting, the child was kept clean and well-fed. I suppose you could say,' Miss Jerome observed, a slight quirk to the corners of her mouth, 'that, from the point of view of the Department, Queenie's trouble was that she loved her father.' The woman looked directly at the detective, a look cool and appraising. 'What a social worker needs, Inspector, to make the wheels run smoothly, is, ideally, apathy. You've probably noticed the same thing in your own line of work. Nothing is more complicating than love.'

Jurnet muttered, 'I've noticed.'

'By that age, of course, we could have made arrangements which would have enabled the child to remain at home with her father all the time. That is, if Mr King had been a different kind of man.'

'And what kind of man was—is—he?'

'Extremely violent. Never to her, so far as we were aware. I never found a mark on her. But the women he brought home—and over the years there was a regular procession of them, not one of a type one would willingly choose for the role of surrogate mother—he treated with hatred and contempt, if not worse. Some of the things he did—' Miss Jerome broke off. Jurnet noticed that her face had become tinged with pink, her eyes fierce. 'I've never actually counted the number of times he was up before the court. But, obviously, not an environment in which to leave a vulnerable child.'

'Drink, was that the trouble?'

'Unfortunately not.' There was a twist of irony to the

young woman's well-shaped lips. 'Unfortunately, because, although drink, of course, is itself a symptom, not a cause, it does give you something to latch on to, you can go on from there. But violence that erupts without apparent reason, that wells up from deep within the personality as an innate part of it—' The social worker shook her head, seeming to find her memories distressing.

To help her along, Jurnet asked, 'Was it back to Auntie, then?'

'I was very young and inexperienced. I knew that, despite the way things were at home, it couldn't be the right thing to separate Queenie from her father when she was so determined to be with him, despite everything; but I hadn't the courage to come out and say so. It's been on my conscience ever since. Not that it would have made any difference, probably, if I had. My case supervisor was all for placing her with a different foster mother or, if that didn't work out, putting her into a home. We had a case conference and everybody said the same.'

Miss Jerome fidgeted with the file, but still did not open it.

Then she said, with the suspicion of a sigh, 'That's about it, really. The next seven years are a record of Queenie being placed here, there, and everywhere, and always, first chance she got, running home to Daddy and all the horrible things that were happening there. The longest time she stayed in any one place was in a children's home whilst her father was in prison for attempted murder. Actually, he had Queenie to thank it wasn't a murder charge. She'd hit him on the back of the head with a bottle as he was tightening his hands round the woman's throat. The day he was released from gaol Queenie ran away to be home with him.'

'Did he return her love, as you remember?'

'I never saw any sign of it. Unless the very fact that he kept his hands off her—and we were particularly mindful, in the circumstances, of the possibility of sexual, as well as physical, abuse—was his way of showing it. In the end, not to mince words, we simply gave up: checked periodically to make sure Queenie was physically OK, otherwise left it at that. I can't tell you what a relief it was when she became too old for our ministrations, such as they were.'

Miss Jerome smiled ruefully. 'Not one of my greatest success stories. Particularly galling, in fact, as I had grown fonder of the girl than, by any purely professional criterion, I ever should have.'

Sounding to himself like the Superintendent, Jurnet said, 'One must never become involved.'

'I couldn't agree more,' said Miss Jerome. 'One day, when you've the time, you'll have to tell me how it's done.'

17

All of a sudden, Jurnet realized, the wind had ceased to
matter. Tatters of grey still scudded across the sky; last
season's crisp bags, defiantly unbiodegradable, still tumbled along the promenade ahead of him. But the wind,
possessing him like any other piece of moveable trash, had
caught him up into its own element. He had become part
of it as a swimmer, after the first shock of cold and wet,
becomes part of the sea. The detective found himself
smiling hugely as he and his companion gingerly negotiated a flight of sand-drifted steps down to the shoe-clogging
grittiness of the beach.

Jack Ellers face lightened.

'Allah be praised! An oasis! Date palms! Minarets! Veiled
houris with emeralds in their belly buttons! Don't tell me
it's a mirage, boyo! Don't tell me it's a mirage!'

Ahead, where the promenade, describing a decorative
semi-circle, provided a certain degree of shelter, a red-and-
white striped Punch and Judy tent bellied in the wind.
From the apex of its peaked roof a white pennon flew
bravely, folding and unfolding itself to disclose lettering
which, as the two detectives drew nearer, could be
deciphered as KING PUNCH. The tiny proscenium arch, with
its protruding shelf or apron and its scalloped valance
edged with gold braid, was shadowy and untenanted.

'Hallo, kiddies!'

Before a startled Jurnet could decide where the piercing, nasal voice was coming from, there was Punch in all
his magnificence, wearing his hump with pride and sitting
on the narrow apron, his white-stockinged legs crossed
above red satin slippers trimmed with rosettes of gold
ribbon, one hand delicately picking at a nose of heroic

proportions, the other extended in regal acknowledgement of his invisible audience.

'Hallo, you little perishers! Back again, are you? And there was I hoping the cold winter, all that ice and snow, would have done for you once and for all, but no such luck. Heigh-ho! Here you are again, snotty-nosed as ever, dribbling at either end—ugh! Why your loving Mums haven't chucked you out with the rubbish years ago I'll never know.

'Well, then!' The puppet, large and prosperous-looking, with a face of utterly engaging malevolence, moved his head from side to side, the beads on his cap catching the light. 'Are you sitting comfortably? Don't worry, it won't last. First your left leg'll go to sleep, then your right. Next, your nose'll begin to itch, then your funny bone. Before you know it, you'll be screaming with backache, toothache, headache, diarrhoea, constipation, and St Vitus' Dance. Oh, we *are* going to have fun!'

Jurnet called out, 'Anybody home?'

At the question, Punch uncrossed his legs, and bent forward, head down, hump up, as he positioned himself for a good look. Then, without warning, a head topped by a black velours hat, wide-brimmed and romantic, appeared on the little stage, all but filling it: opened its gash of a mouth and demanded, in accents harsher but less nasal, 'Whadya want?'

The detective did not introduce himself immediately. Given the overall dimensions of the tent, the owner of the head and the hat must be standing on a step or a box to bring himself up to the level of the miniature proscenium. But had he been as tall as one of Dave Batterby's blanketless Dinkas, the fact of his height would have been less disconcerting to Jurnet than the face presented for inspection. Allowing for differences of scale, the puppet and the puppeteer were identical twins. True, the living man possessed none of the doll's debonair sparkle, but the great nose and the chin curving upward in a crescent to meet it, were carbon copies: the face of one clearly intended by providence to be a Punch and Judy man.

Feeling a trifle foolish, Jurnet said curtly, 'We want a few words with you.'

The mouth opened again. 'What about?'

'Loy Tanner. We are police officers investigating his murder.'

'The best of British luck. What's it to me?'

'We have reason to believe you were with your daughter in her caravan at the University of Angleby following on the concert given by Second Coming in the Middlemass Auditorium, and that, during part of the time at least, Loy Tanner was also in the caravan.'

'That Queenie! Never knew when to keep her bloody mouth shut! What she say then, the silly mauther?'

'I'd rather hear your version.'

'It'll cost you. This bleeding sandstorm, I got a throat you could file your nails on.'

'I don't mind buying you a pint.'

'*Two!*' interjected Punch, in his nasal twang. The man's lips had not moved. '*Whither he goest I goest, and where he drinkest, I drinkest also.*'

'Two it is!'

The man took his time clearing up. Jurnet and Jack Ellers, waiting at the rear of the tent, where the red and white stripes, divided from roof to beach, were tied crosswise like a child's pinafore, found themselves loaded with a number of cotton bags out of which poked, unnervingly alive, the heads of other actors in the unending saga of Mr Punch: Judy and the baby; the dog Toby and the crocodile; the butcher and the baker; the policeman, the judge; the hangman and his gallows. Even the string of sausages, cascading in a fluorescent purple out of its restraining reticule, seemed instinct with a life of its own.

Punchy King himself came out at last, carrying Punch and an old-fashioned work basket, its lid of quilted satin, powder blue. 'Ripped his ruddy pants and had to stitch him up,' he explained affectionately. 'Don't ask *me* what the little bugger's been up to—and *he's* not saying, that's certain.'

Punch, tucked snugly inside his creator's sheepskin coat,

only the head showing, let out a great hoot. '*He's a fine one to talk!*'

Creator? Or was it the other way round, Jurnet wondered, as he unprotestingly helped to stow the bags, each on its labelled hook, in an elderly blue van parked at the kerb. Punchy King, the detective was interested to discover, even had a hump like his star performer. Well, almost. Years of bending, presumably, lest the top of his head be visible to his eagle-eyed young patrons, had set his back in a permanent curve.

Happy among his puppets, he seemed a contented soul: no sign of the violence which had made the family home such an unsuitable environment for young Queenie. At his direction they crossed the road to the Haven Hotel where they found a bar as big as a ballroom, empty save for a barman examining his teeth in a pocket mirror, and an elderly man staring stonily out to sea, an untouched glass of whisky on the table at his side.

Punchy King sat Punch in one of the dralon-covered chairs, arranging his hump comfortably. To Sergeant Ellers, on his way to get the drinks: 'Four, remember!'

Jurnet said: 'Tell me about the old days. You knew Loy Tanner before he made his name?'

'Who d'you think made it for him? Hadn't been for me, there'd have been no first coming, let alone second!'

'How was that, then?'

'Why, there was him and that la-di-da what's-his-name, Johnny Flowerdew, doing the rounds of the places down by the quays for whatever they could pick up, which was strictly zilch. Could think themselves lucky if someone chucked over a fag between the two of 'em. That lot off the rigs, what they want is topless Mother Machree, not what Loy Tanner had to offer.'

'And what was that?'

The little Welshman had come back with four foaming tankards. Before answering the detective's question, King set one of them carefully in front of Punch—'Cheers, me old darlin'!'—and took a long pull at his own pint. Wiped his mouth on the back of his hand, and said, 'Blamed if I can put a word to it. To tell you the truth, nine times out of ten, soon as he got going, I had to run to the pisser or there'd be a nasty accident. Maybe that's how genius gets you—in the guts, I don't know. All I do know is, I reckon I knew star quality when I heard it. And I was right!'

'So how did you help him?'

'Put in a good word where it mattered. Winters, would you believe it, there's not all that much call for a Punch and Judy show on the beach. That's when I do my private engagements. Kids' parties and—' the man sniggered, unpleasingly—'not such kids' parties. Did it ever strike you, copper, there's all life in a Punch and Judy show? All life and a bit over!' King leaned over and put a loving arm round his puppet's shoulders.

'The times we've had together, eh, chummy, you and me! I tell you—' raising his head as if challenging the two detectives to make something of it—'I got a Judy in black leather and chains'd make your eyeballs pop—but there! Got to mind my p's and q's, ha'nt I, when there's Little Boy Blues on the premises! What I meant to say was, I had an agent, see, in those days, and I told him, mark my words that pair o' kids definitely got something. Fix 'em up with drummer, get 'em a couple of gigs an' you won't be sorry.' The man settled back in his seat and polished off the rest of the beer in one long swallow. 'And he weren't, the clever little poofter.'

'That wouldn't be Lenny Bale, by any chance?' Jurnet asked, thinking that he recognized the description.

'Little Miss Clitoris—who else? Everyone made a packet out of Second Coming except yours truly.'

'Tanner must have been very grateful to you.'

'Loy grateful!' The man still smiled, but the resemblance to the puppet in the next seat had faded. Gone the air of jovial knavery. 'Loy Tanner wouldn't give a thank you if he'd been nailed to that cross in Angleby Market Place for real and a platoon of Israeli parachutists dropped out of the skies and set him free.'

'Oh ah. Still, he did give your daughter a job with the group—'

'Who said? It was the roadie took her on. Fell for her like a ton of bricks, can you credit it? The little slut! You seen the way she keeps that caravan of hers? Bloody gippo'd know better.'

Struck by a sudden recollection, Jurnet asked, 'Didn't I see a Punch among her things? A Punch just like this one here?'

The Punch and Judy man looked offended. The puppet, convulsed, as ever, by some secret amusement, preserved his outward composure unruffled.

King said, 'I got fifteen Punches, if you want to know, every one unique. No Punch is just like any other Punch any more than one copper's just like any other monkey, whatever you might think to the contrary. They're all different. As you ask, I've got into the habit, every time I drop in on Queenie, I bring her a Punch for luck. Chop and change about. Not fair to leave 'em too long in that pigsty.'

He leaned over towards the puppet and pushed the tankard of beer forward invitingly.

Jack Ellers said, 'Might as well finish it up yourself before it goes flat.'

'Do the little fellow out of his drink!' the other exclaimed. 'What you take me for? But I won't say no to another, since you ask.'

At a nod from his superior officer, the little Welshman went back to the bar.

Punchy King observed moodily, 'Meant to bring her luck, poor cow, that's a laugh. All she's got out of this Second Coming business, I suppose, is out of a job—unless she can bring herself to shack up with that mini-Frankenstein, Scarlett, heaven forbid.'

The man demolished the second pint as thirstily as the first. Jurnet waited for the liquid to go down, and then said, 'I'd be glad to know what you, Tanner and Queenie were talking about in her caravan, Wednesday night after the concert.'

'I'd be glad to tell you if I could remember what the hell it was. Didn't Queenie say?'

The detective had no intention of letting on that Queenie King had been no more forthcoming than her pa.

'Jest conversation,' she had answered vaguely. 'Like Gawd it's cold, and when are you going to get this bloody place cleaned up. Jest conversation.'

Jurnet said to the Punch and Judy man, 'I'd like to have your own recollection.'

'Jesus, I dunno. The weather, I suppose: how the gig went. If I'd known I was listening to famous last words I'd've paid more attention. Taken a cassette and made myself a million. As it was—I'll tell you this, though—' King sat up as straight as his round shoulders permitted —'there *was* something different, come to think about it. I've seen Loy often enough after gigs to know the way he was, usually—wrung-out like a pair of old drawers. To look at him you'd never guess the fans had just been shouting their heads off like he was a god.'

'And Wednesday?'

'Wednesday he was on a high, over the moon. First go off, I thought, oy, oy, what's he been taking? But it didn't take long to see it wasn't a high at all: more a deep, as you might say. Something so filled him up, whatever it was, something deep down inside him, he didn't seem hardly to listen to what Queenie and me were saying, such as it was.'

'But he was the one who came to the caravan in the first place,' Jurnet was quick to point out. 'He must have had a reason.'

Into the eyes of the Punch and Judy man had come the same sardonic twinkle which was fixed for ever in the eyes of the puppet at his side. He tapped the tip of his great nose with an index finger long and predatory.

'Could be,' he suggested blandly, 'he wanted to say how grateful he was.'

18

Back at Angleby, the air was as still as at Havenlea it had been turbulent. Heavy with a persistent burden of frost, it burned the face like ice-cold steel. In the Market Place, the fancy-goods stalls with their chicks and bunnies, their brightly coloured Easter eggs, looked ridiculous. Plainly, somebody hunting for the Santas and the holly sprigs had opened the wrong box.

Just the same, driving in from the Ring Road, penetrating the city as if through the successive layers of an onion— first the new houses, then the leftovers from the 'twenties; suburbs Edwardian, Victorian, Georgian, and so into the medieval core—Jurnet found his spirits rising in proportion to the changes in architectural style. Partly this was because he could never re-enter his native city, back from a journey however brief, without feeling a *frisson* of love and pride; and partly because of the feeling that he had at last begun to get on terms with Loy Tanner.

And to get on terms with Loy Tanner was to get on terms with his killer.

The duty sergeant greeted the two detectives with, 'Had a good paddle?' And: 'You've got visitors. Two. Been waiting best part of an hour. Mr Batterby spoke to them, but it seems only Detective-Inspector Jurnet will do. They're foreigners,' the duty sergeant said, speaking out of pity, not prejudice. 'Got their names here, if I spelled 'em right.'

Jurnet looked over the man's shoulder, and read in the log-book: *Fatima Valdao. Luis Ferrol.*

'Did they say what it was about?'

'Woman did the talking, what there was of it. Funny how some of those foreign women have a sort of downy

110

skin, have you noticed? Don't go for hair on a bird's face myself as a general rule, but, somehow, it makes them look soft and cuddly, know what I mean? Can't help wondering, eh, if they're like that all over.'

Jurnet said coldly—the duty sergeant was not one of his favourites—'Seems you wasted your time, all those package trips to the Costa Brava.'

'All the birds on the Costa Brava come from Wigan. The joke of it was,' the man went on, unputdownable, 'one of the few things she did say more than once—that's what it sounded like, anyway—was "virgin". You only had to take one look at her to see, whatever else she was, it couldn't be that.'

Jurnet made for the stairs. The duty sergeant, who sincerely believed there was no one on the Angleby force better liked than himself, looked after the tall, dark figure kindly, and remarked to Sergeant Ellers, about to follow, 'Just up his street, eh? Valentino!'

Miss Fatima Valdao had brought along another strip of her apron, together with a jar containing a gritty cream which smelled of the Mediterranean. On the whole it seemed easier to take off one's jacket, roll up a shirt sleeve, than protest. With Jack Ellers looking on with benevolent approval, and the PCs down at the other end of the room shaking with silent laughter, the woman unwound the old bandage with her strong brown fingers.

At sight of the wound, the little Welshman exclaimed with concern, 'You could do with a couple of stitches in that.'

'Is not a sweater with a hole,' the woman observed scornfully. 'Or I bring my needle and darning.' She smeared the ointment liberally over the gash, and rebandaged the arm with a professional competence which, so far as Jurnet was concerned, compensated in some measure for the odour of ratatouille—or was it bouillabaisse?—spreading through the room. 'Two, three day,' Miss Valdao pronounced, lifting her skirt and wiping her hands unconcernedly on her slip, 'and all gone.'

Trusting she did not mean the arm, Jurnet rebuttoned

his shirt sleeve, shrugged on his jacket. If the smell got too much for him, he thought, he could always scrape the stuff off, stick it between two bits of bread, and have it for lunch. But already a delicious feeling of ease was pervading the injured member, making him realize for the first time how much it had been hurting.

'I must say it was very kind of you to come in and patch me up,' he said in all sincerity. 'I'm most grateful.'

'Am come something else,' the woman corrected him, brushing the thanks aside. 'Am come for that someone is asking at Virgin about Mr Tanner, and—' pushing forward her silent companion like a mother impatiently encouraging her child to do its party piece—'this foolish man is see, and says nothing.'

Mr Luis Ferrol, a small man with a face which looked anything but foolish, said, in surprisingly good English, 'The policeman asked who sees Loy Tanner on Wednesday night. I see him Tuesday, so is of no interest.'

'Oh yes, it is!' Jurnet contradicted, a sudden conviction that at last he was on to something tangible sharpening his tone. Sergeant Ellers unobtrusively got out notebook and pencil. 'Take your time, Mr Ferrol. What I want you to do is tell us exactly what you saw, and when, as close as you can make it.'

'I speak of *Tuesday* night,' Luis Ferrol said severely, as if he had no great faith in either the intelligence or the accuracy of the Angleby police force. 'Quite late, I think. I am on night duty and after eleven, about eleven and a quarter, perhaps, I go outside for a cigarette. Very strict "No Smoking" in the kitchen, except for the chef. One day,' the man announced in a voice of dry precision, 'I will be chef, and I too drop my cigarette ash on the *canard à l'orange* to show the fucking customers what I think of them.

'From the kitchen,' Luis Ferrol continued, back to his normal tone, 'is door to the car-park, and I am standing there smoking—not long because is very cold—when white van comes and Loy Tanner comes out.'

'There was enough light for you to recognize who it was?'

'Not enough. At first I think only, crazy young man to be out, the night so cold, in only T-shirt and jeans, no sweater, no anorak. Then he goes to the door into hotel for visitors, where there is plenty light, and I see it is Loy Tanner; and I think to myself, that one, he has his money to keep him warm.'

'You're absolutely sure it was him?'

'I am sure, because he go into hotel and in one minute he is out again, and he come to me more near than you are now. I think he sees the red of my cigarette and know I am there, by kitchen door.'

'What did he want?'

'In lobby of car-park entrance is a single lift which have notice to say "Annexe Only". So he come out again and ask me if lift is OK for taking him to room 317.'

Jurnet's heart leaped. 'You're sure you've got the right number?'

'Sure. Is Fatima's floor, how I know. Sometimes, when I have afternoon off, and Fatima is on duty but not busy, I go to see her in room 317.' Mr Ferrol smiled confidingly, as one man to another. 'I know 317 very well. You understand me? If 317 is taken, we go in 318 or 319 or whatever is empty. All good beds, but 317 best. Very good springs.' Frowning: 'In summer, with many tourists, sometimes all rooms are taken. All morning tourists sightsee. Afternoons they say their feet kill them, they rest on bed. By time they are ready to walk some more, I must be back in kitchen for preparing dinner. But this time of year, no problem.'

Well, well, thought Jurnet, fascinated by this glimpse of the submerged underlife of a four-star hotel rising like scum to the surface. Still, not his business, thank goodness.

'Did Tanner say anything else?'

'Nothing. I tell him for 317 he must go through to the main hall, where is lift will take him to the third floor. He goes and does not say thank you.'

Jurnet and Sergeant Ellers exchanged glances.

Jurnet said, 'Well, Mr Ferrol, I'm sure we're very much obliged to you for your help with our inquiry. Just for the record, Detective-Sergeant Ellers will get what you have just told us typed out, and ask you to sign it when you have read it through and are satisfied that it is an accurate transcript. I'm sure you won't mind waiting a few minutes longer.'

'When you type what I tell about Fatima's rooms, will you show the manager?' The man did not sound bothered one way or the other.

The detective answered easily, 'I do my job, and leave him to get on with his.' Turning to the woman, 'And Miss Valdao—I hope I've got that right—thank you again for bringing Mr Ferrol along to see us.'

'Nothing,' the woman protested: took Jurnet's hand and kissed it.

Ferrol said, 'You come to Virgin restaurant, I see everything is very nice for you.'

Down at the other end of the room the young PCs were killing themselves.

'Thanks very much.' Jurnet retrieved his hand as soon as he decently could. 'One thing's for sure, though. After what you've just let on about the chef, I'll know not to order the duck.'

A slow, beatific smile suffused the sallow features of Luis Ferrol.

'You want I should tell you what he does to the *boeuf en croute*?'

19

'Do you know what Jews do when somebody dies?' Lenny Bale demanded, when Jurnet and Jack Ellers, receiving no answer to their knock, and disregarding the 'Do Not Disturb' sign, entered room 320 with Fatima's pass key. Second Coming's manager evinced neither surprise nor displeasure at the intrusion. 'They sit about on low chairs for a week, and all their friends come round as if they were paying a social call. They bring cakes, and smoked salmon sandwiches, make tea, tell jokes. They call it a *shiva*. I was taken to one once, and it was marvellous. It made you see how it's possible to lose the one person who made life worth living and still go on loving God instead of cursing his guts.'

'My information—' Jurnet spoke with careful detachment, avoiding the sly, sideways glance of his subordinate —'is that it's only done in the case of a close member of the family.'

'And Loy, you mean, wasn't even a second cousin three times removed? Only my bloody life, that's all.'

Bale swivelled round on the stool on which he was perched in front of the dressing table; readdressed himself to the task with which he had been occupied when the detectives came through the door. A mess of cosmetics littered the dressing-table top. A fair sample of them had found their way to his face.

The man looked ghastly. The eyes were smudged about with purple shadow: improbable lashes, heavy with mascara, swept up and down in crazy arcs, depositing a stippling of sooty specks on to a skin powdered to a graveyard pallor. The mouth, deep crimson, was painted in a cupid's bow.

The man wore a sleeveless dress of purple lamé, slashed

115

from hem to thigh and from neck to navel. Bracelets concealed some of the scars on the naked arms. Those that remained visible exactly matched the colour of the lamé.

Lenny Bale said, 'Did I tell you I offered to have a sex change, if it would make him feel differently towards me?' He studied the travesty in the mirror with narrowed eyes, apparently not displeased with what he saw. Two large tears, filtering through the absurd lashes, compounded the ruin of the *maquillage*. 'I'm sorry now I didn't go ahead with it. I ought to've, even if Loy did fall about at the idea. "That titchy chipolata!" was what he said—that boy, you had to laugh!—"What difference could *that* make?"'

'Mr Bale,' said Jurnet, reminding himself, with some effort, that there was a Jewish prayer which thanked God for the marvellous diversity of His creatures—'Will you please tell me exactly when on Tuesday Mr Brown of California telephoned you?'

'Oh—' intent on drawing an ebony line through his left eyebrow—'who can say exactly? Some time in the afternoon.'

'But how is that possible? You were out at the University all day overseeing the preparations for the concert. My information is that it was getting on for dark before you broke up.'

The man put his eyebrow pencil down.

'You're right! Now I think of it, the call came through as I was getting myself a shower before dinner.'

'Between 7 and 8 p.m., would that be?'

The other shrugged. 'I suppose.'

'How is it, then, it wasn't far from midnight when you phoned the roadie to tell him of your sudden change of plan—that you had to be back in London next day?'

'I was in two minds. I'd never missed a gig before except for illness. It took me that long to decide. Anyway, I don't think it was as late as that.'

'Mr Scarlett says it was.'

'*Mr* Scarlett. You don't have to believe every word that midget tells you.'

'How's that?'

'He knows his job, I'll give him that. Only reason I keep him on. He affects me aesthetically. Still, I could give him the sun and the moon, and any harm he can do me, the shit, he'll do it.'

'Why should he do that?'

'Jealousy. Jealous of me and Loy being so close.' Bale swished the split skirt aside to show shapely limbs in spangled tights. 'Jealous of anybody with a pair of gams to set the world on fire. Ask him, why don't you?'

'I just did.'

Guido Scarlett was not in his caravan, the University deep in the peace of the Easter vacation. Eventually a gardener, raking the last of the old year's rubbish from under the oak trees, had pointed downhill towards the little river which formed the University's northern boundary.

The detective's shoes made little squelching noises and left tracks of a darker green on the sodden grass. The landscape had an air of unreality, the trees two-dimensional, a scribble of smoke rising lazily from the chimney of a farmhouse on the further side of the stream up to a smoke-coloured sky. Winter; except that the still air was pierced like an arrow with birdsong and a springtime racket of rooks. Two swans moved silently with the current, the ripples widening behind them.

Jurnet walked on, preoccupied, unseeing. The conviction that, if only he had the mother wit to recognize it, he already possessed enough knowledge to name the killer of Loy Tanner, tormented him with a hurt that was almost physical.

Once he had looked up the word *'clue'* in a dictionary. *'That which guides or threads a way through a maze.'* All right for lexicographers, when every copper knew that, nine times out of ten, it was just the opposite: a will o' the wisp luring you into the nearest bog with its delusive light.

What would have happened to that Ancient Greek bloke back in the labyrinth if the wool, the clue, he'd been unwinding had suddenly broken off and he couldn't find the end down there in the dark?

Maybe he ought to ask Miriam for a ball of her knitting wool to practise on.

As always, the thought, the mere name, of Miriam both lightened and intensified his mood. He looked about him and was suddenly astonished by the beauty of the scene: possessed by an unreasonable joy that even the sight of Guido Scarlett, down on his knees by the river, his face buried in his hands, could not entirely dispel.

Jurnet said, in his jolly-rozzer voice, 'Come along, now! Things can't be as bad as all that.'

The man crossed himself and got to his feet; such a small elevation that the detective was shocked afresh by the disparity of scale between limbs and torso, embarrassed by having to make the man look up to speak to him. Humiliation should be a punishment deserved, not the visitation of a pitiless god.

'What you want?'

'A few words, that's all.'

'Nothing I can tell you.'

'Nothing?' Jurnet shook his head in a friendly way. 'For a start, you could tell me why you're down here carrying on.'

'Law against it, is there?'

'Look,' said Jurnet, keeping the smile in place, 'there's no call to be hostile. No one's against you, so long as your conscience is clear.'

'Not *for* you, neither.'

'That's where you're wrong, then—that is, if you meant what you said about loving Loy Tanner. If you did, you'd want to help us catch the bastard that did for him. But then, maybe, you were only kidding.'

'What nobody understands,' said Guido Scarlett, low at first, then louder, 'was the honesty of him. The rest of you—oh, you got manners, some of you. You lean over backwards to be nice to the poor handicapped bugger whose own mum took one look at him and lit out with a chap come to the door selling life insurance.' The man drew a trembling breath. 'A little kid'll call out, "Look at that funny man, Ma!" and his Ma hushes him up quick, because tha's manners, in't it? But that kid, let me tell you, he's got more sense than all you well-bred shitheads put together. I am what I am!' Guido Scarlett shouted. 'Do I make myself clear? And that's what Loy—Loy out of the whole world—took me for—'

Jurnet interrupted tartly. 'You are what you are all right, chum, which is a self-pitying bugger with a chip on his shoulder the size of a giant redwood. No wonder your legs are bandy, carrying that weight! So now, Mr Scarlett—' with a complete change of tone—'if we've finished with the histrionics, suppose you tell me exactly what you did with yourself Wednesday night, after the ball was over.'

There had been little enough to tell. Once the audience had gone, it had been the usual hassle. Take down the backdrop, disconnect the electrics, take a look that everything backstage had been left in decent order. Check that the lads hadn't left anything behind. 'Only extra job I had to do, Lenny not being there, was to settle up with the programme sellers and the usherettes. I'd brought along the money in case—'

'How was that, then?' the detective interrupted.

'Phoned me the night before, didn't he? Must have been nearly midnight—about having to go up to town on something special that'd come up. He'd try to be back for the gig, but if not, well, I knew what to do.'

'Did he say what the business was in London?'

'You must be joking. I'm only the roadie. Dust beneath the fucking chariot wheels.'

'After the clearing up was done, what then?'

'Helped Lijah with his drums, like I always do. We brought them out to the caravan. Johnny was there already, making cocoa—yuk! I said good-night, went and took a leak, and got myself to bed.'

Jurnet said, 'You haven't mentioned Loy.'

'No one ever went near Loy after a gig, and he never went near nobody.'

'Does that mean I'm to take it he *wasn't* visiting young Queenie in her van while you were eavesdropping outside?'

'Who—' the roadie broke off, and tried again. 'What you buggering on about?'

'Don't mess me about. You were seen.'

The man said, scowling, 'She had her bloody pa in there. Tha's all.'

'That's funny. She says, her pa says, Loy was in there with them.'

'If Queenie says he was there, then he bloody was. Only, never known him do that before.'

'Never known him get himself murdered before either. Never known him get himself crucified. Clearly, not a run of the mill night. As much as you did hear, what were Queenie and her dad talking about?'

'Nothing much. The show. Sir bloody Middlemass's bloody statues. The lousy weather at Havenlea—'

'What I don't understand is why you didn't join them. Why you had to hang around outside.'

'That's easy. Because Mr Punchy King Esquire don't think I'm a suitable suitor for the hand of his daughter. Simple as that. Told me, if he caught me hanging round her one more time, he'd stuff me an' put me in his Punch and Judy show, I'd just the legs for it.'

Jurnet studied the man curiously.

'You're not one to be frightened off by that kind of talk.'

The dark face looked, of a sudden, young and defenceless. 'Queenie. She's turned eighteen. Old enough to speak for herself.'

'And she doesn't care for you either?'

'Who bloody expects her to care? Love's for giving, not taking. When you're made the way I'm made, copper, you're ready to settle for a whole lot less than "care", believe me. You're ready to settle for "tolerate", "put up with", "don't actually kick me in the teeth". To look after her, look out for her—' the yearning in the voice was painful to listen to—'that'd do me. That'd do me fine. And there's times—you'll think I'm making it up, but it's true—when she's glad to have me around. When she gives me a smile, I tell you, it'd melt the ice at the North Pole. And then—' the voice hardened, the face locked itself into its familiar lines of savage pride—'along comes Daddy, king of the creeps, only interested in what he can get out of her, if she was in trouble wouldn't give her a flea's fart—but if the Prince of Wales came hammering at her door and Daddy said no, she'd scream through the keyhole and tell him to arse off home to Di.'

'What would Daddy have said if it had been Loy Tanner?'

The roadie burst out laughing: surprising, unforced merriment.

'Do me a favour!' he exclaimed. 'Coppers! Questions, questions, and still they haven't a clue!'

Jurnet and Sergeant Ellers watched Lenny Bale brushing rose blusher along his cheekbones.

Jurnet said, 'One item of information I didn't have to apply to Mr Scarlett for. On Tuesday night, at approximately 11.15, Loy Tanner asked one of the Virgin staff to direct him to room 317.'

The man in the lamé dress leaned towards the dressing-table mirror. He raised his hands to his cheeks and spread the colour into two feverish discs. The result was to make him look even more ill than had the pallor it superseded.

When he had finished, he clasped his hands in his lap, and said calmly, 'Quite right.'

'Why haven't you mentioned this earlier?'

With a flash of spangled tights Second Coming's manager swung round on the dressing-table stool.

'I also neglected to let you know how many times I went to the loo. Tuesday, for Christ's sake! Loy was alive and singing like a lark on Wednesday night. I can call the entire house at the Middlemass Auditorium to say I hadn't killed him. So what business is it of anyone but Loy and me what he was up to the night before?'

'It is very much the business of this murder inquiry, as I'm sure, upon reflection, you will yourself agree. Half an hour later you used the link-up to his caravan to let your roadie know you were going up to London.' The detective's voice remained unemphatic. Only gradually, still with no apparent alteration of tone, did the steel begin to show through. 'Since, without a far higher standard of proof than has so far been offered, I am not prepared to accept that a Mr Brown of California ever did telephone you, I'm forced to conclude it was Mr Tanner's visit which precipitated the call to Scarlett announcing your sudden change of plan.'

The other shrugged. 'Think what you like. Can't stop people thinking.'

'Very true. So what I ask myself, having that kind of mind, is, first, could Tanner have dropped by at that late hour to go to bed with you? And I answer myself—considering how every one's been at pains to let me know how he couldn't bear to be touched—not very likely. I've heard nothing to make me wonder if perhaps he didn't make an exception of you.'

'Cruel! Cruel!' Lenny Bale burst out, his voice high and vengeful. 'It's easy to see, Inspector, *you've* never been in love!'

'Not your brand, certainly. More Loy Tanner's, by the sound of it. Much more likely, here on his home territory, he had a sweet little dolly bird waiting up for him.'

Lenny Bale screamed. He threw himself about. He threw himself at Jurnet, fingers curved into talons.

'Have to put in for danger money with this one,' Jack Ellers complained some minutes later, as he hauled a bedraggled floozy from under the shower. The streaked face dripped make-up on to the expensive towel in which the little Welshman had thoughtfully enveloped the sopping figure.

'Better go and get a wash yourself,' he advised his superior officer. 'There's a scratch on your left cheek. Don't hold back with the soap. If you think you ought to go and get your rabies jab right away, I'll stay with the Queen of the May here till you get back.'

'So long as it isn't AIDS.' Jurnet helped the Sergeant roll Second Coming's manager on to the bed. He covered the ruin with the bedspread, not without charity. Even the slime at the bottom of the barrel was entitled to the respect due to its residual humanity.

Lenny Bale sat up and said, without drama, 'If I'd thought it could have been for a woman, I'd have killed him first.'

'What *what* could have been for?' Jurnet asked.

'The money. Thirteen thousand pounds.'

20

When the story was told—or as much of it as Lenny Bale, still visibly shaken but with all his marbles back in place, was able or saw fit to impart—Jurnet said, 'You left out the most important thing.'

'I'm cold.' The man snuggled deeper into the bed. 'I don't know what you're talking about.'

'I'll spell it out for you. You tell us you leave Angleby Wednesday before the crack of dawn, you spend the day in London running rings round yourself to get together the £13,000 in cash Loy tells you he has to have in his hands by that night—'

'So?'

'Being who he was, you know as well as I do that if he wanted £13,000 all that bad, all he had to do was walk into the nearest bank at opening time and walk out with ten, twenty times as much, once he'd proved who he was.'

'I told you he never used his own bread, if he could help it.'

'But £13,000! Not quite in the same category, is it, as getting a sudden urge to pee when it's your round coming up at the Goat and Compasses?'

'Loy knew there was nothing I wouldn't do for him.'

'I believe you! £13,000! True love can't come higher than that.'

The detective walked over to the window. It looked out on to the courtyard where Loy Tanner had parked his van. The detective stood looking down, watched a Jag slide smoothly from its place and out of the gate like a sleek black seal. He turned, silhouetted against the light, and said flatly, 'I smell blackmail.'

'Crazy!' Lenny Bale's voice lacked conviction. He had begun to whimper.

'What was Tanner proposing to do if you came back empty-handed? Go to the police and tell them his manager had been putting his hand in the till? Or call out a few of his old buddies from the quays at Havenlea to rough you up a bit?' When there was no reply: 'Look—I'm here to catch a murderer. I couldn't care less about your squalid little fiddles, if that's all they are. But I'll tell you this. You say you managed to get the money together. We can check on that, and we will. You say Tanner called round after the concert and you handed it over—'

The other nodded.

'—which, so far as we know, makes you the last person to see Loy Tanner before he finally copped it for good and all. Apart from the killer, of course.' After a pause: 'Unless we're talking about one and the same person.'

'You're mad!' The other's voice had strengthened. 'I stood at that window both days, just as you did now, only the other room, and I watched him drive in and I saw him drive out again. Both times.'

'So sure? At dead of night?'

'You couldn't mistake that white van. Besides, he was crucified, wasn't he, for Christ's sake! Where'd I ever get the nerve or the muscle to nail up a guy on a cross?'

'Nailed, was he? Don't underestimate yourself, Mr Bale. Over at Headquarters, ever since it happened, we've been crucifying volunteers round the clock, one after the other, to see if it could, or could not, be a one-man job; and, if it could be, does it take a young Hercules. And the answer is, no sweat, provided you take it easy and, like in the instruction books, proceed one step at a time. On the other hand, even in the event you're no handyman, maybe you too had buddies over at Havenlea, ready to give a pal a hand in time of trouble?'

Second Coming's manager hoisted himself to a sitting position. At the renewed sight of the lamé dress, the fitful springs of Jurnet's compassion dried up completely.

The man exclaimed: 'Maybes! Perhapses! Talk—that's all it is. You don't know who did it, so you pick on me. Because I loved Loy, because I tried to help him every way I could, this is what I get for it. Because I'm vulnerable—'

Jurnet interposed cheerfully, 'You're that, all right.'

'You can't keep me here in Angleby unless you arrest me. And how are you going to do that, without a single piece of solid evidence to back it up with? I've got to get back to London—'

'Nobody's stopping you, Mr Bale. Just so long as we know where to get in touch.'

'I—' the voice faltered, the man dropped back against the pillows. With coy abandon, one of the dress straps slipped off the shoulder. Jurnet regarded it with a moody disgust. 'As soon as I feel a little stronger—'

'And the *shiva*'s over, eh?' Jurnet straightened his back, took a deep breath. It was not enough. He felt an urgent need for some fresh air. On a sudden impulse, he picked up the man's dressing gown from the foot of the bed, the cashmere luxurious in his hand, and threw it over the dressing-table mirror.

'What's that for?' Lenny Bale sounded frightened.

'Just another quaint old Hebrew custom. After a death they always cover up looking-glasses.'

'Why's that?'

'Couldn't say. Just that's what they do, so I'm told.'

There was certainly something creepy about the shrouded glass. On his way to the bedroom door, the detective relented.

'Want me to take it down?'

'No. Leave it.'

Jurnet turned the car into Sebastopol Terrace and nearly reversed immediately back into Gallipoli Street. Miriam's red Golf was parked outside number 12.

The detective could not have said whether he was pleased or annoyed to find it there. Rather, taken aback: uncertain how best to deal with this overlapping of his two lives.

As he watched, Miriam, loaded with a pile of sweater pieces, backs and fronts and sleeves all separate and swathed in polythene, emerged from the front door and made her way, carefully with her burden, down the narrow path to

the gate. With her bronze hair, corduroy suit of a golden
colour, and flaunting orange scarf, she looked like a sun of
her own, standing in for that other one obstinately skulk-
ing behind the grey sky. Even at a distance Jurnet could
feel her warmth, or so it seemed to him, and was suddenly
racked with the painful joy of seeing her again.

By contrast, Mara Felsenstein, standing in her doorway
in a shapeless grey sweater and skirt, looked old enough to
be Miriam's mother. There was a droop to her shoulders,
a dowdiness that seemed as much innate as due to her age
or the cut of her clothes. When she saw Jurnet getting out
of his car, a deeper shadow crossed her face, to be followed at once by a determined rearrangement of features
which, with a little wishful thinking, might be taken for a
smile.

Not that man again! The detective could guess very well
what must be in the woman's mind. There were some
mothers of murdered sons who could never stop talking,
as if by keeping their violated children enmeshed in a net
of words, they could keep them from slipping away for
ever into the dark; and others who grudged every syllable.
Once speak the word 'death' and it was unretractable.

Only a few, a very few, faced their loss with the honesty
it deserved.

Miriam, stacking her knitwear in the back of the Golf,
looked up with an ill-concealed flash of joy at Jurnet's
approach.

'Hi!'

'Hello.'

With a significant little flick of the head towards number
12, Miriam murmured, 'Go easy with her. She's very near
breaking point.'

'Thank you for your confidence in me.'

'Don't be like that.' She made a little face, utterly
delicious. Her packages stowed, she turned towards her
lover—ex-lover?

'How would you like to stand me dinner tonight?'

'I've no idea what time I'll be through.'

'That's no answer.'

'I'll try again.' Against Jurnet's will, and out of his control, resentment rose to the surface. 'Dinner by all means,

so long as you don't object to three at table.' She stared at him, uncomprehending. 'That corpse with his skull bashed in—remember? My mate, my dear old pal. As you've so rightly pointed out, we go about everywhere together.'

Mara Felsenstein led the way indoors. In the living-room-cum-workroom the knitting machines were covered, the grate empty, the ashes sloppily cleaned out. A cheap electric fire stood on the hearth, one bar on, scarcely enough to take the chill off the air. The whole room seemed to have lost the spruce appearance which had so impressed Jurnet on his first visit.

Mara Felsenstein said, 'I didn't realize you knew Miss Courland.'

'Miriam?' The detective couldn't bear to hear even her name mentioned so distantly in connection with himself. 'Coppers get to know everybody in their patch sooner or later.'

'How nice to know so many people! Would you like a cup of coffee?'

'Me and the milkman, eh? I wouldn't say no, if it isn't too much trouble. You're looking a bit done up.'

The extraordinary eyes, only a little dulled, regarded Jurnet with a tired honesty. 'Do I? I suppose I do. It's funny. Inside—the me at the middle of myself, if you know what I mean—feels it has come to terms with what has happened. Accepted it. It's the outside, the stupid shell you wouldn't think, would you, had any feelings of its own apart from what your mind puts into it, that's finding it hard to cope.'

'Know what you mean. Why don't you sit down and let me make *you* a cuppa?'

The woman managed a proper smile at last.

'Miriam said just the same. People *are* good! But it's good for me to keep busy.' She nodded at a large carton denting the cushions of the couch. 'She didn't even ask if I wanted to take on a new order. Just brought it in, and dumped it there without a word. She's a wonderful person. So understanding.'

'Is that so?'

A little bemused by this picture of his infuriating love as seen through others' eyes, Jurnet followed Mrs Felsenstein into a small kitchen conspicuously lacking in the gadgetry of modern living. The woman filled a kettle at the stone sink and set it to boil on a stove old enough to make a Gas Board salesman feel he had lived in vain.

The detective remarked with cheerful casualness, 'I heard somewhere you can get grants for improving domestic facilities. City Hall could tell you.'

'Loy wanted to have a fitted kitchen put in. He sent a sheaf of brochures: £2,000 the cheapest! Absurd!'

Jurnet said, 'First woman I knew to turn down the chance of a new kitchen when it was offered. You must be one of nature's puritans.'

Mrs Felsenstein stopped what she was doing, and turned to look at him, her expression surprised, as if she had just been told something about herself she had not previously suspected.

'My father was a lay preacher. Perhaps that accounts for it. Anyway, we have everything we need.' She took two mugs down from a shelf and placed them on a table of scrubbed deal, measured a teaspoonful of Nescafé into each.

Jurnet eyed the two mugs and said, 'Mr Felsenstein not about, then?'

'He's lying down.' The eyes were suddenly brighter—with tears, was it, or anger? Mrs Felsenstein picked up a newspaper from a kitchen chair and thrust it at the detective. 'Have you seen today's *Argus*?'

Jurnet took the paper from her, his first impression one of satisfaction that the violent death of Loy Tanner had been demoted from the lead story. 'What exactly—' he began, when the woman stabbed the page with a strong, square-nailed finger.

There were two photographs: the Hob's Hole Venus before and after, both pictures completely missing the magic of the original. As resurrected in the *Angleby Argus*, the big-bellied goddess from beyond the dawn of chronicled time looked about as charismatic as a garden gnome, and not half as pretty.

Jurnet said, 'I know about this. I was at the University

after it happened, and spoke to a couple of the professors. Shocking vandalism.' He regarded the woman curiously. 'Why does it affect you particularly?'

'I don't suppose anybody told you it was Leo who discovered her. Professor Whinglass knows. He and Leo are good friends.'

'Nobody said a word. How did it happen?'

The water boiled. The woman turned the gas off, brought the kettle to the table and filled the mugs, stirring the liquid so that it sloshed over, a little. Out of a cupboard she fetched milk, a bowl filled with soft sugar, and some Osborne biscuits which she set out on a small plate. All this was done with a closed face, a distant manner which Jurnet found hard to account for. At one point she paused, head cocked to one side, listening for a sound from upstairs.

'I thought I heard—'

'Can I make a cup for Mr Felsenstein?'

Mara Felsenstein looked at the detective; came out of her reverie as if she had made a decision. She smiled, a real smile. A transformation.

'Sit down and drink your coffee while it's hot.' She herself took the wooden chair at the further side of the table, took up the other mug and curved her hands round it, warming them.

'In those days,' she said, taking it for granted the other would know which time she meant, 'Leo was a splendid walker; though, even then, he wasn't strong. Too much had been done to him in Auschwitz for him ever to be really strong again. But he was still young, and youth has its own strength, hasn't it?' With loving pride: 'He was fifteen when he came to England, his whole education ruined by the war, but still he managed to qualify as a librarian. That will give you an idea of his determination, his unbroken spirit.

'Any chance he had, in those years before he knew me, he'd get away alone, walking all over East Anglia. Going to see barrows, following old trackways, things like that. Prehistory was his hobby, you see. And that's how he found the Venus, at Hob's Hole.' The woman was silent a moment, then ended, with the air of one imparting a confidence to a friend: 'He always says—even if he smiles a little when he says it—that so far as he is concerned, finding her justifies everything that happened to him up to that day—Hitler, Auschwitz, even the unspeakable things that were done to him there—because, when you came down to it, they were the very things which had conspired to bring him to Hob's Hole at that precise moment of time. So you can see why we're both so upset.'

Mrs Felsenstein reached across the table and took back the *Argus:* cried a little, her tears dropping on to the whole and the vandalized Venus impartially.

Jurnet said, 'I must have got it wrong. Somehow I'd got the idea the statue was only discovered a little while ago.'

At that the woman went red, discarding ten years in her embarrassment. Flushed, she resurrected a kind of beauty. 'Oh dear! I shouldn't have said anything, should I? I don't know what, as a policeman, you're going to think of us. When it came to the point, Leo simply couldn't bring himself to hand her over to the Museum. I think he fell in love with her at first sight and I—' hesitantly—'I too, once I came to know her—I was very immature and I know it sounds silly—began to find her indispensable. I felt that somehow, in some way I can't describe, she was teaching me how to be a woman. For years she stood on the mantelpiece here, watching us—watching over us.'

'People must have commented.'

The other shook her head. 'Not really. The people we know aren't sensitive about such things. A few who smoked stubbed out their cigarettes in the votive dish, taking it for an ashtray. And I remember the man who came from the Gas Board to mend the cooker asking me if I'd won it playing bingo on the pier at Havenlea. He said it was a diabolical liberty.'

'What made your husband finally decide to turn her in after all?'

She thought the question over. 'I'm not sure. Unless it was really her idea. I'd grown up and she was ready to move on.'

'And what did Loy think of the Hob's Hole Venus?'

'Oh,' she said vaguely, startled by the name into the

remembrance of grief, 'he hardly noticed. You know what boys are.'

Jurnet said, 'I don't know. Not one like Loy, anyway. And I need to, if I'm to find out who killed him. I'm truly sorry to give you pain, but I must ask you to tell me about him. Right from the beginning.'

Mara Felsenstein said, 'Nothing could give me more pain than I feel already.' She got up, picked up the coffee mugs and took them over to the sink. 'We saw so little of him, though, in recent years. Others can tell you much more.'

The detective shook his head. 'I've spoken to the people he worked with. What they've had to say has told me any amount about themselves. But about Loy, not all that much.'

The woman stood by the sink in silence, looking down at the dirty mugs, making no attempt to wash them up. Then: 'You said, right from the beginning. You didn't really mean that.'

'I did. Like I said, I need to know.'

'So do I.' She turned and looked full at Jurnet with those eyes he found so astonishing. 'It sounds so ridiculous, doesn't it? Me, his mother. But he was such a quiet child, so secretive—'

'You see, you're telling me things already.'

'Very loving, though.' She said it quickly, as if preempting contradiction. 'And eager to be loved in return. You always had to show it, mind you—he'd never take it for granted. You actually had to say the words before he would be satisfied, and let you go.'

'Was Mr Felsenstein equally loving?'

'Oh yes! He always treated Loy like a son.'

'And did Loy treat him like a father?'

'They were very good friends. It was lovely to see them together. Leo had unending patience, more than I had. If Loy wanted someone to play Snakes and Ladders with, to make a kite, anything, Leo was always the one he went to.'

'Did the boy never ask you why his name was Tanner, not Felsenstein?'

The woman was not disturbed, only mildly curious. 'Do

the police always keep records about women who give birth out of wedlock?'

'Certainly not. As it happens, Miriam happened to say something—'

The other's face lit up with sudden understanding. 'You're the boy-friend!'

'I haven't yet thanked you for the tickets.'

Mrs Felsenstein said, 'Sad, isn't it, I never heard him sing? Professionally, that is.' Turning on the detective the candid gaze which he found so powerfully affecting: 'I expect you find that strange—suspicious even, from one who calls herself a loving mother. But long before then, when he was still living at home, if he sang, it was always in his room, strumming his guitar, and keeping his voice down. It wasn't that Leo and I weren't both tremendously proud of his gift; just that, for some reason we didn't understand but had to respect, he chose not to let us be part of it. Later on, I suppose, we could have bought ourselves a record player and played his records, but we didn't. It would have seemed like snooping.'

'You missed an experience.'

'We must have, from all that the papers have been writing about him now he's dead. But perhaps it's just as well. Perhaps never having heard him makes it less unbearable. At least there's no voice haunting my memories. That is—' amending what she had just said, with a grave concern for accuracy—'assuming there are grades of unbearable, which I really don't think there are.'

Jurnet said, in all sincerity, 'For someone who has to bear the unbearable, you're making out pretty well.'

'I never knew policemen were so kind. Miriam's very lucky. When I see her again I shall tell her so. Of course I told Loy about his name,' Mrs Felsenstein went on. 'As soon as he was old enough to understand—both about his father, and also what was so special about being a Tanner. One thing more than cancelled out the other.'

'Was there ever any question of your husband formally adopting him?'

'Oh, Leo was terribly keen. I was the one who said no. It didn't seem right to me, after all he had gone through, to load him with the responsibility for another man's child.'

Her voice was bleak but stoical. Jurnet, disregarding the greyness and fatigue, sensed the woman's strength of spirit, and was moved by it. 'You must have been very young.'

'Ye—es.' Mara Felsenstein spoke hesitantly, as if 'young' was a word of whose meaning she was not 100 per cent certain. 'Young and foolish. Maybe, if Loy had been Loy Felsenstein instead of Loy Tanner, none of this would have happened. It would all have been different. I sometimes think, I had the chance to choose and I made the wrong choice.'

Jurnet shook his head.

'Don't let it bother you. The only real choices life offers you are different ways of making a fool of yourself.'

21

'Not *many* friends,' Mrs Felsenstein admitted, in answer to Jurnet's inquiry. 'I suppose he was what you would call a loner.' Adding quickly, 'Not one of those children, though, other children take against, for some reason or none. When there were families still living in the Terrace, there were always children scrambling about on the bomb site. Loy would stand there on the pavement watching them, and often, I'd look out of the bedroom window, my heart aching to see him there, so small and isolated, and all the others rushing about and shouting. But after a while it dawned on me that the solitariness was of his own choosing. Time after time they'd call over to him to join in the game, but he always smiled and shook his head. So of course, after a while they stopped asking.'

'Was it the same later on, as he got older?'

'When he was at the Comprehensive there were one or two boys whose homes he used to go round to, to listen to their records, or they'd get together to play their guitars. He was mad about guitars. Leo always used to say the most post that came through the letter-box was guitar catalogues Loy'd written away for.' Her eyes clouded with tears again. 'The Christmas he was fifteen Leo bought him a beauty, really much too good for a teenager, but there! We wanted to give him pleasure. Only, on Boxing Day he took it round to show one of his guitar-playing pals, and one of the boys there accidentally stood on it. Ruined it completely.'

The heavy lids with their thick lashes of light brown came down, squeezed tight against the cheeks. When she raised them, the tears were gone, the eyes with their dazzling whites as bright as ever. 'Fortunately, it was soon after that that he started going with Francesca, which took his mind off everything else.'

'His first girl-friend?'

'Let's say, the only one I knew about. I can't tell you how pleased I was. Not just because she was a darling, which she was—pretty as a picture in a demure, delicate way, a real little convent girl—but because she was so good for Loy. He blossomed, that's the only word for it. Sometimes, when I'd see them out in the street together, when they hadn't seen me first, I wouldn't know whether to laugh or to cry—Loy so manly and protective, she so sweet, a little nun, just beginning to awaken to the possibilities of what life might hold for a woman—' Mrs Felsenstein was silent a moment. Then finished: 'I should have cried, shouldn't I?'

Jurnet proffered inadequately, 'None of us can foretell the future.'

The woman hugged herself, tight; as if she felt the need of somebody's arms about her, if only her own. Said: 'Falcone. Francesca Falcone. Does the name mean anything to you?'

'There's a Mrs Annie Falcone runs the Red Shirt in Bergate—'

'Francesca was her daughter—the last girl you'd expect to have a mother running a pub. I shouldn't say that, should I?—I'm sure it's a perfectly respectable profession—but the Red Shirt does have a certain reputation here in the town—'

'Not much you can tell me about the Red Shirt,' said Jurnet in a closed, official voice.

'I shouldn't say a word against Mrs Falcone. She looked after Francesca beautifully. I gathered she was never allowed anywhere near the business part of the premises. The living quarters were on top, but the way in was through a courtyard round the side—the girl never needed to come through the bar, or anythng like that. Until she met Loy I don't believe she ever went out anywhere except to school or to Mass.'

'How did she come to meet your son?'

'Loy never said. I can only guess. They go in for a lot of live entertainment at the Red Shirt, don't they? Topless, and all that. And of course there are always groups singing there—new boys doing it for the beer, Loy said, in hopes of being talent-spotted by someone from London. It's the same today, except that I'm told the toplessness stretches further down than it used to. If you go past the Red Shirt at night, as I'm sure you know, Inspector, there's always a crowd of boys, most of them too young to be allowed in, milling about outside—'

'So long as that's where they are.' It was the copper speaking.

'I'm sure that's where Loy was. I imagine that's how he first saw Francesca, coming home from somewhere, and turning out of Bergate into the courtyard—'

'Sounds likely. And was Mrs Falcone, do you know, as pleased about Loy as you were about Francesca?'

'I don't know. I never met her till afterwards.'

'Afterwards?' Jurnet rummaged in his memory and drew a blank.

'After the girl was dead.'

Suddenly, Jurnet remembered. Giving no hint of it, he asked, 'What happened?'

'She and Loy had arranged to meet on Yarrow Bridge. They often met there—it's just down the hill from Bergate, but well away from the pub, and I suppose it seemed a romantic spot, the bridge so old, the rosy red brick, and the river flowing below. Loy told me they used to squeeze themselves into one of those little niches there are on either side—you know?—and talk; perhaps kiss when nobody was passing. I'm sure it was all very innocent.

'The evening it happened, Francesca got to the bridge first. It was July, still light, and Loy, when he came along, saw her waiting there on the upstream side as he came down the hill. The bridge was deserted, nobody in sight. He called out to her, but she didn't seem to hear him because—or so he thought—something in the river had caught her attention and she was leaning over the bridge wall in order to get a better look. Those niches have a step up, so she was quite a bit above the brickwork. Loy called out to her again, partly in greeting, partly because he thought it looked dangerous and he wanted her to come away. Instead, she leaned over even further—as if, Loy told us, whatever it was she was looking at was disappearing under the bridge and she wanted to keep it in sight as long

as possible. The next moment, to his horror, she had over-
balanced and gone over the side, and she could only swim
a couple of lengths, if that. The Virgo Fidelis didn't have a
pool of its own then, and didn't like taking their girls to
the public baths. Loy scrambled down the slope to the river,
kicked off his trainers, dived in, and brought her to land.'

'Good for Loy.'

Mrs Felsenstein shook her head. 'Bad for him. Worse
for Francesca. Either falling, or when she was struggling
in the water, she must have hit her head against one of the
bridge buttresses, and she didn't seem to know what she
was doing. The currents round the piers there are very
tricky—more than one boat has crashed into them, as you
probably know—and Loy had a terrible time. Francesca
was fighting and screaming—it's a wonder she didn't drag
him under with her. When he was back home again and I
saw him naked, I was shocked by the way his chest was a
mass of bruises where she had pummelled him. But he
held on like grim death. He wouldn't let her go.

'By then, other people had come down to the river, and
were getting ready to go in after them: but suddenly
Francesca went limp, and Loy was able to get to the bank
without help. The people there pulled them both out, and
they gave Francesca the kiss of life until the ambulance
came. It was only later, at the inquest, that we heard she
must have been dead already when they took her out of
the water. That blow on the head had killed her.'

'What about Loy?'

'They wanted to take him to hospital as well—he was in
a terrible state, as you can imagine. But—one of the
ambulance men told me about it later—when he heard
that Francesca was dead, he let out a great shout, and he
got up and ran away, just as he was, in his bare feet and
dripping wet. They tried to stop him, they thought he'd
gone out of his mind—which I suppose he had, poor
boy—but he ran like a deer, they couldn't catch him, even
though, by the time he arrived back home, the soles of his
feet were slashed to ribbons.'

Mrs Felsenstein concluded with sombre satisfaction, 'He
came home. It was his first thought. I stripped off his
clothes, wrapped him in a blanket, put him to bed just as

he was, with a couple of hot-water bottles. Leo went for the doctor, but by the time he came Loy was asleep, a sleep so deep I wouldn't let the doctor disturb him. He slept for nearly twenty-four hours, and when he woke up he was a different boy.'

'Different? How do you mean?'

'It's not easy to explain.' Mrs Felsenstein wrinkled her brow, pushed her hair back from her forehead. 'To say he'd grown up is too simple. It was the first time he'd had anything to do with death—and when it's the death of somebody you love! Also, he obviously had a terrible feeling of guilt: that if he'd only put out that little extra effort he might have saved her—from which it wasn't too much of a step, I suppose, to convincing himself that, to all intents and purposes, he was the one who'd killed her. It was Leo who, with infinite love and patience, finally got him to see that he had nothing to reproach himself with. Quite the contrary.'

'You still haven't said in what way he'd changed.'

The woman answered slowly, testing each word to make sure it could bear the weight of her meaning.

'In a way that completely astonished us. He became—harder's the best description I can think of. Dominant: even domineering. From being so quiet and retiring, he became the leader among the boys he knew, and among others he'd had nothing to do with before who suddenly seemed attracted into his orbit. Not that he became loud or pushy; just that, when he spoke, they sprang to attention. It was quite remarkable how they all deferred to him, and even more so how Loy seemed to take it all for granted. Leo said it was like Tamino in *The Magic Flute*. He had passed through a soul-searing ordeal, and emerged tempered steel.'

Falteringly: 'I wouldn't want you to think that overnight he turned into a stranger. When the letter came from the Royal Humane Society to say they were going to give him a certificate for his courageous attempt to rescue Francesca, he tore it up and threw the pieces into the grate. It was summer, there wasn't any fire, and he went and got matches, and didn't move away from the hearth until it was burnt, to the last scrap. And when Mrs Falcone called round to thank him personally, he slammed upstairs, and wouldn't come down until she'd gone.'

Jurnet commented, 'Knowing Annie Falcone, I'm surprised she let a little thing like that stop her. I'd have expected her to be up the stairs after him.'

'Is she like that? She looked like that,' Mrs Felsenstein admitted. 'Very handsome, but overpowering, with her blonde hair, and her clothes, and her shoes with such high heels. What a cat I sound! I'm so dowdy myself, I'm just not used to women who dress like that.' The woman shook her head, correcting herself with that devastating honesty which Jurnet had decided went with her eyes. 'But I don't really think, at the time, I noticed anything about her, except her face. It seemed to have suffered a stroke worse than actual paralysis, a dreadful stoniness which left the features still able to move, but had frozen all the emotions behind them. I remember she sat there on the couch with her skirt very short, her knees showing, and a great big handbag on her lap—alligator, very grand, like a small Gladstone bag—and she kept snapping and unsnapping the fastener on the top. After telling me why she'd come she hardly said anything—just sat there snapping and unsnapping that bag. I don't suppose she even knew she was doing it. It was the only sound in the room. I don't know why, it sounded more terrible than silence.'

'What about you? Didn't you say anything?'

'I tried to. I let her know how much I'd loved Francesca, how happy I'd been for Loy to have her for a friend: how even her short life had made the world a better place. After a while, she snapped her handbag shut, got up from the couch and said, "Tell your son I'll say thank you some other time," and went. At the door she turned and kissed me, so I can only hope I'd given her some comfort. Her lips were very cold, I remember, and when Loy came downstairs again, after she'd finally left, he looked at me, burst out laughing, and told me to go and wash my face. She'd left a great smear of lipstick on my cheek.'

'Did Loy find himself another girl-friend?'

At the sink again, Mrs Felsenstein turned on the tap and began to wash up the coffee mugs.

'From here on,' she said, 'I'm afraid you'll have to ask

those others you were talking about. It wasn't long after
Mrs Falcone called that Loy left home.'

'Some kind of family bust-up?'

'Oh, nothing like that! I told you, he'd changed, knew
what he wanted to do, and how to go about it. To Leo's
regret, he'd never shown much interest in school—all his
reports said how well he could do if he would only try, but
he never did—and he left as soon as he could, and moved
in with a couple of boys—well, it was a squat, really.' With
an indulgent smile: 'I remember Leo saying, if he wanted
to live in a derelict house he'd only to move next door, but
that wasn't the point, was it? The whole idea—and very
natural, please don't think we didn't understand—was to
get away from home, stand on his own feet. After a while, he
moved on to Havenlea, and from there to London and a lot
of other places.' The woman looked at Jurnet with a pride
touched with sad humour. 'The rest, as they say, is history.'

'But he never lost touch?'

'I told you. We were a very loving family.'

'That money he was always on at you to take. How
much was it, at any one time?'

'It varied. £50. £150. That last time, when Mr Scarlett
came round with the tickets, it was over £300.'

'Never as much as £13,000?'

Mrs Felsenstein stared at the detective in astonishment.
'What on earth would we do with £13,000?'

'Just asking.' Jurnet asked further, 'That last time he
came to see you, on the Tuesday evening, was he as
affectionate as ever? Everything the same between you?'

'Everything the same.'

Mara Felsenstein put the mugs back on the shelf. Her
back was to the detective: he could see her shoulders
shaking.

'Loy!' she sobbed. 'Loy!'

22

'Have you eaten?' the Superintendent asked Jurnet with that mixture of irritation and concern which seemed at the roots of their relationship. 'That lean and hungry look you were lucky enough to be born with looks even leaner and hungrier than usual. Do you just forget to eat, Ben, or is it some private bargain you make with that Old Testament God of yours? An ongoing Day of Atonement, not a morsel of food to touch your lips until the moment He sees fit to deliver your quarry into your hand?'

'Actually—' Jurnet gave away nothing of his gratification that his superior officer actually cared about his physical well-being—'I was holding back on purpose. I've got a table booked at the Nelson.'

It was a lie, and Jurnet fancied the Superintendent knew it as well as he did.

'They do a good roast beef and Yorkshire at the Nelson,' said the Superintendent, making his scepticism explicit. 'Also a gooseberry fool which, whatever else I am, I am not. Starve yourself, by all means, if that's what you have in mind, just so long as you don't peg out before you catch whoever killed Loy Tanner.' He turned on his subordinate a look from which all goodwill had been expunged. 'We don't seem to be getting on all that fast.'

'No, sir,' the other agreed with a sunny smile artfully calculated to send the bugger up the wall. Of such small revenges was happiness made. 'It takes a little while to get the threads sorted out.'

'Threads?' the Superintendent echoed sourly. 'We aren't sewing the Bayeux Tapestry.' He got up from his chair at the wide desk which made explicit his apartness from the underlings, and went over to the window. 'You seen the latest, out there in the garden?'

'I saw the flowers.'

'Then you haven't seen anything. A lying-in-state, I tell you, lacking only the body of the dear departed. They've got a youngster of doubtful sex at each corner, got up all in white and standing with bowed head over a reversed guitar. That besotted Mrs Skylark has even had the floodlights turned on.'

'Sounds a bit theatrical.'

'A travesty! No doubt, if this weather gets any colder, we'll have a crucifixion on ice. Mountebanks!' exclaimed the Superintendent, finding relief in the small explosion of syllables. 'At least, whatever else it was when they crucified the real Christ, it wasn't sick. It was part of the everyday pattern of events, the normal Roman way of getting rid of troublemakers.'

Still irate at the limits of his authority: 'In the old days, too, in a city of this size, they turned away travelling players and similar trash—wouldn't so much as let them through the gates. Here in Angleby today, God help us, we not only let them in with hosannas, we welcome them to our seat of higher learning, so-called. Wonder they didn't confer honorary degrees on the three of them while they were about it!'

In the interests of fair play, Jurnet felt constrained to point out, 'We don't know that it was actually one of the group who—'

'How right you are!' the other returned, in a voice heavy with sarcasm. 'The extent of our ignorance is positively mind-blowing. We still don't even know where the murder was committed—no reports of screams in the night, or blood seeping through the ceiling. Nothing as to what happened to Tanner's clothes; nothing in the van except a few lengths of cord which, mercifully, the road manager was able to account for. We have no idea how far Mr Tanner toured in his role of *corpus delicti*. Colton, that eager beaver, tells us the post-mortem abrasions on the body could just as well be due to a mile and a half over the potholes of an unmade-up road as forty on a dual carriageway. We're still not sure whether we're looking for a lone

killer or a conspiracy. And, central to all, we still haven't a
clue as to why, with the whole planet in which to dispose
of the carcass, our murderer-stroke-murderers made the
bizarre choice they did. Exhibitionism, religious mania—or
what?'

The Superintendent drew an exasperated breath, pressed
his back hard against the back of his chair, and suddenly
favoured his subordinate with a smile of astonishing
sweetness.

'Get along with you to the Nelson, Ben. It's been a long
day.'

Disarmed by the smile, as ever, Jurnet ventured rashly,
'Chap today wanted to know how anyone could think him
capable of man-handling a dead body up on to a cross, he
hadn't the physique for it. I told him we were working on
that one—had an experiment going with a corps of volunteers, round the clock, to find out if in fact it could be
done single-handed.'

The Superintendent burst out laughing, exceeding the
detective's expectations. He was a man who seldom laughed
aloud. Even more surprising was: 'That's the first sensible
idea I've heard today! Where can we set it up?'

'I didn't really mean—'

'Then you should have! Let's see—' The Superintendent
got up from his chair again, this time to perch himself on
the edge of his desk, a liberty he seldom took with that
formidable emblem of office, and an infallible pointer to
good humour. 'The cross is over at the lab. There's that
courtyard with the rose bushes we could use to set it up
in—no!' pulling himself up short. 'All those windows!
Can't you imagine what a meal the media'd make of it, if it
leaked out? Or—God forbid—they sneaked in a camera-man?'

He reviewed the options, solved the problem with characteristic dispatch.

'That barn of a place where they play badminton. Only
skylights there, and we could fix some blinds, if we're
scared of helicopters!' The man looked as gleeful as an
urchin planning mischief. 'None of your volunteers, though.
We've got to keep this strictly under wraps. If anything
leaked out, the chief'd have conniptions and we'd all be
out on our ears. You and me, Jack and Sid Hale—what do

you think? Not Dave Batterby. He couldn't resist the chance of getting himself on the front page, even if he had to play Judas Iscariot to do it.'

Jurnet was not sure what to think. Playing safe: 'Who are we going to practise on? Where are we going to find someone long and skinny as Tanner was?'

The Superintendent did not answer. The mischievous grin grew wider. He reached across the desk for the telephone, and lifted the receiver.

'Put me through to Dr Colton, would you?'

On the way down to the car-park Jurnet paused, cocked his head to listen, and changed direction—back to the main hall and thence out into the Market Place. Night had settled down on the city, brooding it without love. Under its chill wings most of the traders had packed it in for the day: only here and there a sad, Asian face still waited for the last purchaser of a brass tray or a cut-price toilet roll.

Above, in the little garden, the floodlights gleamed on the young heads, the thin young necks, bent in homage over the mound of flowers. How still the youngsters stood, thought the detective, despite their thin clothes and the piercing cold. Still as a stone. Never a shiver.

But then they had the beat to keep them warm.

The beat had penetrated Police Headquarters; faintly, but enough to drum Jurnet out into the Market Place and across the road to where Lijah Starling, in a black kaftan splashed with yellow, on his head a round African cap woven with gold and silver threads, sat among his drums celebrating the life and the death of his lost leader.

Polished ebony in the floodlights, the drummer sat with eyes half-closed, sleeves thrown back to reveal his powerful arms moving with deceptive ease. The message of the drums filled the available space, banged against the sky. It bounced off the surrounding buildings, scooping bewildered pigeons off the ledges where they had already settled down for the night. Crowds gathered quickly, belated workers hurrying home to their evening meal and their tellies, but drawn to stand rooted to the cold cobbles, listening.

'*Go back to Africa!*' Jurnet growled under his breath. Yet he stayed. He stayed until the sound died away and Lijah Starling sat quietly, his hands clasped in his lap.

A guitar sounded, fragile after what had preceded it, and Johnny Flowerdew walked into the circle of light, strumming as he came.

The voice that came out of the white, mocking face was not the voice of Loy Tanner; but it was not the voice of Johnny Flowerdew either. Either the cold, or the occasion, or the hovering spirit of the lead singer of Second Coming had transformed it. Or else the drums had prepared the way, programmed the listeners to hear more than was there to be heard.

Whichever it was, they listened, and they wept.

> *How sweet the light,*
> *How dark the night:*
> *Sorrow is better than laughter.*
> *A time to weep,*
> *A time to sleep,*
> *Whatever may come after.*

A cruel whisper of wind had begun to circle the Market Place. Automatically, without any lessening of attention, the listeners drew scarves tighter across throats, fiddled for the top buttons of overcoats. Out of this diffuse, unthinking movement a flash of white caught the corner of Jurnet's eye. Taller than most who stood there, he looked over the heads of the crowd and saw Miriam in the act of pulling the shawl collar of her new white coat high over her bare head.

That she had not seen him the detective was practically sure. All her attention was held by Johnny Flowerdew and his bitter-sweet threnody.

> *The silver cord is loosed,*
> *The golden bowl is broken.*
> *The final song is sung,*
> *The final word is spoken.*

A low moan rose from the crowd, heaven-sent backing for a number bound to make it to the charts. Jurnet worked at his cynicism, without much success; conscious all the time of the white coat away on his right. Conscious of the song Johnny Flowerdew was still singing.

Johnny Flowerdew sang:

> We have come to the end of the world.
> The beginning is less than the end.
> The curtain is down, the flag is furled.
> Oh, my friend! Oh, my friend!

23

Jurnet drove on to the forecourt of his block of flats with the feeling that it had been a long time since he had last seen home. For once he was glad to find that nothing had changed, the black polythene bags poised at the entrance as immutable and imperious as the stone lions and unicorns that graced statelier residences. To his one regret, though, there was no sign of the black cat.

A pity. At the deli where he had stopped off for the makings of his evening meal—baked beans, an expiring salad, and a wedge of blueberry cheesecake—he had picked up six tins of catfood, each of a different brand in case the cat was a choosy eater.

Lacking Miriam on the other side of his front door, he was surprised at this sense of homecoming: but there it was. For once he was glad she had stubbornly refused his pleas to get the flat decorated; to instruct him in the mysteries of deep-freezes and micro-ovens so that he could provide a setting worthier of her. Even a three-piece suite and wall-to-wall carpeting, it seemed, had to wait upon his becoming a Jew.

For tonight, at least, he was grateful to have nothing about his domestic ambiance which required living up to. Tonight, if never again, the slow-simmered underwear on the stairs smelled positively piquant, as if someone had added a soupçon of French knickers. On the landing, to complete his felicity, the cat sat waiting.

The animal did not run to meet him: rose and arched itself indolently, rasping its paws through the tatty bit of coconut matting outside the flat door. The detective, absurdly elated, was fishing in his pocket for his key when the door across the landing opened. Mrs Petherton must have been listening for him.

'I thought you were never coming!' she exclaimed, in the waspish way she had on days when her pension was not quite due and the hombre at the Hacienda Bar was proving less than simpatico. 'I told it to go away I don't know how many times, but it just stared at me as if *I* was the one who had no business here. Naturally, I couldn't bring myself to touch it, nasty, flea-ridden thing!' At the sight of Jurnet taking out his key, she let out a dainty scream. 'You're never going to let it inside!'

The detective answered kindly, wishing that he had some gin in the house to help a neighbour over a bad patch. 'If it looks like it's needed, I'll get some flea powder first thing in the morning, I promise you. Either way, you don't have to worry. I've never heard that cats' fleas go for anybody or anything but cats.'

'How can you be so sure? You're not a vet. And what about my fur jacket? I'm sorry, Mr Jurnet'—in her present mood, she did not sound at all sorry—'if you don't get rid of that disgusting creature this minute, I'll call the police!'

'Oh dear!' said Jurnet. 'And I was hoping, since I'm on my own tonight, you'd keep me company over a glass of sherry. I'm sorry we're out of spirits.'

'*Sweet* sherry?' the other inquired sharply.

'Medium sweet.'

Medium appeased, Mrs Petherton allowed herself to cross the detective's threshold once the cat and its putative fleas had been safely locked in the kitchen. She drank three schooners of sherry and would have drunk a fourth if there had been more in the bottle. Having no cheese straws to offer, the detective proffered the cheesecake, which Mrs Petherton found acceptable, to the last crumb. The little woman was plainly even more skint than usual at the end of the week.

It wasn't much of a sacrifice for Jurnet to suggest she do him a favour; take his salad back to her own flat to consume later. He'd only bought it because Miriam had brainwashed him into believing that lettuce was essential to good health, sound teeth, and a successful sex life. For all he knew to the contrary, you couldn't become a Jew without it.

When Mrs Petherton had gone back to her flat, soothed with wine, Jurnet went into the kitchen to feed the cat.

After opening three different tins of catfood, only to have each rejected in turn, he gave in: opened the baked beans and watched them disappear down the cat's gullet with lightning speed. For himself, he uncovered another tin of sardines in the cupboard; ate them without appetite whilst the cat, pausing in a vigorous toilette which must surely have spelt annihilation to any fleas in the vicinity, regarded him with something approaching incredulity.

Not pity, certainly. And quite right. Anyone who didn't have the nous to hang on to his own beans deserved what was coming to him.

Cats, for example, would have known better than to answer the phone. Nothing but doom ever came through the telephone. The only good news was a wrong number.

When Jurnet picked up the receiver, Miriam began immediately, 'I ran into Cecily Gordon in the street, and as she's in charge of all the organizing, I thought it only right to let her know about the Seder as soon as possible.'

'Let her know what about it?'

'That you won't be coming, of course.'

'Shan't I?' Jurnet asked. Cats, he thought, having been stupid enough to pick up the phone in the first place, would, at that juncture, have had the sense to put it back on the hook. Either that, or throw it out of the window. 'It's the first I've heard of it.'

'Then you've heard of it now.' The voice at the other end of the wire did not disguise its tremulous exasperation. 'We've never had a communal Seder before. We want it to be a lovely, joyous occasion—'

'And you're afraid the sight of my kisser will turn the chicken soup sour?'

'Trust you to make a joke of it! We'll be celebrating the first night of Passover, a festival of liberation and hope. And there you'll be, soaked in death like a baba in rum. It's hard enough to take at any time, but on Seder night of all nights I simply couldn't stand it!' There was a sound, a strangled catching of breath Jurnet could not quite identify.

Miriam said in an altered tone, 'You didn't see me, but I saw you this evening, on the Market Place. I saw your face while Johnny Flowerdew was singing, and I saw—even at that distance I could see—it was all just washing over your head. All you were thinking about was how to catch whoever killed Loy Tanner.'

'I saw you too. And you're wrong. That's what I *should* have been thinking, if I was earning my pay. As it was, all I was thinking about was how much I loved you.'

There was a silence. Then a small voice said, 'You must think me an awful bitch.'

'No,' Jurnet contradicted. 'Though I have to admit there are times when you try hard. That tender, funny girl called Miriam who's the light of my life—let her be our secret, eh? Just between the two of us. I promise not to tell anybody, OK?'

'Moron!' But the tone was sweet.

'And, about the Seder—don't worry. I shan't embarrass you by turning up to be the hindquarter at the feast. In fact, I'm glad you reminded me. I doubt if I'd have been able to make it, anyway.'

'You *do* understand, Ben?'

'No,' said Jurnet. Then: 'It's on Good Friday, right?'

'Yes. Good Friday. It comes out at the same time, sometimes.'

'Funny, that. If I hadn't changed sides, who knows? Maybe the Bishop would have asked me to dinner instead. We could have had a lovely time, the two of us, arguing who crucified whom.'

24

Angleby wasn't big enough to boast of anything you could properly call a foreign quarter. Bergate was the nearest thing to it. There, towards the end of the nineteenth century, in the once elegant Georgian houses which had by then become warrens of the poor, large numbers of Italian immigrants had settled—masons and plasterers, makers of the beautifully finished shoes and gloves which were to earn the city an international reputation.

In the backyards, in the tumbledown outbuildings which had begun life as the coach houses of the rich, wiry little men in rusty black clothing, with names like Raffaelli and Marcantonio, had stored the bags of sweet chestnuts which, in winter, they sold, hot and mealy, from portable stoves set up craftily on corners where the wind knifed in straight from the tundra. As the world turned towards spring, they dragged little carts out of their spider-webbed hibernation, and spruced them up till they looked like a Sicilian fiesta; filled them with a frozen custard yellow as butter, and dragged them to the Market Place, there to dispense cornets and wafers and ice-cream boats until once more the leaves fell, the days shortened, and it was time for roasted chestnuts again.

Hitler's bombers and town planning had, between them, wrought changes in Bergate by the time Jurnet drove along the wide thoroughfare to call upon Annie Falcone at the Red Shirt. It was no longer a residential street: offices, warehouses, car showrooms, several with an Italian name on the fascia. The Raffaellis, the Marcantonios and their ilk, prospering for the most part, had long moved on to the comfortable suburbs: yet, it seemed, a race memory remained, a neighbourhood loyalty.

At lunchtime the Red Shirt was filled with Norfolk

151

businessmen ampler of gesture than the patrons of pubs in other streets of the city. Every 26 October, the anniversary of that day in 1860 when Garibaldi entered Naples in triumph and proclaimed Victor Emmanuel King of Italy, the businessmen of Bergate would be notably late getting back to their places of work. Many toasts were drunk, eyes uplifted in homage to the faded relic which hung in a glass case over the bar—the very shirt in which Great-great-grandfather Falcone had fought his way through Sicily and crossed to the mainland, one of the legendary Thousand who had set Italy free.

At night, the Red Shirt belonged to a different world. Then young people from all over the city crammed in to hear the latest group, to goggle or giggle at the topless singer whose top notes, like her bust, had gone a bit flat with age: a naughtiness the licensing justices and the police were happy to condone, finding it convenient to have local sin housed where they could put their hands on it, if need arose. True, a genuine villain might occasionally drop by to add a touch of class to the place, but by and large the Red Shirt was as innocent as only provincial sin could be.

Over both worlds Annie Falcone, ever since the day her husband Joe had dropped dead of a coronary, presided with tact, humour, and an iron hand. Jurnet, from his days in the uniformed branch, remembered well how any brawling in the vicinity of the Red Shirt invariably took place off the premises, not on; which was more than you could say for a good many other pubs in the town superficially of better reputation.

Dino, Annie's latest live-in barman, if that was the right word for him, opened the door reluctantly to the detective's knocking, and told him, with satisfaction, that Mrs Falcone was not at home. A shit, thought Jurnet, taking in the coarse good looks, the powerful shoulders running to fat. A thug with ambitions. Annie must be slipping. Unless, the years slipping away, she could no longer afford to be choosy.

'I'll wait outside.'

On the pavement next to the entrance to the courtyard, a pile of sand, reinforced by thuds and bangings from somewhere at the rear, advertised bulding work in progress. Jurnet frowned at the obstruction and made a mental note to alert the PC on the beat to see that something was done about it. But the frown was for official purposes only. Within, the essential Jurnet, to the essential Jurnet's surprise, was feeling altogether in lighter mood.

The weather, he decided. The day, though chill as those which had preceded it, was sunny, the air tonic. Instead of waiting in the car the detective walked up and down until, ten minutes later, he saw Annie Falcone turn her Volvo estate out of the road into the courtyard, nosing it expertly past the builders' clutter to a cleared space by the further wall.

Jurnet went to meet her, noting, as she got out of the car and locked it, that she, too, was smiling: noting too that, in his opinion at least, she could still have done better for herself than Dino. For somebody who would never see forty-five again, she looked good. A little too plump, the hair a little too yellow, the line of the chin blurred: but the legs, the eyes, the mouth sensual and humorous, were still such as to set up vibrations.

She came towards him teetering on her high heels, fur-coated, sweet-smelling, everything about her a little overdone, not through any error of taste but as if for the devil of it.

'I declare, if it isn't Ben Jurnet! What can I have been up to?'

'You're looking well, Annie.' Shaking hands, allowing his own to be captured by her two, almost an embrace: 'Well and happy.'

'That's because I've just come from church.'

'A state of grace suits you.'

The woman shook her head seriously.

'Not to confession.' Then: 'I can guess why you're here. In fact, if you hadn't come, I was going to get in touch with you. What d'you think of that for telepathy? It's about Loy, isn't it?'

Startled, Jurnet began, 'But how did you—'

'It had to be. Just as my going to St Joseph's this morning had to be about him.'

Jurnet suggested awkwardly, 'You went to pray for the repose of his soul—'

The smile broke out again, gloriously.

'I went to give thanks that he's dead!'

They didn't go upstairs to the flat because, as Annie asserted, what with the noise of the builders, you couldn't hear yourself think, let alone speak. Downstairs, Dino was on the prowl, with his ears like antennae. And no, she didn't fancy saying what she had to say, sitting in a car. Accordingly, the two of them set out on foot, their steps—though not as if either consciously turned them in any particular direction—tending away from Bergate, down the hill, towards Yarrow Bridge.

They walked in silence, the woman in her perilously high-heeled shoes hanging on to his arm; the detective too preoccupied to notice the passing patrol car which braked suddenly to give its pop-eyed occupants a chance to check that they really were seeing what they thought they saw. They walked on to the narrow pavement of the bridge still arm in arm, Jurnet's right sleeve all but brushed by the passing cars. When they came to the third embrasure along, the central of those minuscule lay-bys where earlier citizens of Angleby had dodged out of the way of ox-carts and prancing chargers, Annie turned aside, taking Jurnet with her up the step into the small alcove which overlooked the river.

'This is where Francesca stood that day,' she began, not in any mournful way, and loudly enough to be heard above the traffic. 'Ever since Guido told me you were on the case, I knew that one day I'd stand here with you, just like this, telling you how it really was.'

'Guido Scarlett, you mean?'

'That's right. Cousin of mine. Scarlatti was my maiden name, same as the fellow who writes music. Francesca had a piece of his in one of her music books. It was Guido's papa changed the name to Scarlett. He wanted to father a real English gentleman, and look what he got!'

'Was it through you Mr Scarlett got to work for Second Coming?'

'How else? My connection with Loy Tanner. And that's exactly what I want to tell you about.'

Annie Falcone turned her face away from Jurnet so that

he could see only her profile, following with apparent
absorption a small ship laden with planks on its way upstream to the timber yard.

'I don't want to look at you,' she explained, 'and please
don't look at me, Ben, any more than you have to, because
what I'm going to say isn't at all nice. Connection I said,
and connection I meant. Loy was Francesca's first boy-
friend and I seduced him. There! It's out and I'm glad. I
was between men and I needed someone. Oh, if I wanted
to justify myself I could say I did it to head him off from
trying anything on with Francesca—acted as a decoy so
that, so far as my innocent little ninny of a daughter was
concerned, he'd be satisfied with a kiss and a cuddle, once
he knew that Mama was always on hand with the hard stuff.

'But I don't need to justify myself. Loy was a virgin kid
of sixteen and I was in my thirties—right?—but all I can
say is, that if I taught him a lot, he taught me a lot more.
He knew things he could only have been born knowing.
Things that came to him as natural as breathing. I can't
begin to tell you. Thanks to him, I discovered uses for my
body I'd never known existed.

'Do you understand what I'm saying!' Despite her earlier warning to look away, the woman tugged at Jurnet,
turned him to face her. Jammed into that small bricked
space, they were close enough for the detective to see the
hairline veins in her irises, the pores beneath the make-up.
'I'm not talking about love, nor lust either, but about war!
We fought each other in bed like wild things, we ate each
other up. And when it was over we couldn't wait to do it
again.'

She sighed, as if even the recollection was a drain on
her resources.

'With it all, it goes without saying, he hated me. Does
that surprise you? He hated anyone to have power over
him, so of course he hated his need of me, and me for
supplying that need. And all the time we were destroying
each other like cowboys and Indians, there was my little
angel Francesca up in the seventh heaven over having her
very first boy-friend of her very own.' For once, the voice
faltered: then, from somewhere, found fresh vitality, even
a sardonic humour.

'Well? That's how it was, my friend, but hang on. You ain't heard nothing yet! I don't have to tell you the care I took that Francesca would have no idea what we two were up to behind her back. I never let Loy come to my room except when she was at school, or gone to music lessons or Sunday School. Never at night. With her room just across the landing from mine, I'd never take the chance. The way we carried on sometimes you'd wonder the bed didn't go through the floor. And even when he did come, I always made sure the bedroom door was locked and bolted. Just in case.

'The afternoon she died, she'd gone for her piano lesson, and Loy and I were going hammer and tongs as usual, when I opened my eyes, and there, over the curve of his shoulder glistening with sweat, I saw Francesca standing at the open door, looking at us. Later on, I found out that the music teacher had been taken sick, and sent her home early.

'The child stood there with a face like a cornered animal. It didn't look like my Francesca. If I'd met her out in the street I'd have passed her by. Her mouth was open, but I don't think any sound came out. What I did, I couldn't tell you. My mind went blank. All I could see was that little animal face, and that open mouth.

'Next thing I knew I could hear her feet thudding down the stairs, and then the slam of the outside door. Loy was already out of bed, cramming into his jeans, pulling his T-shirt over his head. He stuck his feet into his trainers, and before you could say knife he was off down the stairs after her. As for me, I just lay there like a log. I couldn't begin to move, I couldn't begin to think. I was still lying there, not a stitch on, when they came to tell me Francesca was dead.'

25

Jurnet said, 'So, of your own knowledge, you've no idea what happened between the two of them down here at the bridge?'

The bridge. The detective put both hands on the parapet, feeling the ancient bricks powdery to the touch. Here the girl had stood, her hands on the brickwork as his were now.

Francesca's mother turned on him fiercely. 'I know everything that happened! First, he put his arms round her as if he was going to make everything all right between them. Then he tipped her over the wall into the river.'

'Have you any evidence for saying that?'

'I knew that's what you'd say! Once a copper, always a copper! Evidence isn't just a thread on the carpet, Mr bloody Ben Sherlock Holmes, or why the clock stopped at 10.53, not 10.54. It's what people are, what goes on in their heads and in their hearts. They brought in Accidental Death at the inquest because they hadn't a clue what Loy was really like, and because they were too innocent to conceive that a child that age might want to take her own life. But look at this brickwork, the height of it, and remember, she was such a little thing. How could she possibly have tipped herself over accidentally? Never! I've already made it clear that what Loy told the coroner about them having made a date to meet here was a lie. So why should you believe anything else he said?'

'You surely don't want me to believe she did it on purpose?' The detective's voice was gentle.

'By God, Ben Jurnet, you're thick! What I'm giving you is the evidence of a mother who knew her child like an open book. A true religious. They wanted her to become a nun. She could no more have killed herself, committed that mortal sin, than she could have walked down the street with no clothes on. When I went over to Loy's, a couple of days after, his mother said she was sorry, I couldn't see him because he was lying down, still sore from the bruises on his chest. Do you know how he got those bruises? Not from trying to save Francesca, let me tell you! From her trying desperately to stop him from drowning her! And when he couldn't get her to stay under, he banged her head against the arches, to finish her off for good and all.'

'Mrs Felsenstein thought you'd come to thank him.'

'I'd have thanked him all right! She was a nice woman, I took to her. How she ever got a son like that I'll never know. She wouldn't have been so nice, though, if she'd known what I had in my handbag—I had a job fishing out one large enough to take it—the dagger Joe's ancestor used when he was fighting for Garibaldi. The only reason I didn't push my way up to Loy's room and let him have it then and there was because she spoke so sweetly about Francesca, and I suddenly saw that killing the shit wasn't going to bring her back. When I left, I went straight to St Joseph's and lit one of the biggest size candles to Our Lady, and I promised her a new altar cloth for her chapel, new candlesticks and the best crêche money could buy, if only she'd make sure Loy Tanner got what was coming to him. This morning,' she finished with satisfaction, 'I told Father Mullen to go ahead and order them.'

Jurnet said: 'Let's forget about evidence for the moment, Annie. You must see I've got to have a reason why. You and the boy go to bed together, OK—or not OK, as the case may be. Your daughter finds out, poor kid. It must have been a terrible shock—but, for Christ's sake, in what way does it add up to murder?'

The woman looked at the detective with a kind of contemptuous affection.

'I'd expected better of you, I really had! By now, other people besides me must have spoken to you about Loy, you must be beginning to get at least an idea what kind of person he was. He couldn't bear that Francesca had seen him and me screwing. He knew that in her eyes he was perfect, she worshipped him like a god, and he couldn't bear to let her go on living, knowing the truth about him. It offended his vanity. He couldn't stand it.'

'If what you say is true, I wonder he didn't go for you as well.'

'I thought about it a bit, but as I didn't much care, just then, whether I lived or died, it didn't bother me. As a matter of fact, we'd just then finished the restaurant extension—the same as we're putting back at last. It was all ready for the grand opening when there was a fire, and it burned down to the ground. I'd taken some pills and the first thing I knew, I was on a ladder slung over a fireman's shoulder. It was arson all right, they never found out who.'

Annie Falcone shivered. Under the mask of make-up the molecules of her skin seemed to have rearranged themselves into a pattern that was corrugated, old.

'Don't think I'm trying to get out of my own responsibility for what happened; or that, being a Catholic, I've been to confession, performed my penance, and that's the end of it till next time. I may have been absolved by the Church, but, by God, I haven't absolved myself. I don't suppose I ever will.

'Some nights when I can't sleep in spite of the pills, I get up, put a coat over my nightie, and come down here just as I am, to this very step we're standing on, and I kneel down and pray for forgiveness. That time of night, there's hardly any traffic. These little nooks and crannies are full of shadows, and Francesca seems very near. A car did stop one time and a man got out and came to have a look; but when he saw me, bare-legged and in my fluffy slippers, he took fright, hopped back into his car and drove off.

'Another time, I came down here and found a wino sprawled out on the step; a down-and-out, young but already a ruin, stinking to high heaven.' An expression of defiance, almost of pride, came over her face. 'I let him have me, there on the pavement. It seemed a fitter punishment than any number of Hail Marys.' Managing something of her earlier humour: 'Imagine if one of your police cars had come along. What they would have thought! What the wino made of it, God only knows.'

Jurnet could not disguise that he was moved. 'A beautiful dream, I shouldn't wonder.'

The woman looked at him kindly, but shook her head. 'I doubt it. More likely, just one more humiliation to add to all the others. The poor bugger could hardly get it up.'

They walked back to Bergate, away from the chill of the river; together, but carefully apart, even though Annie wrung her ankles over more than once on the cobbled pavement. When it happened, the detective did not proffer a helping hand, nor did the woman seem to expect one. On Yarrow Bridge they had been close, too close. It was a relief once more to put space between them.

They left the gentle ghost of Francesca Falcone and made their way uphill.

Jurnet said, 'Don't take this wrong. Did Loy ever give you any money?'

'I ought to slap your face,' Annie Falcone returned without rancour. The molecules had reverted to their previous arrangement. She could once more have passed for forty. 'In those days, he didn't have two pennies to rub together. If anything, it was all the other way round.'

'Have you ever had anything from him, either gift or loan, since he came into the money?'

'Do you think I'd take a brass farthing after what I've just told you?'

It was, as Jurnet duly noted, scarcely an answer.

'What about recently, very recently? For instance, just before he copped it?'

His companion looked at him in sorrowful disappointment. 'I've been talking to a wall.'

She stopped in her tracks, and stood surveying the Red Shirt across the street, freshly painted and prosperous-looking. On the signboard a curly-haired Italian type, bleeding through several gaping holes in his red shirt, pressed on indomitably, waving a tattered flag.

'Funny, isn't it,' she observed, 'how they both came from the blood of heroes—Francesca from one of the men who fought with Garibaldi, Loy from Robert Tanner. You'd think, if anything, it should have given them some kind of special protection, instead of the reverse.'

The pile of sand was still blocking the pavement. Abreast of it, Annie Falcone stopped again and said, 'I know, really, there isn't anything you can do. In fact, now that Loy's dead and can't do any more mischief, I'm not sure there's anything I want you to do. It's been done for me. It's just that I felt I had to let somebody know what he was really like.'

'What you've told me has been very helpful.'

'In helping you find the murderer, you mean?' The other nodded. 'In that case, I'm sorry I said anything. Unless, perhaps, after what I've said, if you do catch him, you'll let him off more lightly.' The woman brooded on this for a moment, then asked, looking up into the detective's dark Mediterranean face as if there were some answer to be found there, 'when you solve a mystery, is it really the way it is in detective stories, all the loose ends tied up like a well-wrapped parcel?'

'Nothing's ever that simple.'

She said unwillingly, as if until then she had held the words back, but could hold them back no longer, 'That bedroom door, for instance. I can't get it out of my mind. I was always so careful about making sure it was locked and bolted. If I left it to Loy I was always on at him, had he seen to the door, was the door locked, until he'd tell me to stop nagging, for Christ's sake, and get on with it. That afternoon, I *know* I asked him, three times at least, whether the door was locked, and each time he said that it was. He said it.'

'So?'

'So I say to myself, supposing he left it unlocked deliberately, wanting—in fact, willing—Francesca to find us there?'

'Why would he do that?'

'I can't think—except for the reason he did everything. Out of a terrible destructiveness that was in him. For the hateful, mischief of it.'

Jurnet thought about what she had said. 'You realize what you've just set up? A totally different ball game.'

'Not altogether different. The same ending.'

'He couldn't possibly have known that the music teacher was going to be taken ill.'

'Couldn't he?' Under the make-up, Annie Falcone had gone very pale. 'They crucified Jesus. He was God. He died for us. With Loy it was the other way round. He wanted people to die for him, after he'd ground them up small and spat them out. How do you know, when they hung him on that cross, they weren't crucifying the Devil?'

26

Sid Hale was waiting for him when he got back to Headquarters, with him a man in a suede car-coat, a plaid scarf, and a Roman haircut—give or take a bit of decline and fall in the way of a bald spot obstinately resistant to cover-up combing. Hale looked his usual, disillusioned self, only Jurnet, who knew the man well, recognizing the ironic amusement buried deep in the mournful eyes. As for the Professor of Contemporary Institutions, his expression was one of deep shame improbably compounded with a childish self-congratulation.

'Looks like our business at the University's begun to overlap,' was Sid Hale's greeting. 'You've met Mr Culliver, I think?'

The Professor, who had twitched with annoyance at not being accorded his title, put out his hand; then, thinking better of it, put it behind his back as if he feared Jurnet might have his cane handy.

'Well!' Hale said. 'I was looking, actually, for the Archaeology man, to have a few words about the Hob's Hole Venus incident, only they told me he wasn't expected in today, so I asked for Mr Culliver here instead. He'd been seen on the premises, I was told, but where? Somebody eventually said he thought he'd seen the Professor going towards the paddock where the caravans were parked. It seemed unlikely, but still, as I was already there . . . Suffice it to say I strolled over in that direction and discovered him in the act of breaking and entering into Loy Tanner's caravan.'

'Oh, I say!' objected the Professor. 'Not entering. I barely had my foot on the lowest step.' His pride in his achievement overcoming every other consideration: 'You

163

know, it actually is true, what they say about credit cards. I tried the Barclaycard first and it didn't budge, but the American Express Gold slipped in as smoothly as butter.'

Jurnet observed gravely, 'It pays to go up-market. Now, would you care to tell me, sir, the object of this piece of research?'

'All I wanted was to get back the book I lent him.'

'And what book was that—'

'One of my own, as a matter of fact.' The Professor of Contemporary Institutions coloured becomingly. '*The Eschatology of Pop.*'

'Oh ah. And is that the way you normally repossess yourself of books you've lent to people who don't return them?'

The Professor threw Sid Hale a discontented glance. 'I'd have been in and out in two shakes if he hadn't happened to come along, just at that moment. It isn't as if I was going to do anything except take back what was mine.'

Sid Hale lifted a large book from the nearest desk. 'It was there all right. All 620 pages of it.'

'It's a large subject,' the Professor conceded complacently. His brow clouded over, his voice became petulant. 'You're complaining to me. I'm the one should be complaining to you. I'm the one that's been robbed.'

'How is that?'

'Did you find some money on Loy Tanner when you found him? Because if you did, it's mine. There was £150 in notes in that book when I handed it over to him after the concert. I've a right to know what happened to it.'

'What did you give him the money for?'

The question, the stern tone in which it was uttered, caught the Professor off balance. The man squared his shoulders, making a decision. 'He never came up with them so I can't see there's anything you can do to me. I asked him to get me some drugs.'

Jurnet and Hale exchanged glances.

'What kind of drugs?' Jurnet demanded. 'Cannabis? Heroin? Cocaine? LSD?'

'*I* don't know,' Simon Culliver returned, impatient of

this attention to petty detail. 'I left it to him. Whatever they're going in for these days, is what I said.'

'They?'

Irritably: 'My students. You don't suppose I'm fool enough to take drugs on my own account? I just needed to sample whatever they were taking.'

Jurnet made no attempt to disguise his scepticism. 'I must say, it seems conduct beyond the call of duty.'

'Perhaps.' The Professor of Contemporary Institutions sighed, and suddenly looked his age. 'But then you see, Inspector, it wasn't a matter of duty, but of love. I happen to love my students, unwashed, unmannerly and unaware as they mostly are. And I feel—I've felt for some time— that I am failing them.'

'In what way?'

'In every way. Can you imagine a teacher of English Literature, let us say, who can lecture only in Sanskrit, and whose class, in turn, can respond only in a secret language of their own?' The Professor ran a despairing hand through his hair, rendering the bald spot explicit. 'As you know, I occupy the Chair of Contemporary Institutions in the University—a contradiction in terms, if ever there was one, since institutions, of their very nature, cannot be contemporary. They need time and patience to develop and come to maturity, and today there isn't time and certainly no patience. Notwithstanding, my courses are always over-subscribed because young people are attracted by those two words. They think they sound, God help us, relevant. And when at last the penny drops and they begin to understand what a con it all is, I'm the one they blame for misleading them.

'And that's why—' the man looked at Jurnet, fancying, quite mistakenly, that he perceived a dawning sympathy—'I thought that if I could bridge the gap, not just learn to speak their jargon but tune in to their wavelength—for example, since so many of them seem to go in for it, find out for myself what it's like to be high on drugs—I could be of some real service instead of remaining—in their own words, I need hardly say—the silly old nit who likes to pretend he's one of the boys—'

'Silly old nit sums it up precisely, sir.' Jurnet's words

were a cold douche, drowning the Professor of Contemporary Institutions' pitiful little moment of truth. In defence, the man resumed his motley, smoothed his expensive hairdo back into place, sucked in his stomach, brought his dimple out into the light of day.

'Are you going to charge me?' he asked hopefully.

'Boost your standing with the young 'uns no end, I dare say.' Jurnet was stubbornly unco-operative. 'We'll see. In the meantime, and before you leave the building, we shall require a statement from you, setting out what you have just told us, together with anything further which may come to mind as you go along. Incidentally, I can tell you that no sum of £150 has been recovered. If it should come to light, and you can prove your ownership, it will be returned to you in due course.'

'Seven twenty-pound notes, and one ten.'

'Put that into your statement with the rest. Did Tanner tell you who he intended passing the money to?'

'I never asked, and he never said. To tell you the truth—whatever you may think, Inspector, after today—I'm a law abiding bloke by nature and I felt a bit diffident about asking.'

'I see.' Jurnet paused, himself a bit diffident about asking. Then: 'That book of yours, Professor—Eschatology—what is that?'

'It means the study of last things.' The Professor of Contemporary Institutions picked up his *magnum opus* with loving hands.

'The study of last things,' the detective repeated. 'Seems a lot of paper to say pop is the end.'

'Foreshadowings of the Apocalypse—' the proud author seemed not to have heard the intervention—'not just in the words and music, you understand, the philosophy and the body language of the performers, but in the total ambiance: everything from the design of record sleeves to the psychosomatic motivation of the disco—the volume of noise, the strobe lights, the deliberate fostering of disorientation. I can claim in all modesty to have written the definitive work on the subject. It's a good read,' he promised boyishly, 'even if I says it as shouldn't. I'll be happy to lend it to you, Inspector, and promise not to turn up at your address with my American Express card in my hand if you're late in returning it.'

Ending, with becoming grace: 'Although it is, of course, an academic text primarily, it should not be beyond the understanding of a moderately intelligent layman.'

Jurnet, whilst acknowledging the compliment, declined with suitable regret. 'Above my head, I'm afraid.'

At which point Detective-Sergeant Jack Ellers, his chubby face unsmiling, came into the room and announced without ceremony, 'I've got the car out, Ben. It's round the front. The Super's gone on ahead. We're needed at Havenlea.'

27

This time, familiar with the place, they drove straight
along the front, making for the cars already parked in the
distance. Apart from them, Havenlea seemed as empty, as
uninviting, as on the two detectives' previous visit. The
tide was at its peak, three-quarters of the way up the
beach, the air drenched in flying spume. The waves hurled
themselves at the shore and retreated in a rattle of pebbles. The best you could say about the lowering sky was
that there was altogether too much of it.

As Jack Ellers parked at the end of the line, a thickset
figure battled its way along the promenade to meet them.
Jurnet was pleased to recognize Detective Chief Inspector
Herring, stationed at Havenlea; christened Alexander but,
in that place, destined from birth to be known as Bloater.

A huge man, with the gentle strength of many giants, it
did not seem to have embittered him. He greeted Jurnet
and the little Welshman as old friends, and reassured
them, 'We've left everything as we found it.'

'Who found him? You never see a soul about.'

'It *is* a bit parky.' The Havenlea man smiled, sounding
quite proud. 'Last Monday we registered the lowest tem-
perature in the British Isles south of the Shetlands. Pen-
sioner lives just off the front took his dog out to do its
business. Let it off the lead so it could go down on the
beach while he waited up top in the nearest shelter. When
it didn't come back as usual he went to investigate, and
found it behind the Punch and Judy tent, running back
and forth barking like mad. It didn't look as if the dog had
actually gone into the tent: just kept snuffling around at
the base. The old chap had quite a job getting the animal
on the lead again. He himself didn't look into the tent

either. What there was to be seen outside was enough for him. He went across to the Haven Hotel and asked them to phone 999.'

The Superintendent was waiting for them down on the beach, trousers tucked into wellies, and dressed for the wind and the waves in a navy parka laced with white cords, very nautical. Jurnet often wondered where his superior officer kept the apparently inexhaustible wardrobe that was stocked with clothes for every occasion, however unlikely. Somewhere in the depths of Police Headquarters, he felt sure, behind a door to which only the Superintendent had the key, hung everything from a wet suit to lederhosen and funny little hats with feathers in them, all available instanter as the need arose.

'You took your time,' said the Superintendent, not caring who heard him. He was in the usual filthy temper murder produced in him. Jurnet, trying nobly to be understanding, mumbled something inaudible, and turned to the matter in hand.

Punchy King sat inside his Punch and Judy tent leaning sideways, his body supported by one of the corner struts, his wide black hat tilted at a rakish angle. He looked extremely surprised, as well he might have been, that somebody should have stuck a knife into his back, with fatal results.

Amused, as well. Whether it was intended, or whether it was a trick of muscles contracting in a last agony, the face of the dead man looked more than ever like Punch's, full of the puppet's derisive dismissal of the world and all its tomfoolery.

The man, however, unlike his little playmate, had spouted blood, not polystyrene foam or whatever else went to fill a puppet's innards. A lot of blood. Blood had soaked into the back of the tent, obliterating a fair proportion of the red and white stripes. Blood that must have tumbled from mouth and nostrils had turned the front of the dead man's grey cardigan a sticky rust; it had splashed in great gouts over Judy and the crocodile and the policeman, lodged in an arrangement of pockets that hung against the outer canvas; stained the needles and reels of cotton in the open workbox he still held in his lap.

Slumped between the Punch and Judy man's knees, his absurd little legs dangling, Punch stared, full of a malign humour. It looked as though King had been sitting on his stool—which was, in fact, a small pair of folding steps of the type usually found in kitchens, peacefully sewing, when the killer had raised the back flap of the tent and struck. The seam down the centre of Punch's hump was slightly open, a needle and thread still dangling from the point Punchy King had reached in his stitchery. From the narrow aperture, something white and powdery still descended in a last feeble trickle to join the small mound of whatever it was that had already formed beneath the hump on the sheet of hardboard which did service as a floor.

Protected by disposable overalls, one of the scene-of-crime men reached in gingerly and lifted a sample of the white powder on a plastic spatula. When he had straightened up, cautiously, so as not to displace his booty, the Superintendent took the spatula from him, moistened a finger and dipped it in: put it to his lips, his nose.

Jurnet, not waiting for the verdict from on high, pronounced unhesitatingly, 'Heroin!'

'Reason we wanted you here pronto,' Bloater Herring explained amiably, 'was because you'd been in touch so recently with regard to questioning King about Loy Tanner. I must say, unless you've come up with anything pointing the other way, I'd be surprised if it turns out there's any connection between the two killings. My guess is—though it is only a guess—that it's one of those coincidences which occur every now and again.'

The Detective Chief Inspector sat down in a chair which had none of the pretensions of the Superintendent's back in Angleby. Jurnet for one was relieved the man had sat down. On his feet, he filled the small room to the point of suffocation. Seated, he at least left more or less enough oxygen for the rest of them.

A ship's whistle sounded piercingly under the window. Jurnet, close enough to the glass to see the busy commerce along the river, marvelled afresh at the difference between the two Havenleas, the port and the resort: a difference between the quick and the dead.

Outside the police-station window, cranes dipped and rose with a strange, avian dignity; juggernauts, parked along the quay, engulfed or disgorged containers whose contents, so far as the looker-on was concerned, were known only to God and the customs and tally men moving importantly with their clipboards amid the organized chaos all about them. Principally, there was life: men shouting, swearing, spitting; coiling ropes and uncoiling them; slouching on bollards, fag-end in mouth, staring out vacantly over the water; sitting in lorry cabs with the racing editions spread out over the steering wheel. A rough, tough lot from the look of them, with the swagger of men with money in their pockets, and no apparent worries about where the next lot was coming from.

The Superintendent said, 'I get the impression you're not exactly surprised.'

'I am and I'm not,' returned the Havenlea man. 'It'd never have surprised me to hear King had done for one of those beauty queens he shacked up with, he's been so near to bringing it off more than once. On the other hand, I'd never have picked him out as a victim—not, that is, till I saw what came out of that little fellow's hump. Anyone who's into drugs, whether as seller or buyer, has to know the score.

'Ever since they parked those platforms out there in our bit of ocean, we've been aware of an operation building up. In fact, as you know, we've been working on it for some time, and we've got our eye on a couple of chaps who work on one of the rigs. We've reason to believe they've been taking delivery of the goods out there in the North Sea, and landing it at Havenlea. We've been holding off in hopes of catching the big wheel.

'When any of the men come in for rest and recreation, as they laughably call it, we all but give them an enema to see what they're bringing in with them. As for the boats and 'copters, we practically take them apart every trip. But so far—nothing.'

'There could be a link.' Jurnet deemed the moment right to bring his colleagues up to date on the life and times of Simon Culliver. Inured as they were to the infinite diversity of human folly, they still looked a little bemused at the lengths to which the Professor of Contemporary Institutions had been prepared to go to get on terms with his students.

The detective finished, 'Loy Tanner went to Queenie King's caravan after the concert, when her father was still there. Could be that the object of the visit was to pass on the Professor's order for his drug cocktail.'

Addressing himself to the Detective Chief Inspector with that charm he was always so free with to strangers, the Superintendent said, 'What worries me, frankly, is whether the villain who has just put paid to Mr Punchy King hasn't, at the same time, and quite inadvertently, deprived us of our murderer.'

'Look on the bright side,' urged Bloater Herring, the smile on his enormous face positively angelic. 'One suspect less can't be bad, can it?'

Part 2

Answer

28

'Suspects!' exclaimed Sergeant Ellers, winding the car window down an inch or two as if the outer air were a commodity it had become safe to breathe so long as you didn't overdo it. The sun was shining, the wind reduced to a breeze. Suddenly it was to be observed that branches thought winter-bare were, in fact, full of buds, that songbirds were getting their act together, and the new season's no-parking lines flaunting golden along the verges.

Only Sid Hale, sprawled in the back of the car, protested plaintively 'You want to give us all pneumonia?'

'Suspects,' Sergeant Ellers repeated, reporting to his senior officer in the driving seat. 'Scarlett says he and Queenie were in her Dormobile playing—I kid you not—Happy Families. Lijah Starling was in bed, according to him. Says he never gets up before noon, not even to commit a murder. Johnny Flowerdew was in Havenlea.'

'What's that?' cried Jurnet. Sid Hale sat up and took notice.

Pleased with the dramatic effect, the little Welshman proceeded to detail.

'The story is that he did a gig there on the edge of town—a private party to please an old school chum, and they persuaded him to stay over. He gave me a number to call and a woman answered, who, unless she was having me on, said she was Viscountess something or other, and yes, dear Johnny had indeed come down for Orion's engagement party and stayed the night, leaving at about 11.30 after a late breakfast. I checked with Havenlea who said it was all in the local rag, Johnny's name included.'

'I don't suppose they also put in the paper whether he did or did not get up early, whilst everyone else was still out cold after a night of champers and knees-up, tiptoe out of the house to knock off Punchy, and then tiptoe back to his bacon and eggs without a soul knowing, Punchy included? Hm!' concluded Jurnet. 'Interesting!'

'Not as interesting as Lenny Bale who says that at the fateful hour he was in Angleby, down by the river, thinking sad thoughts.'

'Oh ah.'

'No "oh ah" about it. As it happens, he wasn't the only one down there by the Water Gate. There was a youngster too, a good-looking lad, according to PC Nye who, at 9.10 a.m., had occasion to arrest our Lenny for indecent exposure.'

'Christ! What a lot!'

At least, thought Jurnet, Annie Falcone had a respectable alibi, if indeed it was any alibi at all. Certainly, remembering her getting out of her car, the long legs swivelling round from the driver's seat, it seemed unthinkable that she could have just come from a murder. Could she anyway have walked on the beach in those high heels? Unless, of course, all her wits about her, she had taken along flatties to change into, as well as something bloodproof to slip on over her clothes. The detective remembered that she hadn't wanted to sit talking in her car. Was she afraid he might notice sand on the floor, a knife on the shelf under the dash?

She had said that she had gone to church to give thanks. For one death, or two, Jurnet wondered, his face reddening at the memory of his own visit to St Joseph's.

He had inquired first at the presbytery, only to be told by a skimpy-haired housekeeper that Father Mullen was over at the church, a flamboyant brick structure which made the detective feel uneasy before he had even got inside, where the sight of the many painted statues, their poses of exaggerated piety, brought him out in a sweat.

By the time a black-clad figure entered from somewhere at the side of the altar, he had changed his mind about the whole business; was ready to leave with his questions unasked, unanswered.

The priest, however, had seen the stranger and come forward faster than the latter could retreat with decorum.

'Welcome,' the priest said, a greeting which did nothing

to make Jurnet feel any more at home. He fumbled for his card whilst Father Mullen, an elderly man who looked satisfied with his faith, waited patiently, hands folded in front of him, a smile on his face.

When Jurnet stated his business, the smile did not waver, only became quizzical: the kind of smile reserved for children who have done something silly. 'I'm afraid I cannot answer your inquiry about Mrs Falcone.'

'But I understand she spoke to you about some gifts she was proposing to make to St Joseph's.'

'Is that so?' the priest said pleasantly.

Conscious of blundering on, Jurnet nevertheless persisted, 'So it stands to reason you must know, one way or the other.'

'Only God takes note who enters His house, Mr—Mr Jurnet, was it? Fortunately, I am not required to stand at the door taking the tickets.'

At least, Jurnet congratulated himself, he'd been spared one chore. The Havenlea men had broken the news to Queenie. Done it pretty well, by all accounts. There had been no hysteria, and not all that much crying either. It was almost as if—since everything Dad did was OK—getting himself killed was OK too: something which he had arranged to have done to himself for reasons she wouldn't dream of questioning. She had shown no surprise upon learning that a kilo and a half of heroin had been found inside the little wooden windmill whirling merrily away in the dead man's front garden, as well as enough domes of acid to have half the population of Havenlea jumping from their bedroom windows in preference to taking the stairs.

Sure, she knew about the drug-trafficking—that is, in her own words, 'kind of knew'; having finally caught on as to why he kept changing over the Punches, taking back the empties, as it were: but as to the scale of his enterprise, she hadn't a clue. He was a Punch and Judy man, wasn't he, the best in the business? Fixing up a fix for a friend was just the kind of thing you did, if you were the kind of man her Dad was, always ready to do anybody a good turn.

By the time Jurnet had arrived to have his own little word with Queenie, she was back from Havenlea where she had been taken for the formal identification of her father's remains. They seemed to think she would mind it, she told the detective, and Guido had nearly done his nut, but it had been nice to get a last look at him before they started cutting him up proper. She was glad that he hadn't looked as if it had hurt too bad.

Jurnet said, 'You mustn't be afraid to have a good cry. Do you no end of good.'

'Make me look like an old hag, you mean, with me eyes sticking out like gooseberries!' The girl tossed her head. 'Know what's the matter with you coppers? You don't know what being straight is. All that counts is what looks right, never mind what's the truth of it.'

Turning on the detective a look of contempt: 'If I say I'm even relieved he's gone for good and all, you'll either say to yourself *oy, oy, what's she been up to?* or, *the little slag, going on like that, and her dad not even cold in his coffin*. But it's true.' For a moment the childish underlip quivered. 'Ever since I was a kid I've spent my life afraid it would happen that one day I'd run back home and he wouldn't be there, ever.' Daring the other to contradict her: 'Well, tha's one worry off me mind, isn't it?'

Shaken, Jurnet inquired, with some diffidence, 'So what do you intend to do?'

'Marry Mr Guido Scarlett, what else, and live happy ever after.'

'You could do a lot worse.'

'You mean, assuming it wasn't him did for Loy?'

'Assuming that,' the other assented gravely.

'You reckon? No sex, of course,' the girl said, as if it went without saying. 'I told him, and he's willing. He knows I'd never go against me certificate.' Queenie King touched her green quiff, preened herself. 'Loy would've laughed himself silly,' she asserted cheerfully. ' "Imagine," he used to say to me sometimes, "you coming down the aisle arm in arm with that gargoyle. The wedding guests'd fall out of the pews laughing!" '

'You could always go to the Registry Office.'

'There you go again!' the girl cried. 'Let me tell you, Mr

bloody copper, I'm going to have a long white dress and a veil with orange blossom, an' a bunch of roses and lilies done up with satin ribbon. And if you feel like coming along to the church for a good giggle, you're welcome, I'm sure!'

When Jurnet came out of the caravan, Guido Scarlett was there, as the detective had known he would be: dark and threatening, rocking to and fro on his foolish little legs like one of those German clockwork toys, ingenious but unlikeable.

Jurnet greeted the roadie with, 'Congratulations!'

'What you buggering round here again for?' was the gracious response. 'There's already been enough bloody bluebottles buzzin' around to fill the Albert Hall, standing room only.'

'You don't know how lucky you are. One murder in the family, you can always assume it's a one-off, which it usually is. But two, that's an entirely different kettle of fish. It means somebody's found out that murder's a useful tool to have around the house. You'd be surprised how easily two murders can blossom into three, or four, or even more. The more you do it, the more you can think of somebody else who'd be improved out of all recognition by being dead. If I was in your shoes I'd jump for joy every time a copper came within hailing distance.'

Guido Scarlett scowled. 'Still don't give you no reason to drive Queenie round the bend.'

'What's the matter? Wax in your ears? Don't tell me you weren't listening to every word I said. Drive her round the bend! She even asked me to the wedding! Look—' Jurnet said, making a last attempt to get on terms with the prickly customer—'you probably think she's taking her dad's death very well—no screams, no carry-on. So she is, up to a point. Only it's part of my job to have experience in such matters, and you can take it from me, it's too early to tell. It hasn't hit her yet, but when it does, there's no knowing how it'll take her. All I'm doing is warning you to look out for the signs.'

'Don't you bleeding well tell me how to look after Queenie!'

The detective sighed. 'In that case, I'll change the subject—' changing his tone to match—'to one I've raised with you before. Let's see if we can do better second time round, shall we? Namely, what Loy and Punchy King were chewing the rag over, after the concert.'

'Go an' bounce your balls!'

'In that case, I'll have to go back and have another word with Queenie.' Jurnet took a step or two, back towards the Dormobile.

'Leave her be!' The man waited for the detective to stop and turn. Then he muttered, 'What the hell! Can't make no difference now.'

His voice, when he spoke again, was, for Guido Scarlett, conciliatory. 'I didn't want her involved, tha's all. I knew, when those two used to get talking, and it was something she'd rather not know about because it could get them all into trouble she'd shut off—not hear a bleeding word they spoke, innocent as a lamb. But I knew you'd never buy it.'

'So—what were they saying?'

'Something about a boat. Whatever you say, I couldn't hear more than snatches here and there. Punchy said something about the old one being past it, and they'd have to get themselves another, with a better engine. An' then Loy asking how much Punchy reckoned a new boat would cost; and after that, a lot of argy-bargy about money. I couldn't hear the details.'

'What was your impression? That Punchy was trying to touch him for a loan, or that the two of them were in it together?'

The roadie was silent, his brows knit, eyes brooding. Then he sighed. He seemed to be saying goodbye to something, or somebody. 'Anyone knew Loy,'d know it couldn't be either of them things. Loy, he'd never have lent you the dirt under his fingernails. And as for going partners—' The dark face lit up momentarily at the absurdity of the suggestion. 'What gave Loy his kicks was to start things going, stir the pot, an' then stand back in the wings splitting his sides watching the others falling flat on their faces—'

'And yet you say you loved him—'

The dark face twisted painfully.

'We all did. That was the best bloody joke of all.'

In the lab recreation room, the cross, set up on the centre
line of the badminton court, had lost all its magic: merely
two planks of wood, placed so, and so. In that setting, held
upright by an arrangement of blocks and wires, it looked
no more than another piece of PE equipment, on a par
with the vaulting horse and the wall bars.

The room, on the Superintendent's instructions, had
been left unheated. Not so cold as the Market Place on the
night of the murder, but cold enough. Concerned to re-
produce as faithfully as possible the conditions under which
the killer or killers of Loy Tanner had gone about the
macabre disposition of his body, he had commanded his
men to report for duty in such coats, scarves, caps or
anoraks as they deemed sensible wear for a hard frost.
Gloves, too, it went without saying. Whatever else the
murder/murderers had worn that night, he/she/they had
worn gloves.

Jurnet, sorrier than ever to have begotten such a crack-
pot enterprise, made one last try.

'I still can't help thinking, sir, we shouldn't bother Dr
Colton. A dummy would serve the purpose just as well—'

'Absolutely not!' It was the police surgeon himself who
took up the challenge, seeming to take the detective's
suggestion as a personal reflection upon his ability to play
the role for which he had been cast. 'The articulation
would be bound to be unsatisfactory, and the distribution
of weight all wrong. The outer integument, whatever else
it was like, would be nothing like skin.'

'A serious reconstruction for a serious purpose.' The
Superintendent was in high spirits. 'Check that the door's
locked, Jack, will you, and then bring over that ladder.
Now then—' in tones well suited to a games room, the
coach rehearsing the rookies in the ground rules—'since
there's nothing to show us the exact placement of the
ladder, each of us is to feel free to position it any way he
thinks best. And if, in the course of the experiment, you
want to move it from one spot to another, that's OK too,
the one reservation being that, in doing so, you never let
yourselves forget that Dr Colton, however well he may act

the part, is not in fact a cadaver. So whatever you do, don't drop him on the floor from a great height or we may end up with a different kind of case on our hands.'

The police surgeon was busy undressing himself. He took off his clothes, bracing himself against the cold, and put them, neatly folded, on top of the vaulting horse. His body, whilst looking older and less flexible than Loy Tanner's, did indeed bear a remarkable resemblance to that of the murdered pop singer. Neither Jurnet nor the Superintendent had the cheek to point out that, strictly speaking, in the interests of verisimilitude, the doctor ought also to remove the modest trunks which concealed his private parts.

'As for you, Barney—' the Superintendent concluded his exhortation—'you say rigor wasn't established by the time Tanner was, so to speak, elevated, so for heaven's sake let yourself go floppy. Don't forget you're dead.'

The doctor unlaced his shoes and removed them: took off his socks before replying. He tucked them into the shoes and placed the pair, nicely aligned, next to the clothes.

Then he said, with unexpected humour, 'I hope I've met enough of them in my time to know how a properly brought-up corpse behaves in company.'

Half an hour later, all the participants in the serious reconstruction were ready to agree that a single person, acting on his own, could have crucified Loy Tanner, just about. The Superintendent did it with the neat-fingered precision with which he did everything, only his forehead, shining with perspiration, suggesting that any special effort was required to heft a dead man up a ladder, anchor him by his belt to the centre post of a cross, and then, raising the head and the upper part of the torso, secure each arm in turn to the horizontal.

Through it all, Dr Colton, well versed in the gaucherie of death, lolled too convincingly for comfort. To the others, awaiting their turn, it was a relief to observe that he, too, was sweating.

Jurnet, while hating every second of it, managed not too badly, aware that he would have done much worse with-

out the Superintendent's example to follow. Fumbling in
his kitchen-sink gloves, he dwelt with hatred on the sight
of his superior officer's elegant hands encased in operating
theatre issue, a second skin. It came as no surprise that
the Superintendent had not seen fit to requisition a similar
pair for each of the team, nor even to strip off his own for
re-use, once he had no further need of them.

Jack Eilers, instructed, for purposes of comparison, to
wear his normal winter gloves, made a right muck of it and
very nearly of Dr Colton into the bargain. Somehow up-
ended, the police surgeon, still heroically shamming dead,
hung by one leg, the ladder teetering alarmingly.

'Leave them alone!' the Superintendent commanded peremptorily, when the other two detectives started forward
to render assistance. 'Jack can do it!'

And so he could, if a man hanging lopsided by his arms
alone—the silver clasp on the late pop singer's belt having
somehow unlatched itself—could properly be called crucified.

'Take a short rest, if you want to,' the Superintendent
suggested graciously, when the doctor had been helped
down the ladder, his trembling legs refusing to perform
the manoeuvre for him. Once down, he squatted cross-
legged on the board floor, inhaling chestily. Sid Hale went
over to the horse and brought back the man's jacket,
draping it over his shoulders with the exaggerated tender-
ness which he often called in aid to avoid any suspicion of
soft-heartedness.

Even so, listening to Colton's laboured breathing, he let
the camouflage slip, and addressed the Superintendent. 'I
should say he's had as much as he can take, sir.'

'Oh! Do you think so?'

The police surgeon caught the note of exasperation, and
lifted his head, controlling his voice with an effort. 'I shall
be quite all right, once I get my breath back.'

The Superintendent looked closer, and put on his charming face.

'Barney, I'm nominating you for an Oscar! A magnificent
performance! Go and get yourself dressed, man, before
you catch cold. Even lacking Sid's contribution, I think we
can say that we've proved our point—demonstrated that,
at the same time as we are looking for a pair, a trio, a

quartet, a coachload of villains who may have done for Loy Tanner, we are equally looking for a single killer.'

Jack Ellers was looking green—as indeed they all were, in varying degrees, even the Superintendent. It was as if, in placing a man on a cross, they had each received some private intimation of what the real thing had been like. The little Welshman blurted out, 'Whoever did it, whatever else he was, he was sick. Isn't that right, Doctor?'

Colton, fumbling with his shirt buttons, was glad of the excuse to take five.

'Not my field, I'm thankful to say. My clients are beyond such questions. Still, it's a sobering thought that the corpse of Einstein possesses no more reasoning powers than that of a mentally retarded infant.'

'You know what's going to happen once we make an arrest?' The Superintendent spoke with resignation. 'The shrinks will move in from all points of the compass. As if one needed to be told that murder could never be normal!'

Looking from one to another of the little gathering: 'Haven't we all noticed, taking depositions, even where the accused professes terrible remorse, how often a kind of gruesome pride creeps in unbidden—an enlargement of personality which seems to come with discovering yourself capable of committing an act so far beyond the bounds of the permissible—'

From across the room, knotting his tie, Dr Colton nodded agreement. 'A feeling which could even affect physical performance—'

'Are you saying that a person who doesn't ordinarily possess the physical strength to hoist a body on to that cross might, in that temporary state of euphoria, be up to it?'

'As I've said, I'm not the person to ask. But it certainly would not surprise me.'

29

Jurnet was climbing the castle mound.

Crossing the Market Place, below the little garden where kids with reversed guitars still stood guard at each corner of the murdered pop star's symbolic tomb, he had happened to look eastward up Lion Yard, the pedestrian way which cut through to the Castle Bailey, and seen the Norman keep high on its mound above the city.

Probably it was the sun, pale but convalescent, which had tempted the detective's steps away from the path of duty. The great building of creamy stone bulked four-square against a sky of gentle blue. Here and there on the grassy slopes that rose steeply from the Bailey some early daffodils were already trumpeting the spring. Jurnet, moved by God alone knew what vernal madness, had bought himself a doughnut.

Punishing himself for his truancy, he ignored the fine stone bridge which leaped across the chasm which separated the castle from the rest of the city, and toiled up the mound itself, using the track—part path, part stair—which zigzagged up to the plateau at the summit. Halfway there, at a little nook furnished with a wooden bench, he stopped to get his breath back, and partake of refreshment.

There, out of the wind, the sun was warm, the view tremendous. But alas, as with so many things in life, the idea of a doughnut was better than the actuality. It was messy, the jam oozing, the sugar a film of crystalline glue. Even after vigorous rubbing with his handkerchief, the detective's fingers and mouth still felt sticky.

Jurnet's disillusion was not assuaged, either, by the sudden recollection that long ago, on that very seat, he had sat, one summer evening, with a girl whose name he

had forgotten—Sandra Something, was it?—a pretty girl
wearing a dress crackling with the petticoats they were
wearing that year, and shoes with spike heels that made
her legs look almost as good as Marilyn Monroe's. She
hadn't found it easy, in those shoes, to mount to this eyrie
to which he had led her with lecherous intent, but she had
persevered good-humouredly enough, doubtless anticipat-
ing felicities which would make the journey worthwhile.

What had happened was nothing. Jurnet discovered that
twenty years later the memory of that non-event could still
bring a blush to his cheek. He had been afraid to so much
as touch the girl's hand, until at last she had stood up, stiff
with starch and boredom; called out derisively, 'Ta ta,
Romeo!' and gone stumbling downhill on her spindly heels
in search of boys who, if they didn't yet know everything,
at least knew enough to be going on with.

Seen close to, the castle stopped being a picture postcard
and stood forth in all its stony heartlessness—a fortress
built by foreign conquerors, not to potect the city, but to
keep it under. Nasty little shafts of chill, tumbling down
its walls from some polar repository above, sent Jurnet
moving out of their shadow as if out of javelin range,
towards the high railings which protected visitors from the
cliff edge beyond. In all the wide gravelled space which
surrounded the keep, only one person was to be seen: a
woman sitting on a camp stool, a large drawing-pad on her
knees, making a view of the city.

Hunched over her work though she was, something
about the set of her shoulders seemed familiar to Jurnet.
As he drew nearer, scrunching the gravel, the woman
looked up with a wary expression which changed instantly
to a smile of warm recognition.

'Inspector Jurnet! This *is* a strange place to run into
you!'

'I could say the same.' Jurnet shook Mrs Felsenstein's
hand, proffered across her drawing pad. 'Except—' with a
sideways twist of the head, the better to see the sketch she
had been working on—'now that I've seen that, not strange
at all. I didn't know you were an artist.'

'Nothing so grand, I'm afraid. I just felt I had to have

some air, and as I enjoy sketching when I get the chance—'
She let the rest of the sentence go; stood up, closed her
pad, and carefully placed it on her stool.

'Now I've interrupted you.'

'Not at all! I'm so glad to see you, I can't tell you—'

Again the woman broke off, this time apparently in
some difficulty. The detective thought she looked a bit
peaky, though the impression of inward strength which
had struck him earlier was undiminished.

'How can I help?'

Mrs Felsenstein did not answer immediately: she turned
towards the railings and looked out over the city. Then she
said, with a little shiver, 'This is a hateful place, really. I
don't know why I come here. This great pile of earth—did
you know there used to be a hundred Saxon homes on this
spot, before the Normans came and started to build the
castle? And that when some of the home-owners protested, they knocked the houses down anyway, and buried
them and the protesters together?'

She gave a little deprecatory smile.

'Sometimes—I know it's silly—I find myself imagining
that they're still down there, those buried people, living
their Saxon lives as if there'd never been any 1066 and all
that: and that one day, out of all that nice municipal grass,
I'll see a hand sticking up and it's an Anglo-Saxon trying to
get out.'

Jurnet laughed. 'That's a bit morbid, if you don't mind
me saying so.'

'It is, isn't it?' the woman agreed readily. 'I'm afraid I do
have a rather morbid imagination. But this is the place to
encourage it.' This time she looked upward, to the castle
ramparts. 'They say that Robert Tanner's bones hung there
for more than fifty years. Just to remind the citizens of
Angleby what happened to people who tried to make life
better for the poor and oppressed. There's a story that
every time another one of them fell down—sometimes it
was as big as a thigh bone, sometimes as small as the joint
of a little finger—that same night one or other of the
Tanner family would swim the moat—there was water in it
still in those days—climb the castle mound and whip it
away. When, at long last, they finally collected the whole

skeleton, they took it to Wendham, where he came from, and burid it near the church altar.'

Mara Felsenstein, neé Tanner, sighed. 'A hundred years ago, the local squire had Wendham church done over— the old flagstones taken up, and shiny tiles put down in their place. The workmen found some bones: well, old churches were full of old bones, and if you held up work to give all of them a consecrated burial, you'd never be done. So they chucked them out with the rest of the rubbish, and got on with laying the new floor.'

The woman turned back to the detective, astonishing him afresh with the candid beauty of her eyes. A little smile emerged at the corners of her mouth, and retreated again.

'You'll say I'm being morbid again, and perhaps I am. I keep thinking of Robert Tanner, and I want Loy buried, not left dangling from the ramparts, as it were. Not because I'm religious, because I'm not, at all. I just want his life brought to a decent close, one decent, ordinary people can accept.

'Without a funeral and a grave—' she was speaking rapidly now, urgent to get what she had to say over and done with—'without people coming in for a ham tea after the service, there's no ending I can take hold of, only the hateful violence that stopped him breathing. He's not alive any more, I can face that if I have to, but so long as he's lying in that mortuary, he isn't dead either. I can't go on to the next thing. And I have to go on to it. Leo's ill. He needs all my care and all my love, and I can't give him either, not properly, so long as Loy's life and death remain incompete.'

'Buried or unburied, that's the way they'll stay till we catch whoever killed him.' Moved by the sorrow in her face: 'Don't fret yourself. One thing's not dependent on the other. I'm afraid there's nothing I personally can do about advancing the date of the inquest; but once it's over the body will be handed over without messing about.'

'Will it? Oh, I hope so.'

'I'll tell you one thing, though.' No good, Jurnet thought, the woman deluding herself. 'You'll have a job keeping your son's funeral quiet. And once the media cotton on to who *you* are—'

'I shan't care about that,' she replied with surprising nonchalance. 'It's the way of life he chose. If he leaves it with all that show business and publicity I can only suppose that's the way he would have wanted to go. I can put up with it, if I have to.

'Once it's over,' she continued, with that devastating honesty which went with her eyes, 'Leo and I can settle down, not as if nothing had happened, but to some semblance of peace and quiet again. After all,. we saw him so seldom, once he'd left home. In time, it will all seem like a dream. We'll be asking each other if it really happened.'

'You're not likely to be left in much doubt about that. Don't forget your son must have been a very rich man.'

'That's nothing to me.' The woman stared at the detective in sudden alarm.

'Naturally, we've been making enquiries, if only to see who could have had a vested interest in wanting him out of the way. I don't think I'm letting you into any secrets when I say there's a strong likelihood that, whoever else may benefit—depending on whether a will does or doesn't turn up—you must be in line to come into money, a lot of it.'

'No!' Mrs Felsenstein cried out in distress. She had become very pale. 'I don't want it! I don't have to take it if I don't want to!'

'Absolutely correct!' Jurnet said soothingly. 'Sorry if I spoke out of turn. Don't often come into contact with somebody who actively doesn't want to be rich—in fact, this is my first time ever, and probably my last! If you really don't choose to benefit from Loy's estate, I'm sure the Treasury will be only too glad to take it off your hands. I was thinking more of Mr Felsenstein, actually. How you'll be able to provide all sorts of comforts for him, take him on holidays—'

'We *do* go on holidays! Every May we hire a car and we have the most wonderful week driving round Norfolk and Suffolk visiting all the sites Leo used to be so interested in—'

'With your own car, if I may say so, you wouldn't be

restricted to just one week in the year. But there! You don't need my advice on how to live.'

'No,' she returned stiffly. Then, melting: 'I'm sure you mean well. It's just that—' faltering a little—'I don't know how much longer Leo and I have together. I don't want anything to disturb it.'

In a rather agitated way, unlike her usual air of quiet containment, she folded up her camp stool, tucked her pad under her arm, and bade the detective good-bye. Jurnet thought it better not to suggest accompanying her. He watched her move away in the direction of the bridge, walking fast. In motion her body possessed a distinction not apparent in repose. If she'd lived in one of those countries where women went about with pots on their heads, Jurnet reflected, she'd have managed fine.

As he turned to leave, back down the steps and past the bench where nothing had happened, something lying on the gravel caught his eye: a small tin of dull metal which Mrs Felsenstein must have dropped without noticing.

He picked the tin up and opened it. Inside were a stick of charcoal and a number of pencils beautifully sharpened, only one point beheaded by the fall. The name *Mara Tanner* was scratched roughly, as with a compass point, on the inside of the lid.

The detective put the tin in his pocket. He would be seeing Mrs Felsenstein again, that was certain.

30

Jurnet came up the stairs carrying a carton packed with two dozen cans of baked beans. He hoped it wasn't the same with cats as it was with people. For himself, he had only to fall for a special offer, the large economy size, two for the price of one, for him to go off whatever it was that was being offered for the rest of his natural.

Approaching his landing, sounds from Mrs Petherton's flat across the way informed him that this was one of those days when that lady's Happiness at the Hacienda Wine Bar had prolonged itself beyond the appointed Hour. Her gramophone was on.

Mrs Petherton's gramophone, a massive construction wound up by a handle with the kick of a Kalashnikov, was encased in a mahogany cabinet pockmarked by shrapnel, its lower half opening by double doors on to a record store, 78s all of them, their surfaces corrugated by time and war and steel needles used too many times over, but once as blackly shining as the brilliantined hair of the young men who had long ago danced to them, partnering girls with tiny breasts.

The gramophone stood on its own circular rug in the centre of Mrs Petherton's living-room, at once a cenotaph and a phoenix, the sole survivor of Mrs Petherton's furnishings, blitzed together with the building which gave them shelter on a night of 1942. Amazingly, as its grateful owner never tired of recounting, not only had the machine itself survived intact, but the records equally.

Mrs Petherton did not often mention that the same providence which had miraculously preserved her gramophone had at the same time seen fit to obliterate her

husband and her five-year-old daughter, dug out of the
rubble three days later.

'I'll see you again, (sang the record on Mrs Petherton's
gramophone)
Whenever spring breaks through again.
Time may lie heavy betwee-twee-twee-'

Jurnet sighed. He was familiar with *'betwee-twee-twee-'*. On
ordinary days, within a second or two, Mrs Petherton's
neat little heels could be heard clicking across the floor,
and *flick!* the needle was over the hump and running in
the groove again as sweetly as anyone could wish. Today,
obviously, it was a matter of waiting until the spring unwound itself, *'twee-twee-tweeeeee-ing'* down to ginny silence.

The cat was not on the doormat. Not that the detective
had expected it there. He had got into the habit of leaving
the bathroom window open, and the cat of availing itself of
the facility.

Indoors, it was—not waiting, for that would have im-
plied a need of him which Jurnet would never have had
the conceit to presume—but there; coiled in the armchair,
not moving when the detective sat down on the edge of it
to take off his shoes, except to raise a desultory paw and
claw a few strands out of his jacket sleeve.

Jurnet slipped out of the coat, and said, 'High time I got
myself a new one,' only to blush for his foolishness. If
things had come as far as talking to animals, things had
come a sight too far.

The cat did not even have a name, or if it did, it was a
secret, not to be advertised to every Tom, Dick or Harry
who chanced along. Somehow, Jurnet felt obscurely, if
ever he came to deserve knowing the cat's name, it would
be vouchsafed to him.

He opened a can of the beans, set it out in a bowl, and
filled the cat's saucer with milk. 'Cat's saucer': he liked
that. Of such trifles was home made.

It gave him the courage to ring up Miriam and ask her
why Jews in a house of mourning covered up their mir-
rors. It was a point which had bothered him off and on
ever since his visit to Lenny Bale.

Miriam sounded pleased to hear from him, but annoyed to be asked; but perhaps that was only because she didn't know the answer.

'If it's that important, why don't you ring up Rabbi Schnellman and ask him yourself?'

'I would,' Jurnet replied, not without malice, 'except I thought it might be a bit awkward if he asks me about the Seder. If he wants to know why I'm not coming tomorrow after all, I'll have to say, won't I, that you told me not to?'

'Sod you,' said Miriam, 'and happy Passover.'

She rang off.

Half an hour later, she phoned back.

'I spoke to the Rabbi, and he says it's nothing to do with anybody having died, it's to do with praying. He says you must never pray in front of a mirror because, even if you don't consciously intend it, it's as if you're bowing down to an image—to that most potent of false gods, is how he put it—an image of yourself. Well, you know how many people can turn up at a *shiva*—often by the time they're ready to say prayers the living-room's jammed to the doors. Without meaning to, you could easily find yourself staring straight into a looking-glass.

'And so they cover them up—only where people happen to be praying, not anywhere else in the house—just to be on the safe side. Is that what you wanted?'

'Exactly what I wanted. Ta very much,' said Jurnet. 'A happy Passover, and sod you too.'

Later, in the bathroom, shaving in front of the mirror in the ever delusive hope that, for once, the rampant stubble would not require an additional pruning back next morning, he surveyed his own reflection and decided you would have indeed to be hard up for a god, if that was the best you could come up with.

Gods should be cool and inscrutable. That was why the Ancient Egyptians had worshipped cats. Strange squeaks and mews summoning him back to the living-room, he found his own cool and inscrutable feline rolling about the floor enmeshed in knitting wool. From some crevice it had unearthed one of Miriam's samples, and from some place still more submerged a memory of its own kittenhood—if indeed it had ever had one, streetwise as it was. It tumbled about the room in ecstasy, the velvet fur rumpled into fluff, paws shadowboxing, eyes hugely staring: a moment of complete relaxation, collapsed like a spent balloon, and then it was off again.

For a little, Jurnet watched entranced. Then, not sure he was doing the right thing, he found some scissors and carefully cut the animal free. It seemed neither pleased nor sorry to be back to the inscrutability bit again.

Gorged on baked beans, and wondering if the cat felt as flatulent as he did, the detective went to bed early, setting the alarm of the bedside clock, but turning its hateful, spastic display away from him.

One day, he promised himself, when he had solved the Loy Tanner murder case, he would drive out with it to the country, open the car door, and set it free. Jurnet lay back in bed, picturing the clock as it disappeared into the distance in little hops, skips and jumps *tic, tic, tic*—until it was out of sight and gone for ever. Only the possibility that it might find a mate, multiply like mink, of digital displays winking like mad from every burrow and hedge bottom, held him back.

Mrs Petherton had found the strength to wind up the gramophone. She had put on an old favourite which Jurnet, who knew the record only too well, had rechristened 'Tiptoe Through the Hiccups'. Detective and gramophone belched in unison.

It was not the most encouraging milieu for logical thought, so that it was not surprising that Jurnet found it hard to marshal his thoughts on the death of Loy Tanner into anything approaching an orderly progression. Instead, they fluttered about him like butterflies, just out of reach. They settled with wings folded, pretending they weren't there at all; though he knew, with an almost obsessional certainty, that they had only to spread themselves out in the sunlight—stay still for a moment, blast them—for him to read there all he needed to know.

Sinking turgidly towards sleep, he found himself thinking of a woman. Nothing unusual about that, except that, in some way his tired brain could not unravel, he seemed still to hold the dead pop star in the forefront of his mind;

and the woman, for once, wasn't Miriam, but a stumpy figure with dugs down to her what's-it—the Hob's Hole Venus.

There was nothing erotic about his fantasy: on the contrary, the Venus scared the pants off him with her fierce, all-consuming concentration on the life growing inside her. Jurnet, who often thought about the children he and Miriam would one day make together, tossed uneasily on his bed. Was the message that once he had performed his crude, biological function he would lose her; not as at present, for a few days, or weeks, but for good—the child to be born not the visible consummation of their love, but its sworn enemy?

On the edge of oblivion he wondered blurrily why on earth the yobbo who'd mucked up the Venus had gone for her breasts when what she was crying out for was a bloody great boot in the belly.

31

'And one Good Friday, after a hundred years had passed, a bloke called Prince Charming hacked his way through the undergrowth and woke up the Sleeping Beauty with a kiss—' Jack Ellers broke off and looked about him with qualified approval. 'Pity there only seems to have been one of them. Beauties, I mean. The wicked spell may have been broken, I've still only seen one pair of legs worthy of the name since we started walking.'

'It's a family resort. Kids and grannies.'

Jurnet screwed up his eyes against the sun. He at least was in no mood to be critical. Havenlea had awoken from its winter's sleep. The wind was still distinctly nippy, wrack littered the beaches, the strong light rendered cruelly explicit the shabbiness of the sea-front shelters and bathing huts, but what the hell! The season had begun, and for once the sun and a public holiday had made it together. Dogs were barking, children running, mothers calling: families down on the sands staking out tribal encampments with windbreaks of striped canvas.

Early in the day as it was, cars were already cruising slowly along the front in search of a parking space.

'If you really want to see a sexy pair of legs,' Jurnet suggested, 'take off your shoes and socks, stroll down to the water, roll up your trousers, and give everyone a treat.'

They had wasted a couple of hours, but Jurnet bore no ill will for that. It was the kind of courtesy to be expected from a man like Bloater Herring that he should have invited the Angleby detectives to sit in on the Havenlea conference with the regional drug squad; and to have declined the invitation would have been churlish in the extreme. Jammed into the room which was barely large enough to house that giant of a man on his own, let alone in conference, Jurnet would have regretted his own politeness had not the Detective Chief Inspector been such a likeable man. As it was, he had listened with every appearance of intelligent interest with, this time, not even a glimpse out of the window to divert him, to an hour or more of the obsessive statistics which, with such specialized units, as he knew from experience, passed for conversation. Just as he had expected, neither the regional squad nor the Detective Chief Inspector himself had had a single thing to contribute which might bring them closer to either Loy Tanner's or Punchy King's murderer.

Now, nearing the place where the Punch and Judy man's tent had stood, he was not surprised to find a sizeable crowd, constantly replenished, gazing down at the patch of sand where a life had come to a violent end. One cheeky little boy, greatly daring, jumped down from the promenade on to the fatal spot, where he stood shifting from one foot to the other, looking up at the rest for their admiration. Proud of himself, but suddenly fearful.

'You come back here this minute, Darren!' his mother commanded; and Darren, for once obedient, dashed for the nearest steps, thankful to be delivered without loss of face.

Convenient to the scene of the crime, the bar at the Haven Hotel was doing sensational business. Enormous as the room was, it was packed wall to wall. At the sight of the crowd, Jurnet nearly retreated. He had been hoping for a quiet drink in a room as empty as on his earlier visit, with, given a bit of luck, occasion for a word with the barman—not enough to constitute a questioning, which would have been quite improper without prior clearance with Havenlea, but, well, a word.

Sergeant Ellers asked, 'Shall we try somewhere else?'

'Might as well.' Then: 'Hold on a minute! What's that?'

The detectives painstakingly worked their way to the bar where two large-bosomed ladies of mature years were helping out the barman. One of these asked Jurnet, 'What's yours, love?' and looked understandably put out when he

ignored her, edging away along the counter to where the
barman stood drawing a pint.

Jurnet pointed and said, 'Where did that come from?'

Punch sat at his ease, high on one of the shelves at the
back of the bar. Legs crossed, one hand affectionately
cupping the great hook of his nose, he leaned nonchalantly
against a cluster of Johnny Walkers, surveying the crowded
room with a bright-eyed insolence. In the smoke-laden
atmosphere of the place, Jurnet, for a ridiculous moment,
had the impression that the puppet had favoured him with
a nod.

The barman, too rushed for chat, rang up the money for
the beer, and said offhandedly, before turning away to the
next customer, 'Another one of Punchy's.'

'Just a minute!' The detective intervened with enough
authority in his voice to bring the man back, face red with
annoyance. 'How and when did it come into your possession?'

'Who the hell wants to know?'

Jurnet took out his ID card.

'Christ! Not another one! What is this, a persecution? I
already spoke to you lot. Told you everything I knew,
which was strictly nix.'

The man was overdoing it. Jurnet took a chance, and
said, 'You never showed the police officer that.'

'Yeah—well.' The man changed tone, became ingratiat-
ing. 'Punchy only left it night before he was done in,
didn't he? And when those other guys came round it
completely slipped my mind. When Punchy give it me, I
just stuck it in the cupboard, way I always did, and never
gave it another thought. It was only this morning, looking
for some extra space for the tonic waters, that I came on it,
and thought to myself, now Punchy's gone, this here's
what they call a conversation piece, and stuck it up where
you see it now. Punchy's never coming back for it, poor
sod, that's for sure.'

'What's this about "as I always did"? Were you in the
habit of providing accommodation for Mr King's puppets?'

'Not a crime, is it? Or should we have been charging
VAT?' The man heaved a sigh of exasperation. 'Look—if
you'd known Punchy you'd have known he was a funny

bloke—and that's the understatement of the year. You never knew what he'd say, or do next. Sometimes he was just going on somewhere from here—down to the quays, maybe, to screw a slag, and didn't want to take Punch with him. Said it might put ideas into the little chap's head. He'd ask me to take him and put him away, and he'd pick him up next time. Other times he'd come in and say Punch had misbehaved himself something dreadful, and would I shut the perisher up in the cupboard till he'd learnt once and for all who was master. It weren't always the same Punch, you understand. He had any number of 'em.'

'We're aware of that. I shall have to take this one along with me for examination.'

The other looked mutinous. 'Am I to get it back?'

'Shouldn't think so—but not for me to say.' Jurnet took out his pad. 'I'll give you a receipt.'

'Stuff it.' Reaching for the puppet and plunking it into the detective's arms: 'On second thoughts, stuff him as well, while you're at it. Punchy hung out here much longer, he'd have had us all round the twist. From now on, nothing goes into that bloody cupboard that don't come in a bottle.'

'Good thinking,' Jurnet said, 'so long as it isn't a genie. We'll have a couple of bitters, please. Halves.'

By the time they got back to Havenlea HQ the air in Detective Chief Inspector Herring's office had replenished itself, more or less. Space again, Jurnet was happy to note, to see out of the window and down to the quayside, where a middle-aged woman in a kaftan, over-painted and under-corseted, was exchanging pleasantries with a couple of bashful youths from the rural hinterland.

The enormous man, seated in solitary modesty, welcomed back the two detectives with an unaffected pleasure which Jurnet found quite touching. 'So long as you haven't come to pick a bone with me for wasting valuable police time—'

'A very useful meeting—' Jurnet demurred, not to be outdone in politeness.

'Don't tell me! They're very good fellows,' the man, who

obviously found it hard to think ill of anybody—anybody on the right side of the law, at any rate—earnestly assured his colleagues from Angleby. 'God knows what the local drugs scene would be like without them. But I don't have to tell you how it is when you go regional—regional anything. The organization takes over. You're so busy taking an over-view it's hard not to lose track of those little ants scurrying about at ground level.'

'Or, even harder, the ones that aren't scurrying any more, but are lying squashed flat on the pavement.' The two men exchanged glances of perfect understanding. Jurnet continued, 'So long as you don't think we're back to say, look what we've got and you missed. Jack and I stopped by at the Haven Hotel for a drink, and by the purest chance—'

The little Welshman opened the carrier bag he had rescued from a litter bin, and hauled out its contents. Punch emerged smelling of Chinese takeaway, but as serene as ever.

The Detective Chief Inspector reached across his desk for the puppet and took hold of it gently. He might have been receiving a baby. But then, thought Jurnet, with hands the size of hams you were either tender with everything you touched, or a complete disaster.

'I'm growing quite fond of the little fellows,' Herring confessed. Ending with a certain regret: 'I suppose we'll have to open him up, like the rest.'

Punch stared impassively out of the window whilst Sergeant Ellers did things to his hump with a razor blade. Severing Punchy King's fine stitching with careful labour: 'He'd have made somebody a wonderful wife. My Rosie'd give her eye teeth to sew like that!'

At last the opening was wide enough for the insertion of a hand. 'Lot of that foam stuff we found in the others.' The little Welshman scrabbled about, bringing out some flat padding and a handful of plastic nodules which spilled over the desk and on to the floor. 'There's something there! Let me make it a bit bigger—'

A moment later, the Sergeant straightened up with what he had found: ten £50 notes secured with a wide manila band on which somebody had scribbled some figures.

The three detectives studied the haul in silence. Then

Jurnet said, 'I can see we're going to have to have another word with Mr Lenny Bale.'

After Havenlea, Angleby was quiet: quieter than Jurnet could remember. Missing the liveliness of the resurrected seaside resort, the detective nevertheless approved of the silence engulfing the city. In Angleby, he reflected with a perverse satisfaction, it no longer being any business of his anyway, people knew what was due to a dead god. They knew how to conduct themselves on a Good Friday, unlike some he could mention . . .

As they threaded the silent streets towards the city centre and Police Headquarters, he said as much to Jack Ellers, who hooted. 'Decent respect! It's because everyone's gone where we've just come from, if they aren't at Yarmouth or Cromer!'

Within doors, Headquarters was kept on the go much as on any other day, break-ins and wife battering, as usual, largely replacing other business which had fallen off on account of the holiday. More than one conference at high level had been convened to discover why those particular forms of lawbreaking had become as traditional to Angleby over Easter as bunnies and Easter eggs. The break-ins were explicable, given that many people had gone away for the weekend leaving their property undefended; but for the extraordinary jump in the statistics of wives with black eyes, broken noses and worse, no reason had been deduced other than the rather unsatisfactory one that spring had sprung, the sap was rising, and what more natural than to take a swipe at the old woman?

By evening, Jurnet, called in to lend a hand with the press of complainants, was ready to turn it in, aware that the day had been flatter, the toil less rewarding, by reason of the absence of his superior officer. The Superintendent had taken the day off. True, without him on the premises one breathed more easily. But equally, with him there, either invisible or a looming presence fraught with threat, life in Angleby CID acquired an extra dimension.

Sergeant Ellers brought in a Lenny Bale looking much improved, wearing his grief with the same sharp attention he had paid to his clothes and his jewellery. He had been

to the morning service in the cathedral, and it seemed to
have done him as much good as a fix. It had been fabulous,
he proclaimed: out of this world. He spoke as if he had
discovered some new form of spectator sport out of which,
with the right kind of hype, there was money to be made.

Jurnet said coarsely, 'Don't go getting any ideas about
those choirboys. Remember you're out on bail.'

'The nerve of that blue-arsed ape!' was Bale's rejoinder.
'Equating me with some dirty old man in a dirty old mac!
Indecent exposure! It's humiliating! If he'd only contained
himself for a few minutes, the randy twerp, he could have
copped me on a charge worth pleading to.'

He eyed the detective with a look of stern dissatisfaction.

'Regular Sodom and Gomorrah you got down there by
the river, anyone ever tell you? Did you hear they've
remanded me for medical reports—me! Not that sweet
little cherub who led me on, looking like butter wouldn't
melt in his mouth, nor anything else either. He's the one
the shrinks need to talk to, they'd learn something. Fishing? Oh, he was out fishing all right!'

Jurnet said, 'We'll look into it. In the meantime—' he
opened a drawer, took out the bundle of £50 notes and
tossed them on to the desk top—'take a look at these.
Don't touch!'—as the Second Coming manager stretched
out a joyous hand to take possession. 'Just tell me if you
think you recognize them.'

The detective saw no reason for letting on that Fingerprints had already confirmed the man's prints on the wrap-
ping, as well as those of King and Loy Tanner.

'Of course I recognize them! Those are my figures on
the wrapper. I distinctly remember jotting them down to
see how much of the £13,000 I still had to go. Where's the
rest?'

'All in good time,' returned Jurnet, less than frank. 'If,
when the inquiry is concluded, you can prove that you are
the owner of these ones, they will be returned to you.'

'Can't you at least tell me where you found them?' The
man stammered a little, then asked, 'Was it a woman,
after all?'

The detective picked up the wad of notes and returned

them to the drawer, turning the key with deliberate ceremony.

'You'll have to contain your soul in patience.'

When the man had gone, leaving behind a trace of perfume disturbingly reminiscent of something Miriam sometimes used Jurnet sat chewing on a ballpoint.

'Seeing that Tanner left Queenie's caravan ahead of her dad—everyone's agreed on that and I can't see what they have to gain by lying—it stands to reason Punchy must have met up with him again that night after he'd been to the Virgin and collected his £13,000. I can't see how else Punchy could have come by that £500—'

Jack Ellers went to the heart of the matter. 'Come by it *how*, that's the question.'

'Fair means or foul, eh? If Guido Scarlett heard aright, Tanner wasn't at all receptive to the idea of forking out for that boat. But who knows? When they did meet up again, Punchy may have finally persuaded Loy to shave a bit off that £13,000 in his favour.'

The little Welshman shook his head.

'I don't buy that. If it had been £10,000 say, or twenty—a fair round number—I might have, but not thirteen. It's an odd sort of figure, as if it was the cost of one definite thing Tanner had in mind to use it for. Like the down payment of a house, say—'

'Or,' amplified Jurnet, an image of the sand heap outside the Red Shirt coming into his mind, 'the cost of some building work.' He considered further what the other had said. 'I think you're right, Jack—that Tanner asked Bale to get him £13,000 because £13,000 was the exact sum needed.'

Jurnet unlocked the drawer and took out the notes again. He stared at them as if they could tell him something.

'In which case—'summing up—'how else could Punchy have come by this little lot, except by means of a blunt instrument?'

'That still leaves that business of the corpse on the cross unaccounted for.'

'Are you asking me or telling me? Think about it. Exactly the kind of crazy caper you might expect from a nutter like King.' Jurnet once more returned the notes to the drawer, slammed it shut. 'The more I think about it, the better it fits.' He pushed back his chair and stood, tall and morose. 'Maddening!' he pronounced, 'not being able to get at the bugger, not even to ask him the time of day.'

'If we can turn up the remaining £12,500, we won't need to.'

'Hell, I don't know!' Reaching for his coat, hanging from a peg on the wall, Jurnet announced, 'I'm going out to eat.'

'Isn't today that Passover feast you were telling me about?'

'Er—yes, that's right,' the other said, too quickly. The little Welshman, too practised not to notice, was too tenderhearted to let his doubts show. 'Got to get over to the synagogue. They can't start without me. Know what? We were slaves in Egypt, today we are free.' Jurnet smiled bleakly. 'Turn yourself into a Jew, Jack, you don't just get yourself a new religion. You get a whole new set of ancestors thrown in.'

'So long as it doesn't include a mother-in-law!'

Jurnet thought, I should be so lucky.

Just to prove to himself that he didn't give a damn one way or the other, he went to the new place in Shire Street, and, the sole customer in the pink, candle-lit ambience, ordered scampi and gammon, followed by something gooey with whipped cream. He ate fast, too fast for his digestion, fancying the waiters angry with him for being no more than one; tipped enough for four and went back to his car feeling—not for the first time nowadays when he ate forbidden food—that he had lost that round. It had long ago dawned on him that what he was engaged in was a contest rather than a conversion, one in which his opponent held all the aces, to say nothing of making up the rules as he went along.

By the time Jurnet reached the quiet suburban street which housed the synagogue, the shellfish and the ham, with the dessert on the sidelines egging them on, were engaged in a life-and-death struggle which could have only one outcome. The detective drew up a little down the street from the modest, stuccoed building, hopped out fast and jettisoned the lot in a forsythia bush.

One game to God.

The sound of singing was coming from the synagogue hall—one of those happy Hebrew melodies that were still pierced through with melancholy, as if to celebrate the impermanence of joy. Jurnet stood on the opposite pavement listening, wondering why he had come. Or rather, knowing and not knowing.

There was no window on to the street to which he could press his face like the Little Match Girl out of Hans Andersen; no possibility that Miriam, moved by some irresistible telepathic urge, would come out, see him standing there under the street lamp, and draw him back inside with both hands. All the same, he waited a little longer, if only to prove beyond doubt that miracles never happened; then shivering a little, for the night had become cold—walked back to the car and drove away.

The thought of his empty home hateful to him, he drove to the Chepe, parked the car and went through the FitzAlain Gate into the Cathedral Close, dark after the city streets, the lamps low-powered in their cast-iron lanterns. The enormous bulk of the cathedral, that great stone ship becalmed in the water meadows, loomed above him: no moon to catch the tips of the pinnacles, or strike a silver reflection off the golden weathercock which swung against the sky at the point of the steeple. All was in mourning for the dead God. Never a hint that anyone, not even the bishop, had to know the plot-line from past Easters, if nothing else: that, give it a couple of days, everything would be coming up roses.

Only a couple of days, after all He'd been through! Jurnet felt a genuine pang. He had a sudden vision of God the father whipping the grave cloths off God the son with 'Easter Sunday, lad! Time to get the show on the road!' And God the son, poor bastard, hanging on to the covers with his mutilated hands, and pleading, 'Just another ten minutes, Dad!'

Confused as to where he belonged, and to whom, Jurnet thrust his hands deep into his pockets and turned to go. One hand closed over something hard and metallic. He fished out Mrs Felsenstein's tin and opened it, read the name *Mara Tanner* scratched on the inside of the lid; noted that, in its time in his custody, the stick of charcoal had fractured in several places and another pencil point had gone for a burton.

He shut the tin, lowered it back into his pocket with elaborate care. Went back to the car, and drove to Sebastopol Terrace.

32

The first thing he saw when he turned the car into the narrow cul-de-sac was Miriam's red Golf parked outside Number 12.

Miracles did happen, he thought for a wonderful moment before his habitual caution intervened to suggest a dozen alternative reasons for the car being where it was. Even so, he parked a little further up the street and approached the house with a stealthy step, just in case, behind the flimsy curtains which let the light through but prevented him seeing who was in the room, Miriam was there to be taken by surprise; just in case she would greet him with a kiss full on the lips. Just in case she would say cheerio to the Felsensteins and go with him lovingly, back to the synagogue and the singing.

The woman who opened the door to his knock was a stranger. All he could make out of her, indistinct in the dim little hallway, was that she had on some long garment, housecoat or dressing-gown, and wore her hair spread loosely about her shoulders. Only when the extraordinarily brilliant whites of her eyes caught a reflection from the street lamp did he recognize Mara Felsenstein.

Taken aback by her unwonted appearance, all his senses poised to call 'Miriam!', he stammered feebly something about it being unwise to answer the door to nocturnal visitors without first ascertaining—

'I know!' She cut the policemanly rebuke short with a contrite smile. 'Leo's always saying we must get a chain.'

She brought him through to the living-room where, in the stronger light, he saw with astonishment that, dressed as she was, in a straight housecoat of some dark blue material with a slight sheen, and with her hair, damp from washing, curling in delicate tendrils about her ears, she looked still a girl, a girl worth looking at.

Not that he had all that much attention to spare for her. Miriam was not there. Was she in the kitchen? Or upstairs in the bedroom, asking Mr Felsenstein how he was feeling?

'The car!' Mrs Felsenstein exclaimed. 'You thought Miriam was here! I'm so sorry—'

'I was coming here anyway,' said Jurnet, sternly relegating his fantasies to their proper place, wherever that might be. 'I just happened to notice—'

'What a shame! She left—oh, it must have been an hour ago, at least. She's really too good, and she makes so little of it, doesn't she, she won't take no for an answer. She brought some work round, and then she said that as she hadn't any use for the car over the weekend, she proposed to leave it outside. She said it looked like being a fine Easter after all, and, if Leo was feeling up to it, why not take a drive out into the country? Go out each day, if we wanted to—she wouldn't be needing the car back till Tuesday.'

Mrs Felsenstein crossed to the hearth, carefully keeping her housecoat away from the one-bar electric fire standing in front of the empty grate, and reached over to the wooden mantelshelf for the car keys. Holding them up in evidence: 'Wasn't that lovely of her?'

Jurnet nodded, a little jealous that Miriam could be so nice to other people.

'Is Mr Felsenstein all right, then?'

'If he doesn't feel well enough, we shan't go.'

'Your husband seems to have to spend so much time in bed, I couldn't help wondering—'

The woman sighed, fiddled with the keys before returning them to the mantelpiece.

'He's going through a bad patch, poor darling.' She looked at the detective, her face shadowed by concern. 'You aren't here to speak to him, are you? He was up until twenty minutes ago. When he saw how much wool Miriam had left, he even tried to do a little work—' she nodded in the direction of one of the knitting machines where a few rows of green ribbing, rigidly held to a straight edge, hung below the needles—'but he had to stop and go up. He's had his pills, so he's probably sound asleep by now.'

'Not to worry.' Jurnet smiled reassuringly into the worried face, and found himself surprised afresh at the woman's transformation. It was the hair, he decided. Not beautiful hair like Miriam's: quite ordinary hair, but soft about the face for once, instead of being pulled back severely like an old time school mistress.

Jurnet felt suddenly embarrassed that he had called. Such people went early to bed, and he must have interrupted her bedtime preparations. All the more foolish of her to have opened the door to him in the first place. When she moved, he became aware that underneath the rather flimsy housecoat she had nothing on.

He put his hand into his coat pocket and brought out the tin. 'Actually, I just popped over to bring you this. I found it at the castle, after you'd gone.'

Mrs Felsenstein clapped her hands with pleasure, like a child. She took the tin from the detective, opened it, read the name scratched inside the lid as if to check it was really what she thought it was.

Jurnet said, 'Sorry about the charcoal. I think that was my fault.'

The woman looked up, radiant.

'It's nothing. Charcoal's always doing that. I can't tell you how glad I am to have it back. I know it's silly, but it happens to be just about the only thing I have left from when I was a child—sometimes, I think, the only thing that convinces me I ever was one.'

'Glad it caught my eye.'

Mrs Felsenstein exclaimed gaily, 'I'm going to make some cocoa. It ought to be champagne, a celebration, but cocoa's the best I can offer. You *do* drink it!' she added anxiously.

'Hooked on it,' replied Jurnet, who couldn't stand the stuff. Wrily he wondered if he'd have found it easier to say no if Mrs Felsenstein had pulled her hair away from her face and pinned it up in the frumpish bun she normally went in for. On the other hand, tonight, still a slave in Egypt whilst Miriam escaped into the wilderness singing, even cocoa with a middle-aged woman with her hair in a bun was better than home with only an alley cat for company.

A prick of conscience accompanied the thought of the cat. The baked beans were going to be late tonight. He'd make up for it with a double portion.

Waiting for the cocoa to arrive, he wandered across to the knitting machines and, his back to the window, sat down at the one he designated as Mrs Felsenstein's. A piece of blue knitting, patterned with white sheep processing nose to tail—the front or the back of a sweater, he guessed—hung down from the machine, the design programmed by the plastic-coated punch-card he spied behind the rack of needles. After a little, he turned on the switch and listened as the machine began to hum pleasantly. User-friendly, he nodded approvingly, wishing he had the nerve to move the carriage, produce his very own row of fleeces growing from the hooves up.

'You do it like this,' said Mara Felsenstein, reaching over his shoulder to move the carriage. The detective could feel her breast, generously rounded, pressing against his upper back as she leaned forward. 'It's terribly simple— not, perhaps, to do well, but to do well enough. The machine does it all for you. All you have to do, really, is keep track of when to increase or decrease, or cast off.'

'Joining the pieces together can't be easy.'

Jurnet would have liked to get up, but felt it would be not only impolite to do so, but worse: an implicit snigger.

'Not my headache.' The woman moved away. 'That's a job for the linkers. You should ask Miriam—she's got everything organized down to the last stitch. They're the ones who take the separate sections and turn them into a finished sweater. It's more interesting work, as well as better paid, but it requires a degree of concentration I can't be sure of—I mean, Leo may suddenly need me, and then I'd have to get up and leave whatever I was doing, no matter what.'

'I suppose so,' said Jurnet vaguely. He switched the machine off, feeling, for no sufficient reason, that he had somehow escaped a situation fraught with some peril.

He sat on the couch where Mrs Felsenstein indicated, and accepted the proffered mug of cocoa. She chose the floor for herself, on the hearthrug close to the electric fire, whose glow made her skin look downy, young.

Jurnet steeled himself to take a sip of the drink, and found it less revolting than he had feared.

'Did you, by any chance,' he asked, first sucking in his lips to trap the pinkish froth which coated them, 'ever know a man named King, had the Punch and Judy show at Havenlea?'

'The man who was killed? I saw it in the *Argus*.' Mrs Felsenstein set her mug down on the floor and looked up at the detective. 'No—I never knew him—why? Except that when Loy was a child and we used to go down to Havenlea for the day, we always had to make a beeline for the Punch and Judy. Nobody ever saw who was working them, of course—there was just a woman who came round with a wooden box for the money. Whether the man inside the tent in those days was the man who was murdered, I couldn't tell you.'

'Him or his father, I reckon, depending how long ago it was. I gather the Kings have run the Punch and Judy show at Havenlea for generations.' Jurnet smiled. 'That hardly constitutes knowing.'

'Sometimes I felt I did,' she replied seriously. 'Know him, I mean. It was all so cruel and heartless—the things Punch did to everybody, always getting away with it, and acting as if it was all a great joke.

'I always had to be the one to take Loy. Leo couldn't stand it. He'd take a deckchair down by the sea and wait for us to come back. But Loy loved it. All the children did, I suppose because it was so—well, anarchic. The one place in their small world where right didn't triumph, where honesty wasn't the best policy. Punch got away with everything, and I sometimes felt—quite wrongly, I'm sure—that the man out of sight moving the puppets about must be the same, or he could never have gone on doing what he did year after year.'

Jurnet said, with a slight emphasis on the last word, 'He didn't get away with everything.'

'No, of course not, poor fellow!' Mara Felsenstein drank some of her cocoa, and asked, a frown of worry instantly

ageing her, 'What made you ask whether I knew him? Is
his death connected with Loy's in some way?'

'I just wondered if your son had ever mentioned him to
you.' Jurnet evaded the question. 'Mr King's daughter works
for Second Coming, and he and Loy had certainly met.'

The woman got up with a neat, economical movement
and set her cocoa mug down on the mantelpiece. The glow
from the electric fire penetrated the fabric of her housecoat, outlining the legs beneath, well-shaped but on the
heavy side. She stood looking down at the detective with a
troubled gaze.

'Please don't think I'm badgering you,' she said, a little
breathless. 'I'm sure it must take an awful lot of time to
put all the clues together. More than our linkers! Only, it's
so hard on Leo, this limbo, the way everything drags on.
It makes me so afraid for him—'

'Not easy for you either, I'm sure of that.' Jurnet did not
need to simulate sympathy. 'I wouldn't want you to think
that over at Headquarters we aren't only too well aware of
the strain you're both under. The best I can say is, we
aren't hanging about, I can assure you of that.'

'I didn't mean—' Mrs Felsenstein rearranged her thoughts,
and began again. 'It's only, with time passing, doesn't it
get harder, less likely you'll ever find out who did it?'

'We're nowhere near that point as yet.' Jurnet got up
from the couch, handed over his cocoa mug. 'Delicious!'
he pronounced, almost meaning it. Mrs Felsenstein turned
away to set the mug on the mantelpiece next to its fellow,
the detective drifting back across the room to the knitting
machine and the piece of fabric patterned with sheep, one
after the other.

The woman joined him there and said, 'Another row
and then there's a repeat, same as the others but with one
black sheep among all the white ones. Miriam says it's one
of our best numbers.'

Jurnet laughed.

'Be truer to life to have all the sheep black and just the
one white one. Not such a good seller, though.' He looked
down at the woman. Even away from the fire, he thought,
she looks young tonight.

He said, 'I want you to believe that we're making progress. We've been listening to what people have had to say, and even more, if you follow me, listening to what they haven't.'

'You mean they've been lying?'

'Not necessarily. I mean that everybody has secrets—everybody, you and me included, if you don't mind me saying so. Sometimes they are secrets we can hardly bear to reveal to ourselves, let alone to others; and sometimes they are secrets we long to share, even though, some-times, we know the sharing will get us into bad trouble.'

Jurnet said, 'I believe profoundly that whoever killed your son, like any other undiscovered murderer, finds the burden of the knowledge of what he has done almost impossible to bear, alone. Yet how, knowing the conse-quences, can he come out with it? That's his problem, and ours too. That being so, we have to move on to the facts, to the mistakes he has made.'

'Supposing he hasn't made any?'

'Impossible!' the detective stated with confidence. 'He may think he hasn't, but he has; because, underneath it all, don't you see, subconsciously, that's what he wants—to be found out. All the time he goes about painstakingly covering up his tracks, deep inside he wants passionately to be rid of that intolerable load which is wearing him down. That's why, invariably, he leaves clues that are unknown to his conscious self, sometimes little slips so silly even we, the police, pass them over, don't recognize them for what they are; but clues that, sooner or later, have to lead us to him and him to us, his pursuers who are also his only rescuers.'

'You make it sound like a Greek tragedy.'

'I wouldn't know about that. What I haven't mentioned yet, though, is the third side of the triangle.'

'What is that?'

'Not what: who. The victim. Where does he fit into the picture? Because he has to, or there isn't one. That's why a police officer investigating a murder has to spend so much time asking nosey questions about what kind of bloke was he; reading other people's letters, going through old school reports or the files of old newspapers.

'Your son—forgive me—was killed by a blow on the

back of his head. He couldn't have seen the arm raised or the weapon descending, or he would have ducked, tried to dodge. There would have been a struggle, and there's no evidence of anything like that. But I have a crazy theory—' Jurnet went suddenly bright red at what he had already revealed of himself, and at what he proposed to reveal further; yet, under the almost mesmeric scrutiny of those wonderful eyes, the whites so pure, the pupils so brilliant, could not, or did not choose to, stop—'that every murder victim, even if death comes in the dark or while he's asleep knows the identity of his murderer.'

Mrs Felsenstein whispered 'Poor Loy!' and covered her face with her hands.

Jurnet, furious with himself, said awkwardly, 'There I go, rattling on. It must have been the cocoa.'

'No, no! I'm very grateful—'

'Don't know what for.' The detective settled his coat on his shoulders. 'I must be getting along.'

The other took her hands away from her face. 'Thank you again for bringing back my tin.'

'My pleasure.' The detective took a few steps towards the door; turned as if remembering his manners, and shook hands. Inquired: 'Is there anything else I can do for you?'

'There is one thing,' Mara Felsenstein said. With thumb and forefinger she took hold of the zip fastener at her neck; pulled on it in a sweeping gesture that split the edges of her housecoat apart like a dehiscing seed-pod, revealing the naked fruit beneath.

'If you don't mind, that is. You can go to bed with me.'

33

Jurnet drove home through the dark Good Friday night. The city was very quiet. Lucky for him, the detective thought, none of his tribe were on the prowl with their little bags ready to be blown into.

'*Cocoa!*' he could hear their incredulous laughter. 'Tell us another!'

It had been wonderful beyond words, beyond wonder. Beyond guilt, beyond regret that it had happened. He drove homeward, filled with gratitude and a measureless joy that it had happened to him.

'Was I all right?' she had asked tremulously, when at last, on the bumpy old couch, they had drawn apart from each other, not too far apart.

She had sounded like a virgin, she the mother of a grown son. She had made love like a virgin, assuming there to be such a thing as a virgin without timidity, possessed of perfect discretion, and a delicate and instinctive knowledge of all that there was to be savoured in the coming together of a man and a woman. There had been a freshness, a radiance—Jurnet had to stop the car, draw in to the side of the road and sit quietly for a little, until the world returned to its accustomed orbit.

'When can we do this again?' he had demanded, transported; yet scarcely surprised when she had answered, with a loving finality that left no room for contradiction: 'Never!'

Jurnet swung the car round into the entrance of the block of flats, enjoying, in his new-found awareness of the possibilities of existence, every movement of the car and of his own body mastering it. He parked, as usual, next to the resident rubbish, switching off the ignition and sitting still in the driving seat for a moment longer, neither thinking nor feeling, simply being.

Even so, ecstasy—if that was what it was—was a perishable quantity, short-lived as a spark. It was replaced by knowledge he could not stifle, nor pretend it was not so.

Coming into the driveway, the headlights, describing their turning arc, had briefly illuminated something.

Something.

Jurnet got out of the car, shut the door, and walked back to the street. In the gutter, slammed against the kerb where some passing vehicle had hurled it, lay the body of the cat. Its black coat was sticky and repellent, the left side of its face laid open in a grin of such manic ferocity that the detective's eyes shut of their own volition.

What did you do with a dead cat beside light a candle to its memory, do penance for the rest of your days because you had got home so late that it had got tired of waiting; and, watching for you, for you alone, had forgotten for one fatal instant the street sense programmed into it from kittenhood?

Load it into one of the black plastic bags to await the dustman? Leave it where it was, for the street cleaners to clear away? Fling it over the hedge into somebody else's garden and let them worry about it?

Jurnet went up to his flat, looked up the number of a vet and dialled it. '*Mr Harvey Chance*,' the recorded message replied with a certain standoffishness, '*is not available at the moment except for emergencies, in which case he may be reached at Angleby 37462. Surgery hours are 9 to 10.30 a.m. daily except Sundays. If you have any message, first give your name, address, and telephone number. Speak when the signal tone ceases. Thank you.*'

When the signal tone ceased, Jurnet did not give his name, address and telephone number. He said, 'My cat is dead. It was run over because I was too busy screwing to get back home and feed it. It was black, and it liked baked beans. I did not know its name. Thank *you*.'

He got the dialling tone again and phoned Dr Colton at his private address.

'That'll be all right,' said the doctor, when he heard

what Detective-Inspector Jurnet wanted. 'Leave it outside
the back door and I'll see one of the mortuary attendants
deals with it first thing in the morning.' Despite the late-
ness of the hour, his voice was unexpectedly gentle. For
once, he did not ask for any forms to be filled in.

Jurnet put the phone back and went into the kitchen.
He fished about in the cupboard under the sink, and
found a carrier bag with 'Harrods' printed on it. It pleased
him to have found such an upmarket winding sheet. Across
the landing, Mrs Petherton's gramophone had begun its
evening recital: *Love is the sweetest thing—*'. Reminded
of a job undone, the detective picked up the carton of
beans, what was left of them.

He crossed to Mrs Petherton's door and rang the bell.
He had to wait a long time. When Mrs Petherton finally
appeared, she looked at him with glazed eyes, and said in
a haughty voice, 'I never purchase anything at the door.'

'Not selling—giving!' Jurnet put on his jolly voice, plunked
the carton down in the passage, and, with a hand firmly
gripped under the woman's elbow, propelled her back to
the living-room.

It was a long time since he had been invited in, and the
squalor of what had been a bravely bright little place
appalled him. The gramophone shone immaculate on its
special rug, everything else looked as if it hadn't been
touched for months. On the little tables and whatnots,
thinner areas of dust among the thicker areas traced the
bases of china crinoline ladies and the china gentlemen
who had bent over their hands; now, no doubt, perform-
ing their elaborate courtesies on the shelves of the friendly
bric-à-brac dealer. The grate was full of gin bottles, several
of them broken. On the floral covers that swathed the sofa
and the armchair, the chrysanthemums were greasy as
from some unidentified blight. Mrs Petherton looked stoned
and ill.

And hungry.

'Got a tin opener?' Jurnet asked, still doing the cheery
bit.

He settled the little woman on the least awful part of
the sofa, and went into the kitchen, which was, for a
wonder, fairly clean, probably because such little use had

been made of its modest facilities. He put some coins in the meter, went back to the hallway for the carton, found an opener and a spoon; opened two tins of the beans and set them to heat in a saucepan on the stove.

'I hope you like beans—' back in the living-room. 'A couple of bowls like this and we'll have you entering for the marathon.'

The little woman sat exactly as he had left her, the faded blue eyes that must once have been so pretty now fixed on the detective's face in bemused conjecture, now sliding away as if the problem he presented was too difficult to be contemplated. 'Love is the Sweetest Thing' had long ago declined into a leaden *thump, thump, thump*. Jurnet went across to the gramophone and silenced it.

He brought a little table up to the sofa and placed the hot bowl of beans on it.

'A mat!' Mrs Petherton commanded imperiously. 'A table mat! You'll ruin the polish!'

'No damage done.' Jurnet snatched up the bowl with exaggerated haste. The table top was already deeply scored with a pattern of interlacing rings, an artefact of years of solitary tippling. He found a mat doing nothing on the mantelshelf and set the bowl back in place again.

Mrs Petherton began to eat, first delicately, like the cat, and then with an appetite painful to watch. Just the same, Jurnet steeled himself to stay and watch it. The dead cat in the gutter wasn't going anywhere. It had, though.

Gone somewhere.

When, eventually, Jurnet came down, carrying the Harrods bag, the body had disappeared. Only some tags of fur and tissue, and a dark stain where the skull had cracked against the kerbstone, were there to convince the detective he had not dreamed it all.

He went along the street a little, on the chance some other vehicle had nudged the corpse to a new resting place: but nothing. Bizarre possibilities crowded Jurnet's tired mind. A fox slinking into town had carried it off for its cubs. Some bright little Fascist slob, full of the joy of spring, was even at that moment nailing the dead cat to a ducky little cross, to be left outside Rabbi Schnellman's door for him to find first thing in the morning.

Anything to blot out the possibility that the cat might be alive, after all; that he, Jurnet, had not merely been criminally late for its supper, but, repelled by its ugly death, as he had supposed it, had abandoned it without mercy or proper examination, leaving it to drag itself off painfully in search of succour or, at least, a softer place in which to die.

He went up and down the street, poking about in hedges, looking over railings and fences. A man who must have been watching him for some time came out of a house and asked him what the hell he thought he was doing. When Jurnet explained that he was looking for a dead cat, the man exclaimed, 'Now I've heard everything!' and went back indoors.

Jurnet returned to his flat, treading the landing quietly for fear of waking Mrs Petherton. Replete with beans, the little woman had fallen asleep on the sofa, and he had gone through to her bedroom, found blankets, and tucked her fragile form in cosily. Tomorrow, he supposed with sinking heart, he would, as a matter of duty, have to alert the social services. What would they do? Get her off the booze for a start. No more Happy Hours in the Hacienda Wine Bar. Put her in a home for the elderly and confused, where they would be ever so kind, but never let her take her gramophone.

The first thing he did when he got indoors was to go into the bathroom and shut the window. Enough was enough.

He put away the Harrods bag, undressed and took a shower. Mara, he thought, soaping the flesh that had clothed their passion, rinsing the passion away with the soap: a strange and lovely name.

It seemed a long time ago.

It seemed to have nothing to do with Miriam.

He wished that he had known the cat's name.

Who was it had said love was for giving, not taking?

He went to bed, twisted and turned, sleep eluding him. Found himself reliving, not that coupling on the Felsenstein's couch, but one in which he had not even participated: Loy Tanner in Annie Falcone's bed, and the girl Francesca standing at the door with her mouth open.

Conscious of his own freshly laundered cleanliness, the black hair damp on the pillow, he spared a disparaging thought for the reddish locks which had hung dankly to the dead pop singer's shoulders. Tomorrow, he promised himself, he would go over the picture file once again, refresh his memory of what the shit had looked like. Not the pictures of Tanner dead, but the *Argus* shots of Tanner triumphant. It would be interesting, to say the least, to see whether screwing his mum gave you a new perspective on Loy Tanner.

Sliding deeper towards sleep, Jurnet could have sworn he heard Mrs Petherton's gramophone start up again, not in the next-door flat, though—in his own. In the very room where he was lying.

'I'll see you again,
Whenever spring breaks through again.
Time may lie heavy betwee—twee—twee—'

On the edge of oblivion he suddenly knew that Mrs Petherton had something very important indeed to tell him. For a second, he sat up in bed, hugging the knowledge to him as if it were a favourite teddy bear without which he'd never settle: then fell over the edge and forgot all about it.

Next morning, last thing before he left the flat, Jurnet opened the bathroom window dreading what might come in but feeling he could face it. The day outside was wild and gusty, empty crisp packets bowling along the pavements. The sensation that everything out there was on the move made Jurnet feel vigorous and optimistic. A day for new beginnings.

To his astonishment and relief—bracing himself as he had been to plumb the depths of self-disgust—the only pangs of conscience which assailed him related to the cat; a regret, he accepted, which would haunt him as long as he lived. That he had been unfaithful to Miriam scarcely troubled him—but then, whatever a superficial reading of the events of the night before might suggest, he had not, in any essential meaning of the word, been unfaithful to

Miriam. You might as well assert that by going to the South Pole you were being unfaithful to the North one.

Jurnet wrinkled his nose at the absurdity of his thought. Who did he think he was kidding? That must be the kind of guff all faithless lovers fed into their personal computers to get themselves in the clear. *Mea culpa*. Metaphorically, over his cornflakes and cup of instant, he beat his breast, calling himself all the right names—a lecher, a swine, a dirty old man.

A waste of time. He still did not feel guilty, only great.

Mrs Petherton was on the move too. When the detective came out of his front door he found her there, on the landing, trying to coax a clapped-out shopping trolley to attempt the stairs.

'It used to be so good.' She regarded the reluctant piece of junk, which was stuffed with soiled, chrysanthemum-patterned slip-covers, with the slightly dazed surprise which seemed to be her characteristic response to a world in which nothing was as good as it used to be. 'It used to be *very* good.'

She made no reference to the previous night, unless the slip-covers were themselves a reference. Perhaps the rumbustiousness of the weather had got to her too: perhaps there was something to be said for baked beans, after all.

Jurnet carried the trolley downstairs for her. Outside the front door, the little woman thanked him prettily; then said quickly, keeping her face turned a little away so that what Jurnet saw under the pale blue cloche hat, only a little shabby, was a tender curve of cheek which seemed to belong to an earlier self that hung on regardless, 'Silly me! I thought I'd run out, and do you know? When I looked in my pension book I had two weeks not even used!'

Jurnet said carefully, meaning, don't blow it all on gin, love, for God's sake: 'One does have to budget these days.'

'One does.' She nodded seriously, meaning, Jurnet feared, gin first and then manage as best you can on what's left over, assuming anything to be left over. 'Today it's the slip-covers' turn. I'm taking them to the launderette. They've got a little soiled, and it *is* spring.'

'Can't I drop you off with them? Save you trundling that thing along the street.'

'How kind! Only I have to go to the Post Office first— you have to pay in advance, you know—and that's in the other direction.'

'Why don't I take the covers in for you, then, and get them started? You can settle up with me later. That way, you won't have so long to wait.'

'Oh, I never mind waiting,' Mrs Petherton said. 'I spend a lot of time waiting. And waiting in the launderette is very pleasant and soothing. I often think the world would be a better place if only everybody would take time off to sit and watch the washing going round.'

As she spoke, something stirred in Jurnet's consciousness; rose and promptly dropped back into the primeval ooze. Still, something must have remained in suspension because, when he finally reached the launderette, having persuaded Mrs Petherton to do as he suggested, instead of clearing off to work as he undoubtedly should have done, he slumped into a chair and, eyes fixed on the window in the machine door as if it were a spyhole into a secret kingdom, waited for the washing to go round.

He was feeling a little uncomfortable. The girl who looked after the washing machines had been embarrassingly ready to get the covers loaded for him, to add the detergent, perform any other little service she could think of for the tall, dark and handsome male fate had sent along to the launderette that morning together with the usual raggle-taggle of old age pensioners and mums with sticky young.

Jurnet, who had lived long enough to know the effect of his looks on the young and simple-minded, had—out of kindness, not vanity: he hated the outward, delusive foreignness of himself, inwardly so English, so Norfolk—given her one of his Mark 2 smiles, only slightly smouldering. However, when the girl, neat and bright in her fresh green overall, saw the state the slip covers were in, her expression changed to a point where even the Mark 4 smile, unashamedly sexy, was useless to retrieve the situation. At his weak disclaimer, 'Actually, they're not mine,' the girl's lip had curled disdainfully, and she had slammed off, blonde hair swinging.

Feeling disloyal to Mrs Petherton who, poor soul, deserved better, he waited for the washing to go round and scothe his ruffled ego as the little woman had promised it would. The effect was quite the opposite. The chrysanthemums were rust-coloured and yellow on a dark green background, and the colours jangled his eyes, his thought processes. He shut his eyes to get away from them; concentrated on the woman next to him telling her neighbour on the further side how to make a bread pudding what *was* a bread pudding; on the modish electronic *ting!* of the cash register, the clink of milk bottles, and the comfortable, village voice of the girl in the green overall, 'Just the one pint today, please.'

He got up and blundered outside, into the windy air. Christ, it was cold! Yet a cold spring day, not a cold winter day. The world coming alive, and he, Ben Jurnet, with it.

Deeply ashamed of the exultation which possessed every atom of his being, he ran back to the car, unlocked it, and got in.

Got on to Control and gave the appropriate directions.

34

They came into the forest as into another country, not a friendly one. True, there were no candy-striped barriers, no floodlights, observation posts nor men in uniforms demanding passports; but there might as well have been.

Without warning, the placid, farmyard Norfolk of small villages clustered about the parish church like chicks about a hen, had yielded to a parade ground where trees marched in regiments to the horizon, closing in the road, closing out the rest of the world, the sky the sole escape.

Driving, Sergeant Ellers shuddered with exaggerated Celtic sensibility. 'Time we drew lots, boys, to see who gets chucked out first if the wolves attack.' High up in the sky two fighters from the American air-base a few miles to the south, sprang across the gap between the trees, leaving behind fraying vapour trails. 'Vultures as well!' exclaimed the little Welshman. 'It's as good as being on telly.'

The intention was good, as Jurnet, in the front passenger seat, acknowledged with a sideways smile; but it was clear from the driving mirror that Blaker and Nye, the young constables, were in no mood for jokes. They sat in the rear of the car looking stiff and stupid: no one more urban than your provincial townee, his precarious sophistication threatened by the wilderness only minutes from the city centre.

The detective took another look at the map spread out on his knees.

'I make it the third drove road along, on the left. A shade under two miles. The local lads and the bloke from the Forestry Commission are in a roadmenders' lay-by couple of hundred yards this side.'

'Oh ah. Wonder how long His Nibs'll take.'

'Depends how long it took him at the University.' Jurnet leaned forward and peered through the windscreen. 'Time to keep your eyes peeled.'

It was easy enough to find the lay-by: harder to find parking space behind the mini-mountains of aggregate. Two vehicles were already occupying all that was available.

The Superintendent, looking military in his Burberry, came up to the car before Ellers had brought it to a halt, and demanded, 'What kept you?'

Jurnet looked at his superior officer in astonishment. 'We didn't see you pass us—'

'For the very good reason that we didn't. We came the shorter way.'

Jurnet did not think it worth his while to point out that the map over which the two had pored together had shown no alternative route short of swinging in a wide arc round the perimeter of the air-base, thereby adding a good fifteen miles to the journey. If the Superintendent said there was a shorter route, then there was one, even if—as, given the circumstances, seemed probable—it had involved a cross-country dash under the noses of NATO transports lifting off for Europe.

If Blaker and Nye looked a bit off, it was as nothing to the dishevelment of the Superintendent's passengers. Even Sid Hale, who rose each morning in the confident expectation of Doomsday, and retired each night a little put out to find it had been put off yet again, looked in a state of shock.

'The important thing is, I was able, as you suggested, to get hold of the Professor,' the Superintendent went on. The Head of the Department of Archaeology at the University of Angleby, his complexion pastier than his morning muesli, nodded unhappily at Jurnet. 'And I am relieved to tell you—' the voice, perfectly modulated, contrived nevertheless to infuse the surrounding air with the threat of what might have happened, had it turned out otherwise— 'that, according to Mr Flotman, the Forestry Commission man they've laid on for us, our journey is not in vain. You would appear—' the admission seemed to be wrung from him with positive physical hurt: in no way, despite the extravagance of its terms, could it be taken for a compliment—'to have made the right deduction from that combination of evidence and intuition which is so uniquely your own. They're here.'

Mr Flotman, a young man in a knitted cap topped with a red pompom, and glowing with good health to the point of offensiveness, led the little party to the beginning of the drove. He seemed to be having difficulty not to regard his secondment to police duties as a great lark.

'A bit churned up,' he announced, cheerfully sloshing about in the puddles in his high-laced boots. Of their own lot, Jurnet noted that, as was to be expected, only the Superintendent had thought to come kitted out with wellies. 'We've been working this compartment best part of the week, moving out some Scots pine, grand stuff. Up to nine o'clock this morning we had hurdles strung across here, hopefully to discourage any of the travelling fraternity with ideas of picking up a bit of timber on the very cheap—so I can guarantee that these are brand-new, or as near as makes no difference.'

The Superintendent bent over the tracks indicated. They were deeply incised in the mud, emerging fainter but unmistakable higher up the slope, a double trail that surmounted its gentle rise and disappeared out of sight down the further side.

'Couldn't be one of yours, I suppose?'

The Forestry Commission man shook his head.

'No way. Standard tread. The few we run this size are all Town and Country.'

'Ah.' The Superintendent straightened up and looked about him.

'I've studied the map,' he said, 'so I know the general lie of the land. What I want you to do is describe to me in detail what there is to be seen over the brow of this hill.'

The young man looked puzzled. 'I'll walk up there with you if you want.'

'Not so much as a topknot is to show over that rise. Just tell me, if you please.'

'Well—' the other considered: then, mentioning first things first, 'There's the trees, of course, either side. Norway Spruce, just coming up for brashing.' At the expression on the Superintendent's face he quickly explained, 'Cutting off the lower branches that'll be dying off anyway by now for lack of light. That lets us get in to mark the trees up for thinning, and—'

'Tell me what else there is.'

'Yes, sir,' said Mr Flotman, looking hurt. 'Not much. Just the drove, straight as a die, a long gentle slope till it gets to Hob's Hole—about half a mile, I reckon. And that's as far as it goes, thanks to a conservation order on that bloody great hole in the ground. Left to us, we'd have taken it on for another three miles at least.'

'Can you actually see the Hole from the top here?'

'A sight better than you could a week ago. Then, there was still the old fence up, you'd hardly know it was there, it had got so buried in bramble and bracken and I don't know what. When we came in this time we thought we might as well do a bit of tidying up while we were at it. Matter of fact, if I say it myself, we did a damn good job. Only when we cleared the trash away, the fence itself just fell apart. We've put up warning signs, and we'll be putting in a concrete and link job soon as we get the go-ahead from the Ministry. In the meantime it's wide open, like a bomb or a meteor just dropped out of the sky.'

Correcting himself: 'What you'd see from the top of that rise, to be accurate, is not the edge of the Hole proper, but which I can best call its rim. If you can imagine a beaker with a very wide lip—say, twenty-five, thirty meters—going all round, that's more like it: the gradient quite gentle, then suddenly there's the real edge, going down more or less sheer to the old flint workings. And that's about all I can think of. There's a footpath the other side, but you'd have a job finding it. Unless those fellows you're after try to get out under their own steam, there's nowhere else for them to go except back the way they came.'

The Superintendent said, 'I'm relieved to hear it.'

Jurnet exclaimed, 'That's terrible!' The young forester, affronted, went as red as his pompom. Jurnet addressed himself to his superior. 'We've been reckoning on having the time it'd take them to get through that fence and all that scrub. We'd been reckoning on them having to get out of the car. But now—'

The Superintendent asked, 'Then what are we waiting for?'

Under the trees it was terrible. Not a forest at all, Jurnet decided: a man-made timber factory that contravened every Act ever passed relating to health and safety at work. Beneath their feet, pine needles slimy with more than wet; above, an armoury of spikes and skewers that tweaked at their coats, their pockets, inserted themselves up sleeves and down trouser legs too many times for it not to have been done on purpose. Overhead, branches programmed with micrometric accuracy dropped small bundles of needles into the space between collar and neck.

Worst of all, thought Jurnet, was the smell. The next person to give him a bottle of pine bath-essence for Christmas was going to get it right back, in the kisser.

'See that you move without noise,' had been the Superintendent's parting injunction as the different parties moved off—Jurnet, Ellers, and the Professor to the left; the Superintendent, Sid Hale and PC Nye to the right. The two local men were left to guard the exit to the road, and to be on hand to receive and forward messages.

They must have been in those woods before, Jurnet decided, to be standing there, grinning like hyenas. The Forestry Commission man, pleading for a role, had been sent, together with PC Blaker, to work round to the further side of the Hole and join up with some reinforcements arriving from Swaffham.

But, without noise! So quiet to outward appearances, the forest, once you were inside, creaked and rattled like an old tram-car on its way to the knackers. Elderly pine cones, trodden underfoot, cracked like bullets.

The three moved along unspeaking, each cocooned in his own cares, until Jack Ellers, who was in charge of the telemetry, tapped Jurnet on the shoulder, and jerked a thumb to the right; whereupon they turned at an angle and made their way thankfully towards the ragged fringe of daylight in the distance.

Jurnet found his throat suddenly dry. Not long now, he thought.

God.

* * *

When he could see the side of the drove, where some long, elegant trunks of Scots Pine were laid out to season, he gave the order to get down. Not until the three were safely on their stomachs did he venture to raise his head.

Even then the trees mocked his intention, their reflections masking the car windows so that he could not make out with certainty who was sitting where; only that it was indeed there, as everything that had happened had predicted it would be, and that both front seats were occupied.

The car was parked at the very end of the drove, its rear wheels on grass, the front ones on the rough marl of that rim which Mr Flotman had described so accurately. A finger of wind, channelled by the surrounding trees, brushed teasingly up the drove road and back again, bending the long grass about the car's rear wheels now this way, now that.

After the forest it seemed very quiet. Too quiet.

Jurnet whispered, straining his eyes for movement on the further side of the road, 'The Super's going to have a go at speaking to them.'

The sun was trying to come out. Professor Whinglass took off his glasses and put them away with donnish precision.

'Reflections,' he hissed briefly. 'Can't be too careful.'

The sun burst out in full glory, as if to applaud his foresight. The wind subsided. Coiled springs, poised for action, the three waited: when, without warning, out of the trees higher up the slope, tumbled a scrum of children, boys and girls with rosy faces and packs on their backs, pleased as puppies to be out in the air again after the dark of the wood.

They came down the slope shouting, singing.

> 'My old man's a dustman,
> He wears a dustman's hat.
> He wears gorblimey trousers,
> And he lives in a councilflat—'

For a moment the three watchers stayed, petrified. Then Whinglass, with surprising, athletic speed, was on his feet, running into the road.

'Leo!' he shouted. 'No!'

Quietly, with only a whispering crunch of wheels over the marl, the car had begun to roll gently downhill towards the edge of the Hole, gaining momentum as the Professor came up with it. Yet somehow, by a superhuman effort, the man got the front door open, dragged out the passenger within. Bundled together, dust flying—impossible to say if they were clinging or grappling—the two disappeared over the edge a moment before the car followed, without fuss, its bright red coachwork giving it the look of a clockwork toy tipped carelessly off a table.

Contained by the side of the ancient mine, the resulting crash sounded muted, nothing much. The explosion which followed was of a different order. By the time Jurnet and his companions arrived at the Hole, the car, up-ended, was well ablaze, its bonnet wedged into the opening of a rudimentary tunnel where, long before history, miners wielding reindeer picks had scrabbled for the floorstone, the hardest flint. Plumes of flame emerged from beneath the chassis to curve upward and inward with deadly grace until the entire car was enfolded in fire as into the petals of some exotic flower, dangerous and devouring.

Jurnet ran along the edge of the Hole, the heat on his face, smoke acrid in his throat and his nostrils.

'There has to be some way down!'

The Superintendent's hand on his subordinate's arm was iron-hard. Jurnet pulled away in vain.

'Nothing you can do. Nothing anybody can do.'

'There has to be!'

'Nothing,' the other repeated, mouthing the syllables as if to one hard of hearing. 'It's all over.' The Superintendent's voice held a cruel finality. 'Now will you stop being sentimental, Inspector Jurnet, and come and lend a hand where you can be of some use!'

Fifteen feet below ground level, caught in a tangle of briar which threatened to give way at any moment, Professor Whinglass, blood dripping into his eyes and down his chin, held grimly on to his unconscious prisoner.

'Sid better be the one to go,' the Superintendent ordered, uncoiling the rope with which, farsightedly as ever, he had thought to festoon his Burberry. 'PC Nye,' he commanded abruptly, 'get those children away from here and off Forestry Commission property.' Keeping his face deliberately turned away from the car, the column of smoke and flame: 'There's nothing anybody can do in that quarter.'

It was no easy operation. The soft walls of the crater offered few holds. Soil and pebbles rained down on the stranded pair, red-hot shrapnel shot up from below. At one point, unwisely putting his trust in a gorse bush that looked as if it had been growing there since the Ice Age, the roped detective swung twirling into the smoke as the great, dusty mass, with its load of prickles, plummeted down an inch from the Professor's unprotected eyes.

Jurnet, the anchor man, hung on to the end of the rope and felt the skin scorching off his palms.

Only some unsuspected physical and moral resource, perhaps reserved to those who measure the survival of man in Ages rather than calendar years, enabled the Head of the Department of Archaeology to hold on to his burden until he was at last relieved of it.

When it was all over and they sat about awaiting the arrival of the ambulance, the Professor settling his glasses back on with trembling hands, Sid Hale limp, head on chest, Jurnet got up and walked over to the unconscious figure which had so narrowly escaped the holocaust: stood looking down at the hurt face, not knowing whether to be glad or sorry.

Part 3

Question and answer

35

I love you. Have you ever had a murder confession which began with those words? I hope my saying them won't embarrass you or get you into trouble with the Chief Constable, or whoever it is who has authority over you. But I have to say them, and say them before I say anything else, because, of all the words I have to say, those are the most important.

Note that I say nothing about your loving me, even though—I don't think I am deluding myself—I believe you did love me a little, for a little while. A police officer can't be expected to love a murderess, I accept that. All I ask is that you don't hate me, or, if you do, hate me gently.

Have you so much pity for the killed that you have none left over for the killer?

For you to understand why I am that monster, I have to go back to the beginning—if there ever is a beginning, or an ending, for that matter—to the little town of Runstowe. I don't know if you know it?—in the corner of the county, between the fens and the forest; very isolated, very inward-looking, very much affected by its geography. A strange, ugly little place, inhabited by strange, ugly people who worship strange, ugly gods in underheated buildings of yellow brick with roofs of corrugated iron. I don't think, in all of England, you could find, in a town of that size, anywhere with as many chapels.

We—my parents, that is, and I, I was an only child—belonged to the Conventicle of the Elect. If you haven't heard of them before, you're lucky. I hardly know what they believed in, except that it was the opposite of everything that meant joy, or beauty, or laughter. My father was the lay preacher there, as well as maths master in the local Comprehensive, my mother taught remedial handicrafts to physically handicapped children, of whom—but that may be my imagination—there seemed to be an inordinate number in the town.

You have no idea how tender my mother was to those poor human accidents. How often, down on my knees beside my bed at night, I used to pray that I too might shake with palsy, or have to clump about in leg irons, so that she would take me in her arms and kiss me the way she did them! But for me she had no mercy. Not for nothing had they named me Mara, which means bitterness. To the Conventicle, life was one long struggle with Satan, and another name for Satan was sex. I was the ever-present reminder that they too, my mother and father, had once fallen headlong into that pit where men and women, lost to all sense of shame, coupled like animals. To have shown me love—even had they felt any—would have been to throw away all hope of eternal life.

I was brought up in the most perfect ignorance—no radio, let alone a television—and dressed in clothes that, anywhere else but Runstowe, would have had my contemporaries in hysterics. There was one girl who did laugh. She was a year or two older than I was, and she and her family had moved into our street quite recently. They not only didn't fit in, they didn't seem to care. To me, they seemed visitors from another planet, the father with his flowered shirts, the mother and daughter with their permed hair, their mini-skirts—yes, even the mother!—and their loud, happy voices.

Every evening Marilyn—that was her name—would come out of her house, with black on her eyebrows and around her eyes, and a new mouth painted in crimson over her own. Naturally I was not allowed to have anything to do with her.

When I was sixteen my grandmother died, the weekend before I was due to sit my 'O' levels. She had been living in Newcastle with my aunt, my father's sister, and my mother and father went up north for the funeral. I'd have gone with them, if it hadn't been for the exams. Full of oblique warnings whose import was quite beyond me, they left to catch the bus, leaving me alone in my home for the first time in my life.

It was May, a long summer evening heavy with the scent of blossom, and I felt excited. I was bright at school and the coming exams did not frighten me. I only wished I knew some better way of celebrating my forty-eight hours of freedom than going down to the corner shop and buying an ice-cream with a chocolate flake stuck in it. I wasn't ordinarily allowed to have chocolate flakes. I wasn't even sure that when I actually got to the shop I'd have the courage to ask for one, in case word of my sinful gluttony got back to my mother.

On my way down the street I met Marilyn. She had seen my mother and father going off with a suitcase, and she asked if I was on my own. She was a large girl with big, floppy breasts and, I think, a careless, generous nature. I think it was because she was sorry for me that she told me there was a dance on at the air-base that night, and her father had said she could have the car, and why didn't I come too?

To my own astonishment, I said yes without hesitation. It was as if all my previous life had been a preparation for that moment. A couple of hours later, to guard against anyone from the Conventicle seeing me, Marilyn picked me up on the edge of town, and we drove to the dance.

It was a disaster from the word go. The heat, the lights, the noise of the band, quite disorientated me. I couldn't dance, I couldn't make small talk, my Sunday-best dress looked ridiculous. Even so, there being far more men than girls, I was asked to dance, at first. Then the word must have got about that I was a dead loss, because I spent the rest of the evening sitting against the wall, tears pricking my eyelids, praying silently for the moment when Marilyn would come up to me and say it was time to go home. When she did put in an appearance, all giggly and hanging on to the arm of a tall airman, she said that she and Jerry wanted to ride around a bit, but it was OK, there was a bus outside the admin. building laid on specially to get girls home who hadn't other transport, and she was sure I understood.

I found out where the admin. building was, just in time

to see the rear lights of the bus disappearing through the gate.

I set out to walk the five miles home. I wasn't a country girl and the darkness and the night noises terrified me. My feet were killing me, and what would my mother say when she saw what a mess I'd made of my best shoes? Whenever a car came along, temporarily lighting up the road ahead, tired as I was I ran like a hare until it had passed, leaving the blackness blacker than before.

I must have done about a mile and a half when a car stopped, somebody in the driver's seat reached over and opened the nearside door, and a man's voice asked out of the darkness, 'Care for a lift?'

I knew, though nobody had ever told me why, that one must never on any account accept a lift from a stranger. But I was sobbing with fatigue. I knew I'd never make it to Runstowe on my own two feet. I whispered, 'Thank you very much,' and got in.

I told the man where I lived, and after that sat rigid, eyes on the road ahead, as if that would somehow preserve me from danger. I couldn't tell you what the man looked like, except that his eyes—but probably I dreamed this up later—were bright red. He drove on for another half-mile or so, and then he turned the car off the road into a field and raped me.

No need to go into that, except to say that the pain and the disgust were as nothing to the utter confusion which seized me. *What was the man doing? Why was this happening to me? Was he a devil sent by God to punish me for going to the dance?*

When he had finished, he drove on to Runstowe and pushed me out of the car into the road. When I got home I stripped off what was left of my clothes, washed myself, and put on a sanitary towel. Then I wound up the alarm and went to sleep. In the morning I went to school with a story of having been knocked down by a hit-and-run driver, to account for my bruised face. I stuffed the clothes into a carrier bag, and got rid of them in a builder's skip. Surprisingly, I sat my exams without difficulty. In fact, I got the best marks of anybody in my year, and won the Governors' Prize, a book token for £5.

Are you wondering what all this has to do with killing two human beings? It has everything to do with it.

This will show you what an ignorant little fool I was. It was nearly five months before I knew anything was the matter. I was quite pleased to have stopped menstruating, and hoped that the messy business wouldn't start up again. My clothes were beginning to feel a bit tight round the middle, and I occasionally wondered if, after all, I was going to grow into a large woman like my mother. That was all, until one day, out of the blue, in the living-room, as I stood at the french window, the light behind me, my mother suddenly screamed and then ordered me to take off my clothes that instant, every last stitch of them.

Whilst I was undressing, she went out into the garden and shouted for my father, who was picking runner beans, to come in at once. My father had never seen me naked since I was a baby, and I cowered trembling behind the big armchair. My mother must have told him something because when they came back indoors together his face was mottled with purple patches.

They hauled me out from behind the chair, and made me stand under the electric light fitting while they pulled and prodded me as if I were a cow up for auction. They never said a word. Then my father told me to get dressed and get out.

Just like that. I wasn't even allowed to go upstairs for my coat.

It was on the bus that I first realized I was pregnant. I had found the rest of my lunch money for the week in my blazer pocket, and so—for no particular reason: I was beyond thought—I had taken a ticket as far as Newmarket. But when the realization came to me, I can't think how, that I was going to have a baby, I asked the conductor to put me down at a lonely crossroads called Hob's Cross. One of the four arms was no more than a footpath through the forest, signposted to Hob's Hole, the old flint mine. I knew that Hob was an old name for the Devil, so that it seemed an entirely fitting place for me to kill myself.

There was no carry-on. I don't even remember sparing a thought for that awful God who looked after the Conventicle of the Elect. It just seemed to me the sensible thing to do in the circumstances. One thing was abundantly clear to me: that life was a whole lot simpler if you were dead.

I followed the trail between the purple heather and the dying bracken until I reached the mine, where I had a bit of trouble getting over the fence. But at last I managed it, stepped to the edge of the Hole and, without thinking any more about it, jumped.

36

How annoyed I was to find myself in the Norfolk and Angleby Hospital still alive!

Instead of falling straight to the bottom of the mine, I had—by a miracle, as they said—landed on a kind of ledge, merely breaking a leg instead of my neck. It took me a little longer to realize that the miracle consisted of the pleasantly ugly man with the foreign accent who came daily to visit me, bringing me gifts of fruit and flowers. My rescuer, Leo Felsenstein.

On holiday from the dyestuffs company in Angleby where he was employed as a translator of research material, he had been on his way along the drove road towards the Hole and saw my efforts to climb the fence. He told me later that he had shouted out to me, but that I'd paid no attention. Well versed, after years in Auschwitz, in detecting signs of desperation, he had said nothing to contradict the ambulance men when they assumed that he and I were together. He gave my name as Mary Felsenstein.

So that it was only necessary to change one letter, the 'y' to an 'a', when I came out of hospital and moved into his flat over a chemist's shop in Mountergate. The first day he considered it safe to leave me on my own, he went back to the Hole, and brought back the statuette they call the Hob's Hole Venus, which had apparently lain in a niche behind the ledge, unseen until he had clambered down to help me. He set it up on the mantelpiece in the little sitting-room, and turned to me with a smile I shall never forget.

'Our patron saint and protectress.'

Let me make it clear that Leo Felsenstein and I have never lived together as man and wife. What the Nazis did to him left him incurably impotent. Dreadful as it is to say it, I could almost be grateful. After what had happened to me I could never have stayed on any other terms.

As to the child growing daily larger in my womb, if I had known about abortion there would have been no Loy Tanner. Well, I didn't know, and I'm sure it never even occurred to Leo to tell me. The years he had spent cheek by jowl with death had given him an almost mystical reverence for human life. He could not have looked forward to the child's birth with more joyous anticipation if it had been his own.

What Leo really wanted was that we should get married before the baby was born, so that it would be born legitimate; but I wouldn't have it; just as, when we did marry—I was eighteen by then—I wouldn't let him adopt it either. I could never bring myself to tell Leo about the rape, preferring him to think of me as a silly, promiscuous teenager rather than have to speak about that night, the red eyes glowing in the darkness. Deeply as I knew I hurt him, I couldn't saddle him with responsibility for a human being with that heritage.

The boy was born soon after we moved to Sebastopol Terrace. I called him Loy after Robert Tanner's youngest son, hoping that to be doubly named after the most honourable Norfolk man who ever lived might be a charm against the red-eyed darkness. Leo was wonderful with the baby. And I? I did for him all the things a mother does for her child. I took him in my arms, kissed him, rocked him to sleep.

All useless. You can't love when you're afraid, and I was deadly afraid of my son.

I'm sure Loy sensed it, even at that age. He hung round me like a forlorn puppy, begging for the love which, to all surface appearances, I was providing in abundance. I was dreadfully sorry for him—sorrier than I was for myself: it wasn't his fault he was who he was. On the night he left home—the day Mrs Falcone came round and wanted to speak to him about Francesca—I even convinced myself that I was sorry to see him go.

But once he had gone—particularly after the money

began to arrive as he started to make a name for himself as a pop singer—the old, ambiguous feelings returned. I knew that, whatever else I did, I mustn't accept money from him. It was too dangerous.

Yet, in the end, I did just that. The years in the concentration camp had undermined Leo's constitution, and he began to get more and more unwell. He had to give up his job, and I gave mine up too—I'd been working in a nursery school—so as to stay home with him. When Miriam took us both on as outworkers, it was a godsend.

Financially, then, things were very tight; but if it hadn't been for the progressive deterioration in Leo's condition we could have managed very happily. Time had only deepened our passionate—yes, passionate!—attachment. I couldn't face the prospect of life without him, and I ran about everywhere, from one specialist to another, spending money we couldn't afford, looking for a cure.

Then I heard of a new operation they were doing in America, still in its experimental stages, but offering hope beyond anything we'd been offered before. Here in England, the doctors said, 'We're evaluating the procedure. In two or three years' time, maybe—' But Leo didn't have that long to wait. I found out that the cost of taking him to the United States and getting the operation done there was £13,000, and when Loy come round to see us the night before the concert at the Middlemass, I repressed all my doubts and fears, and asked him to give me the money.

When I did that, his face went empty, the way it did sometimes, as if he had retreated deep inside himself. Then he said, with no expression in his voice, 'When you finally want something from me, it's not for yourself, it's for him.'

I replied that it was for me, too. 'You know how much Leo means to me.'

'Yes,' he said, 'I know.'

This is the difficult bit.

He brought the money round late at night, in a black case, after the concert was over. Leo, sedated to relieve the pain, had been asleep for an hour or more. Loy opened the case and I saw the bundles of notes packed inside. I saw Leo, by their magic, restored to health again. The vision impelled me towards Loy, to kiss him, for once, without reservations.

'Hold on a minute,' he said, backing away. 'There *is* a condition.'

'Condition?'

'That first you go to bed with me.'

You don't want to know how I felt, do you? Only what I did. What I did was go to bed with Loy Tanner my son, there on the couch in my own living room. Was it rape? You policemen will probably say no. After all, I was—wasn't I?—a consenting party.

Let me tell you, what my son did on that couch was worse, much worse, than what his father did to me in that field on the way home from the dance. For the first time in my life—me, a woman who had lived in complete satisfaction with an impotent man—was made to understand the meaning of physical love. Have I made myself clear?

I had an orgasm.

When he had done with me I left him lying there, face down, one arm trailing. He seemed drowsy, if not actually asleep. Feeling the burden of my own body unbearable, I dragged myself across the room to Leo's knitting machine, where a piece of ribbing hung on the needles, weighted down by some of those weights we knitters use to keep the bottom edge straight. They're quite small, and I don't suppose you've given them a second glance; but heft one of them in your hand after you read this, and you'll be surprised how heavy they are, solid metal under the plastic coating.

I took one of the weights off its hook, went back to the couch, and hit Loy over the head with it—hit him until I was sure he was dead. He made very little trouble about dying: one might almost have thought he welcomed it.

For a moment, no longer, as the blood came out of his mouth and nostrils and his eyes glazed over, I felt a piercing love for him. Then I went and opened the black case, took out the lovely crisp notes, and, bundle by bundle, burned them.

* * *

Is murder a drug, do you know? I ask because of the effect committing one had on me personally, quite the reverse of what I'd have expected, had I ever given any thought to the subject. No regrets or feelings of guilt, no panic as to what was going to happen to me. On the contrary, everything seemed beautifully calm and simple.

First I went and put on my washing-up gloves, and then I went to the cupboard under the stairs and fished out the enormous polythene bag the knitting machines had come wrapped up in, and which I could never bring myself to throw away. I felt foolishly glad that at last I'd found a use for it.

Loy went in quite easily, once I'd bent his knees a little. He had told me that he'd parked on the bomb site, so I took his keys out of the jeans he'd discarded on the floor, quickly put my own clothes back on again, put on my coat, and went out to the van and unlocked it. I left the rear doors wide open. Then I went back to the house to fetch his body.

He was a skinny boy, not at all heavy. I trussed the polythene with some cords I'd found lying in the back of the van, and heaved him on to my shoulder without difficulty. The art was in manoeuvring him through the narrow doorway into the hall, and then out of the front door without banging him; though why it was important not to bang him I couldn't tell you. The possibility that somebody might be watching never occurred to me, and even when a voice that sounded full of suppressed laughter sounded out of the darkness, 'Need a hand, love?', I wasn't seriously perturbed. Nothing was quite real that night, the speaker included.

Yes, as you've probably guessed, it was Mr King, the Punch and Judy man. Well, that was our introduction—quite chivalrous, in an odd way: a gentleman offering to help a lady with a bulky package.

If you knew him, you'll know that everything about Mr King was odd. I myself only knew him for a very little while, but it was long enough for me to know that. What he told me was, that Loy and he had fallen out over a business deal and he had followed Loy from the University because he wanted to have it out with him once and for all. What with one thing and another, he said, he wasn't at all put out to find Loy dead, though he doubted he'd have gone as far himself, if it had been left to him. However, what was done was done, and might he ask how I proposed to dispose of the body?

I answered, truthfully, that beyond getting it out of the house, where the sight of it might upset my ailing husband, I hadn't given it any thought. Mr King tut-tutted, and said that was the trouble with women, they never thought things through. He seemed quite exhilarated. I fleetingly wondered if he had been taking drugs, but as I had never, to my knowledge, actually seen anyone under their influence, I was unable to come to any conclusion. I was only aware that I was beginning to feel very tired—to remember, if not with my mind, then with my violated body, why I had committed murder; and when Mr King suggested that he take over from then on, I was only too happy to comply.

Under his direction, we first shifted Loy's body from the Second Coming van to his own dark blue one, less conspicuous; and I went back to the house and fetched Loy's clothes, stuffed into the case which had contained the money. At the last moment I found I'd left one of the packets of notes unburnt, but there wasn't time to do anything about it, so I just left it in the case along with the clothes.

The Punch and Judy man following, I drove the white van down to the Chepe, and left it there.

I got into the blue van, and suddenly I knew where I wanted to go: Hob's Hole. Hob was the Devil, and the Devil should have his own.

Mr King said he was quite amenable, so long as I did the navigating. He had a figure of Punch on the front seat which he hung up in a kind of pocket at the side of the windscreen to make room for me.

'Move over for the lady.'

There was hardly any traffic on the road. I must have fallen asleep. When I woke up I realized that we had overshot the turn-off, and I was glad. What could I have been thinking of? Hob's Hole was sacred to the Venus. Our saint, our protectress, Leo had called her. True, it wasn't until later that I saw the pictures in the *Argus* and knew, although I couldn't prove it, that it was Loy who had broken her breasts off in the Middlemass Auditorium. Even as a child, when she had stood on our mantelpiece he had hated her, and I had had to put her for safety on top of a bookcase, out of reach. All I knew then was, I couldn't pollute her shrine with the body of my satanic son.

Mr King didn't seem to mind at all that I had changed my mind. 'Women!' he exclaimed cheerfully, turning the car round. He drew into the side of the road. 'Where to now?' he demanded. 'Any other bright ideas?'

'Yes,' I said, as if it had been in my mind all along. 'I want to crucify him in the Market Place.'

37

Well you saw for yourself the result of our labours. Having only one ladder between the two of us made it awkward. If I hadn't thought of using that belt of Loy's, I don't know how we'd ever have managed it.

I'm sure, all those years ago, they did a more professional job with Jesus. For one thing, they weren't wearing gloves then, I don't suppose, in case of fingerprints. Yet it was funny, really. Apart from the gloves, we took absolutely no precautions—there, almost in the shadow of the police station! Anyone who happened along couldn't have failed to see us.

But nobody did come along. The Market Place and the surrounding streets were as quiet as the grave. Mr King seemed to take it all as a great joke. When we had finished, he drove me back to Sebastopol Terrace.

I didn't ask him in. After what had happened already that night, I wouldn't have let even you in, Mr Jurnet, if you had come knocking. I got out of it by saying I still had the room to clear up. I added, meaning it, I suppose, that I couldn't think of how to thank him for all he'd done.

'I'll think of something,' he said: took the Punch out of its pocket and settled it comfortably on the seat beside him, and drove away.

It was light before I had the house back in order. Not that Loy had died all that messily: simply that I suddenly felt so tired in all my bones, it was all I could do not to drop down on to the couch, on to that horrible, stained loose cover, and sleep forever. I forced myself to brew some really strong coffee and, having drunk two mugs of it, set to work: stripping off the cover first of all. The upholstery beneath was no problem, being a nasty plastic stuff you could sponge off. When it was dry I put on my spare cover, washed the other one in the kitchen sink, wrung it out, and left it by the back door in a bucket, ready to hang out after breakfast, along with some other household things I already had waiting.

Very little blood had dripped on to the floor. Still, just to be on the safe side, I scrubbed the boards all over, and polished them afterwards with a polish scented with lavender. Leo would be astonished. I would tell him that I'd suddenly felt inspired to do some spring-cleaning in honour of Easter. The only job I left undone was the fireplace, choked with ash. I was simply too tired. I would make the fire early, before Leo was up, and he would never know that I had burnt his life away in that mingy little grate.

You came next day, Mr Jurnet, with your Sergeant, and told us the news. You won't believe this, but it's true: shocked me as much as if I were indeed hearing it for the first time. I wouldn't want you to think I was pretending. Yesterday had happened to someone else. Today, I was a woman who had lost her son in a ghastly way.

Poor Loy! Poor Leo, who had loved him so!

A couple of nights later, long after Leo had gone to bed, Mr King came back. This time I offered him a cup of tea, but he refused it.

'One good turn deserves another,' he said, still as full as ever of that spooky laughter. He said he'd been turning over in his mind what I'd said about showing my gratitude, and he'd come up with something.

'Some time soon,' he said, 'you're going to be a very rich lady, has that ever occurred to you?' And, when I stared at him, dumbfounded: 'Loy, that boy of yours. He had a head on his shoulders. Thousands, hundreds of thousands—millions, I shouldn't be surprised—salted away here, there, and everywhere. The lawyers'll know where to put their hands on it, they always do.

'And who's it all going to go to, if not his mum? If he's made a will, you're bound to be the chief one to benefit; and if he hasn't, you'll get the lot. Even if he's gone and left it to the cat's home, you'll be bound to get what they call "reasonable provision".' He got up from his chair, did a funny little jig, and sat down again. 'Take it from me, Mrs F.—good times are just around the corner!'

I thought of the £13,000 burnt in the fireplace. Any other time I could have laughed my head off.

As it was, I said, 'You're mad if you think I'd take a penny of Loy's money.'

'*I'm* mad!' Mr King burst out laughing. His large nose became bright red. When he had calmed down, he said, 'What you do is your business. If you don't choose to be an heiress, all the more for me.'

It was blackmail, of course. Either I handed over to him an unspecified sum of money from Loy's estate, or—There was no need to complete the sentence.

'No hurry,' the man said, smiling. I must say, I never saw him out of temper. 'You don't have to go running after them. They'll be getting in touch with you. You'll see. No need to act pushy—it makes a bad impression. Just bear in mind, that's all, that I still have your polythene bag put away in a safe place, and that case with the lad's clothes—'

'I'll bear it in mind.' I too smiled, as I shrugged my shoulders. 'Since I don't want Loy's money, what does it matter to me who has it?'

We parted the best of friends. The first day after that, that I felt Leo could safely be left on his own for a few hours, I took my shopping bag, went down to the station, and took a cheap day return to Havenlea. In my bag I put my plasic mac and my French cook's knife, which Leo took pride in always keeping beautifully sharp for me. On top, for the look of the thing, I put a net of oranges.

I hadn't been to Havenlea since the last time we'd taken Loy there. It had always been later in the year when there were plenty of people about. Now, the emptiness of the place dismayed me. People would be bound to remember the solitary woman walking along the front with her shopping bag over her arm; her height, the colour of her coat, her eyes, her hair.

On the other hand, if I were indeed the solitary woman, then there was no one else to see me; or, if anybody did, it would not be a real remembering. I looked so ordinary.

The wind slapped strongly at my face, and I felt better.

I have always enjoyed the wind off the sea. Suddenly certain that the Punch and Judy tent stood where it had always stood, and that the Punch and Judy man would be inside, waiting for me, I walked briskly along the promenade until, sure enough, there it was, the same as ever, red-and-white striped, with the little pennon flapping. There was a shelter a little before, into which I stepped out of the wind to unfold my mac and put it on. I took out my knife and held it carefully in my right hand, close against my side. Then I went down to the beach.

A tuneless humming came from the tent, a sound with that unmistakable undertone of amusement, so that I knew it was Mr King at home. The fabric of the tent was pushed out of true, following the outline of a rounded back. Without stopping to think about it, I nudged a flap apart with an elbow, and plunged the knife in, knowing instinctively that once was enough. I didn't get a proper look at Mr King at all, only a fleeting glimpse of a Punch as it keeled over, looking quite amused, I thought.

I went back to the shelter, took off the mac and folded it back into its pouch. As it turned out, I could have done without it. In spite of all the blood, not a single drop showed on the plastic.

Before catching the train back, I tried to find the café the three of us always used to go to—Loy had been mad on their pastries, and I could have done with a cup of tea. But where it had been there was now an amusement arcade.

I didn't get my cup of tea till I got back home, and then I had it with Leo, which was much better.

Do you know, Mr Jurnet, what it means to be raped? Of course you don't, so I'll tell you, because I've been giving the subject a lot of thought.

It's a hateful and nauseating act of violence, but when you come down to it, it isn't important. It doesn't count, because it doesn't touch you any way but physically. It isn't at all sexual.

Does that surprise you?

I'll go further and say that when you're a virgin, as I was, and then you're raped, as I was, first by Loy's father and then by Loy's father's son, you are still a virgin in the only sense that has meaning. I tell you this because, apart from those two, you are the only man I ever slept with, and I would like you to feel that you went to bed with a virgin, untouched, even if she did offer herself to you like a whore.

How I envied Miriam when I saw the two of you together! No: envy isn't the word. I was happy for you both. I was just a little sorry for myself.

I knew what had to happen to me sooner or later; that somewhere in His yellow-brick, tin-roofed heaven, the God of the Conventicle was lying in wait for me. Even before you told me about the way every murderer makes mistakes, conscious or unconscious, I was sure that if the police didn't find me out, sooner or later He would. I'd go over everything I'd done, or said, again and again. It was like those picture puzzles they have in children's books—how many mistakes can you spot? How many had I made? Not that it mattered, except in so far as I mustn't be caught, so long as Leo had need of me.

That's how things would have gone along, until they came to the inevitable end, if you hadn't happened to call round with my pencil box, the one thing left from my childhood that gives me pleasure. Now, it is doubly dear to me. Though, all said and done, it wasn't so much after all—was it?—to want, just for once, to know what it was like, as a woman, to lie with a man in perfect love.

I love you.

Are you revolted at the thought of having made love to a woman who has killed three people? Yes, three. By the time you read this there will be, as they say, three notches on my gun. I'm going to kill Leo.

Everything has come together so pat, I have to take advantage of it. The opportunity may never come again: Miriam lending us the car (you never thought to ask whether I too could drive, Mr Jurnet, did you? When I worked at the nursery school they paid for me to have lessons so I could pick the children up in the school minibus and drop them off home again); having to face the knowledge that there's no longer any hope for Leo; and that you're close on my heels, ready to move in any minute.

Principally, though, I want to make an end because I haven't the courage to tempt Providence all over again. Thanks to you, dear Mr Jurnet, I have learnt what happiness is, and I am, frankly, afraid to stay around longer in case I should discover that it is flawed like everything else.

If the Law is really just, you won't say I murdered Leo. You'll class it as a mercy killing, which is what it is. With me locked up in prison, what's the best he could hope for? A few weeks or months in hospital, no one to cherish him as I have cherished him. Truly, I am simply taking him with me for his own good.

Please tell Miriam thank you for all her kindness, and how sorry I am to have to take her pretty car and risk messing it up. It all depends on whether it proves possible to do what I have in mind to do. I hope the car's insured. She will understand, because she is that kind of person. Tell her about us if you want to: don't, if you think better not. Either way, I promise not to haunt you, except as a happy ghost.

Whatever you do, don't pity me.

38

The Superintendent placed the pages of Mara Felsenstein's statement face down in a pile on the desk, fidgeting with them a little to align the edges. When the task was completed to his satisfaction, he sat back in his chair, his face carefully blank. The other detectives in the room stood about, waiting for a sign.

When it came, it was both more and less than they had expected.

'At the time you went to bed with Mrs Felsenstein, had you any reason to suspect her of the crimes to which she has since admitted?'

The silence was prolonged. Inspector Ben Jurnet was to have all the time in the world to examine his conscience and come to a conclusion.

At last: 'I—I don't know, sir.'

'Rubbish!' At the mini-explosion, Jurnet's mates relaxed. If the Superintendent was blowing his top instead of talking icily about disciplinary procedures, all was not lost. 'What d'you mean, you don't know?'

'What I say, sir,' Jurnet maintained doggedly. 'At the time I'm quite sure I didn't—not consciously, that is—or I'd never—' He broke off, red-faced.

'I never supposed you would,' the other admitted with ill grace.

'But subconsciously . . . I don't know. I think there may have been something. Not so much to do with Mrs Felsenstein herself, but whether she wasn't covering up for her husband. He was hardly ever about, and I don't like what I can't see. Was he as ill as she made out? Little things I couldn't put my finger on bothered me. A bit like raffle tickets inside the drum, swirling round too quick to read the numbers—'

'Until you put in your hand and drew out a slip-cover?'

'I suppose you could say that. There it was, hanging on the line in the back garden, one of the first things that caught my eye the first time Jack and I came into that room of theirs. That and the floor, clean as a whistle and smelling of polish, the scented kind. I should have guessed something was up.'

'Some people are in the habit of keeping their homes clean.' The Superintendent, who had once had occasion to call at Jurnet's flat, and had not forgotten it, was not without bitchiness. 'To say nothing of the fact that it was Easter, spring-cleaning time.'

'Kind of you to let me off the hook, sir.' But Jurnet shook his head. 'We didn't know where Loy Tanner had been done in, and we should have kept our eyes peeled. Murders are usually a messy business, and here was his mum, just cleaned up. I should have been on my guard, especially as there was the fireplace, choked with paper and ashes. I can't believe any woman really house-proud would leave a grate in that condition.'

Sergeant Ellers, anxious to share any blame that might be going, observed, '*She* knew it looked fishy, because she went out of her way to make some comment about how she ought to have left the fire for Mr Felsenstein to make—'

They all fell silent, remembering the blazing pyre at the bottom of the flint mine. Then Jurnet went on, 'She said something about having told Loy he ought to get his hair cut for the concert, but, as usual, he'd paid no heed. How could she possibly have known unless she'd seen him after the concert was over? That picture of him in the *Argus* appeared two days before: so, whatever she said, she couldn't have known it from that.'

'It's no good,' he continued, scowling at his own inadequacy. 'Easy enough to find the loose strands once you know where to look for them. We should have cottoned on when she called out, taking us for the milkman—or, if not then, the minute she told us she'd been expecting Tanner to drop by any time that morning. She sat at that knitting machine of hers with her back to the window, unable to see who was coming to the door. Yet she never gave a

moment's thought that it might be Loy coming up the
garden path. It had to be the milkman, because she already knew, without being told, that it could never be her
son, ever again . . .'

On Jurnet's instructions they had driven to Sebastopol
Terrace: found Miriam's car gone and the bright red door
to Number 12 wide open as if awaiting them. They had
found Mara Felsenstein's confession stacked on top of her
knitting machine, held in place by one of the weights
which kept the ribbing even. Jurnet had held the small,
plastic-coated object, elegant with its fluted rim, astonished at its heaviness in proportion to its size; but not
wondering until later, when he had had time to read the
blue-ruled pages covered in a painstaking schoolgirl script,
whether he held in his hand the actual instrument of Loy
Tanner's undoing.

Without Mara Felsenstein's presence, the room had
looked discarded. Somebody had taken the loose cover off
the couch, leaving it neatly folded over the back. The
upholstery revealed was truly hideous. No wonder the
Felsensteins had covered it up: roses that looked more like
jellyfish, swimming in a sea of sick. Without warning,
Jurnet's body remembered its chill slipperiness under the
cretonne cover, sensed amid the ecstasy but unnoticed
until that moment.

A fine ending to a grand passion!

The Superintendent was saying, 'King! That's the one
really sticks in my craw. How could the woman take his
threats seriously? He was in as deep as she was.'

'Not quite, sir.' Sid Hale, who had, until then, stood
quietly by, put in a rueful demurrer. 'King was a gambler.
He banked on Mrs F. not knowing that a convicted person
couldn't inherit anyway, so there'd be no percentage in
shopping her. But it's a rum turn her ignorance cost him
his life.'

'Hm!' The Superintendent considered this contribution,
and apparently found it credible. 'Gambler he certainly
was. The way he ran that drugs racket of his! If the cargo
weren't so filthy one could almost admire the reckless
disregard of precautions, the brazen cheek of the man.

Boat from Holland making regular deliveries of butter and
Dutch cheese to the rig. Butter and Dutch cheese! The
fellows who run those oil platforms—what do they call
them, for goodness' sake, captains or station masters?—can't
have the sense they were born with. D'you know what the
chap, whatever he's called and I could think of a right
name for him, said to regional drug squad when they told
him what had been coming aboard his rig hidden in those
nice red balls of Edam and wheels of Gouda? Bloater
Herring told me. "It was very good cheese!" '

Sid Hale, always cheered by evidences of human folly,
smiled without difficulty. 'I gather the word is that Tanner
put up the money for the operation, took his cut, but took
no part in the actual pushing?'

'So it seems, if you discount the £150 he took off the
loony professor and presumably passed on to King for
processing. Pure kindness of heart, or couldn't bear to
turn down business? Either way, it accounts for Tanner's
presence in Queenie King's caravan after the concert.'
The Superintendent transferred his attention back to
Jurnet. Placing a hand on Mrs Felsenstein's testament
with the solemnity of a hanging judge reaching for his
black cap, he pronounced, 'You understand, Ben, that I
am not in any position to let you know what, if anything,
the Chief proposes to do about this.'

Jurnet, silently noting the promise of that 'Ben', said
nothing. Jack Ellers, the court jester, chanced his arm.

'Publish, of course! Call a press conference! You tell the
Chief, sir! Do us a power of good!' A cherubic smile
spread over the little Welshman's face. 'With our public
image, it can't be bad to let the world know somebody
loved a policeman!'

Jurnet drove out to the University, taking a ridiculously
long way round by the Castle Bailey; stopping on a double
yellow line at a point from which, looking upward he could
see—past the flowery mound and the keep crenellated
against the sky—the rampart from which Robert Tanner
had dangled in air until the last of his bones fell to earth in
the first year of the reign of King James I.

A traffic warden, advancing gaily with her pad and pencil at the ready, clicked her teeth in annoyance when she recognized the car's number, and returned her weapons to her coat pocket.

No Anglo-Saxon hands signalling 'Help!' waved wildly among the daffodifs.

The caravans had gone from the University, leaving disagreeable shapes on the grass where they had stood. A gardener who saw Jurnet looking down at them, came over and said kindly, 'Another couple of weeks and you won't know they've ever been.'

In the foyer of the Middlemass Auditorium, blinds made of green-dyed rattan were drawn across the skylights to shield the idols from foreign parts from the insidious English sun. The Hob's Hole Venus was still missing from its pedestal.

Back in the city, the car, as of its own volition—'my lap of honour', Jurnet congratulated himself ironically—headed for Sebastopol Terrace, where, for a wonder, the largest of the estate agents' boards proclaimed one of the ramshackle houses to be 'UNDER OFFER'.

The detective parked outside Number 12, and opened the garden gate, diverging from the path to cross the handkerchief of starved grass outside the front window. The first thing he saw, shading his eyes against reflections, was the couch with its slip-cover back on. The second—

He went to the front door, found that the handle turned at his touch. In the living-room, a plaster on one side of his head, but otherwise no sicklier looking than usual, Leo Felsenstein sat at his knitting machine, working. The carriage moved smoothly backwards and forwards along the bank of needles. Sheep grew white and woolly on a field of green.

'Inspector Jurnet!' The man did not get up: nodded in excuse towards a pair of crutches leaning against his chair. 'You must forgive me. I am not yet as mobile as I could wish.'

'Please—' Jurnet, embarrassed, stammered, 'I didn't expect to find you here.'

'Where else should you find me but home?'

'I meant—I didn't know they'd discharged you from hospital.'

'They didn't. I discharged myself. They were killing me with kindness and I, as you must have guessed by now, am a survivor. Don't search for words,' Mr Felsenstein added, with a gentle inclination of the head, as the detective cast about desperately for something to say. *Did the man know, or didn't he?* 'There aren't any. Let us be content to understand each other.'

'Saw you go out,' said the duty sergeant. 'Seeing it was marked personal, thought I'd better hang on to it.'

'Ta.' Jurnet took the large, expensive-looking envelope up the stairs with him, away from the man's curiosity. Back at his desk, having slit it open with due respect for its rich creaminess, he read the contents, and laughed aloud.

On double card, embellished with much silver, Detective-Inspector Jurnet was invited to attend the wedding of Miss Regina King to Mr Guido Scarlatti, the nuptial mass to be celebrated at St Joseph's with a wedding breakfast at the Red Shirt to follow.

There were two enclosures beside the prepaid postcard for RSVP; one a typed slip headed *'Press Release'*.

> This is to announce that Mrs Queenie King-Scarlatti, of the famous King family of Punch and Judy fame, in partnership with her husband Mr Guido King-Scarlatti, will be operating the ancestral Punch and Judy show on Havenlea beach from the Spring Bank Holiday on. Mr and Mrs King-Scarlatti are also happy to announce that the Punch and Judy show is also available for hire for children's parties, Masonic functions and etc. For further information ring Havenlea 37629 any evening after 7.30.

The third enclosure was a sheet of notepaper which had lost the crispness it had possessed on the day that Angleby's leading gynaecologist had solemnly attested to Miss Queenie King's virginity. In a bold diagonal across the page a childish hand had scrawled in red crayon: 'CANCELLED.'

Miriam had agreed to meet him in the little garden at the

top of the Market Place. Dusk was deepening to dark as the detective, well ahead of the appointed hour, hurried across the road and past the cupressus, only to find that she was there even earlier, hands in the pockets of her white coat, her hair flaming orange in the orange light of the street lamp.

> *The woman clothed with the sun—*
> *The one!*

Jurnet's heart leaped with love. All day long he had mentally rehearsed the words he would say to her, words to be said in their first moment of meeting, before he weakened under the powerful attraction of her presence and settled for self-interest rather than the more ambiguous rewards of a clear conscience. Confessing to sin was difficult enough, but it was as nothing to confessing to being still unrepentant.

A murderess! he had kept on reminding himself, to no avail. Miriam or no Miriam, the memory of what had happened between himself and Mara Felsenstein would, he knew, enrich his life for the rest of his days. Still and all, love was giving, not taking; and seeing that there was now that much less on offer by way of gift, Miriam had to be told. There had to be truth between them or there was nothing, he told himself so many times that he almost believed it.

Not quite, though—his sense of the feasible taking over at the last moment. You couldn't be an Angleby copper without acquiring some saving apprehension of the inherent imperfectibility of any human relationship. So that when, against all likelihood, Miriam ran to him and kissed him on the mouth, stifling his confession at birth, he surrendered gratefully, lost in a surprise of happiness.

'Miriam—'

Her face wet with unregarded tears, she burst out, 'I've been speaking to Leo. Oh Ben, you can't imagine what he told me! He's told me everything—'

Everything?

Jurnet said awkwardly, 'We did question Mr Felsenstein ourselves—'

Miriam calmed down and said, 'Of course. I wasn't

thinking. You know it all already.' Voice breaking: 'Poor Mara!'

'Poor Loy. Poor Punchy King,' added Jurnet, taking a risk that had to be taken.

'Yes,' she responded soberly, passing the test first time. 'When Mara told Leo what she'd done it almost killed him.'

'At Hob's Hole she nearly added him to the score anyway.'

The other nodded. 'What made it even more terrible— did he tell you?—was that, right up to the time they got into my car, he still thought they were just going for a drive in the country. It was only on the way that she told him everything—'

Everything?

'—and then, when she took the brake off, and they began to move towards the edge of the Hole—' Miriam's eyes widened with horror, as if she too had been among those who, aghast on the drove road, had watched the little car begin its last journey—'if he hadn't already un-done his seat-belt, had his hand on the door handle, Professor Whinglass could never have got him out in time.' Miriam shuddered, shrugged her white coat closer. 'What he said to me was, "I loved her and I left her to die alone." Oh, Ben, you should have seen his face! I'd always thought of him before as an invalid, a shadow who hardly existed without Mara, but he isn't like that at all. He's stronger than any of us, with a sense of life that's like a great river pulsing through that poor twisted body. When he spoke, it was as if he spoke for all the people he saw die in the Holocaust, speaking out against the waste of them, and the pain. I'm explaining it very badly—'

'No. You're doing fine.'

'He said, "If you can kill one, you can kill six million." He said, "How do you think the Nazis began? First they killed one, and then another one, and then another one." Oh, Ben!' Miriam broke off and looked at her lover, her large, lustrous eyes brimming. 'I feel so ashamed, the way I've behaved. Can you forgive me for everything?'

Everything?

Jurnet pulled her towards him, tilted her face upward. 'So long as we make it mutual!'

*　　*　　*

Arm in arm they moved slowly across the small garden where the crosses had stood as reminders of death and rebirth.

Miriam asked, 'Were you lonely?'

'A cat came to keep me company.'

'A cat?' Jurnet suppressed a chuckle at the feminine suspicion in her voice. 'A real cat?'

'I'm not sure.'

Somebody had cleared away the flowery mound erected to the memory of Loy Tanner. Not made much of a job of it either. Bits of shrivelled greenery lay about untidily. The boys and girls—even, it might be, Mrs Lark of Parks and Recreation—had taken their tears elsewhere; or else, youth being what it was, too short for sentimentality, had wiped their eyes, given their noses a good blow, and were already offering up their adoration at another shrine.

Good on them.

Suddenly, Jurnet squatted down on his haunches, moved aside a scatter of petals that had once been red. A thorn stuck in his hand, making it bleed.

Out of the battered earth, the buried daffodils had pushed their way into the air. A solitary golden flower stood up, indomitable.

'They made it! They actually made it!'

Miriam smiled at Jurnet's excitement. She reached for his hand, felt the warm stickiness of blood.

Turning the palm upward, she lifted it to her mouth, and, the tip of her tongue showing cat-like between her lips, licked the wound clean.

About the Author

S. T. HAYMON was born in Norwich, England, and presently lives in London. *Death of a God* is her fourth mystery featuring Detective-Inspector Ben Jurnet.

BANTAM MYSTERY COLLECTION